BURNED

AN ALEX DRAKE NOVEL

LEXXI JAMES

Burned: An Alex Drake Novel
Copyright © 2021 Lexxi James
www.LexxiJames.com
All rights reserved. Lexxi James, LLC.

Edited by the Utterly Extraordinary
Pam Berehulke
Bulletproof Editing

Independently Published.

Cover by Okay Creations

No part of this publication may be reproduced, distributed, or transmitted in any form or by any means, including photocopying, recording, or other electronic or mechanical methods, without the prior written permission of Lexxi James LLC. Under certain circumstances, a brief quote in reviews and for non-commercial use may be permitted as specified in copyright law. Permission may be granted through a written request to the publisher at LexxiJamesBooks@gmail.com.

This is a work of fiction. Names, characters, places, and incidents are the product of the author's imagination. Specific named locations, public names, and other specified elements are used for impact, but this novel's story and characters are 100 percent fictitious. Certain long-standing institutions, agencies, and public offices are mentioned, but the characters involved are wholly imaginary. Resemblance to individuals, living or dead, or to events which have occurred is purely coincidental. And if your life happens to bear a strong resemblance to my imaginings, then well done and cheers to you! You're a freaking rock star!

To my mom and dad.

PART I
THE PRESENT

CHAPTER 1

MADISON

Manhattan

CROUCHED awkwardly in the small space between the watercooler and the wall, Madison couldn't help looking up at the half-filled tank in disbelief.

They're actually gossiping next to the watercooler? How horribly on the nose.

Deflated, she flinched at the sting of each rumor she overheard from her unintended surveillance spot. And the question she mentally kicked herself over wasn't how could this have happened, but how could it not?

Somehow, she'd managed to convince herself that the news of her upcoming nuptials would be barely newsworthy in the engagements section of the *New York Times*.

Ha!

She'd even helped craft the matter-of-fact snippet, certain it would be buried beneath the actual full-blown wedding announcements, not to mention the reports of stock surges and gripping national news.

Her best friend, Sheila—the up-and-coming reporter

Madison had promised the story to—had made every change Madison requested. In the end, the announcement was limited to a single line.

BILLIONAIRE CEO ALEX DRAKE AND DGI ANALYST MADISON TAYLOR
TO WED

Sheila had been promised the scoop, and Madison Taylor was a woman of her word. She held tight to her integrity, no matter how uncomfortable it was. And it was definitely uncomfortable . . . hiding in a corner behind the coffee bar in the break room of Drake Global Industries.

Madison sucked in a silent breath, taking in this long, exhausting day had begun well before the crack of dawn. Glancing at row of international clocks on the wall, the one set for New York time hadn't yet hit eleven a.m.

Awesome.

Texts had begun blowing up her cell phone about five a.m., a total of several hundred, because apparently her number was splayed across the Times Square Jumbotron.

How do I get my number unlisted from the world? Just a small-town girl engaged to a billionaire. Nothing to see here, folks. Nothing to see.

Madison wiggled her toes, afraid they were falling asleep. *I should've called in sick.*

Sick. Or freaked out. *Tomayto, tomahto.*

None of this was as bad as she'd imagined. No, it was so horribly, awfully, painfully much worse.

How this should have gone down was with her busting out a magnanimous can of whoop-ass on her slanderous coworkers the moment she heard the first barb. But this was Alex's company, not hers. And temper tantrums at the office from his new fiancée wouldn't be a good look for either of them. Confronting her detractors would create a situation the press would undoubtedly blow completely out of proportion.

Instead, the women's incoming voices with her name on their lips as they approached the break room had rushed her ass to retreat to a corner that, between you and me, it barely managed to squeeze into.

And there she remained, wedged between the wall and the watercooler. In competitive hide and seek, this space would have rated a C+ at best. But if she were very quiet and still, her secret hideaway would work.

"Madison Taylor," one of them said with disdain. "Who would have thought it? All sweet and innocent, and fucking the boss the whole time."

Madison peeked out as best she could, eyeing the trio of women she'd never even met. After all, over a thousand DGI employees worked at the headquarters here in Manhattan.

Who cares what they say?

Annoyed at herself, she stifled a snort. That was a stupid question. She cared. Way more than every brain cell in her ducked-down head said she should.

I don't even know these women.

But if middle school had taught her anything—other than how to use a tampon, that hair gel and eyebrow tweezing should be done sparingly, and that the little boy you crushed on so hard and wished you could marry someday was batting for the other team—it was that where a trail of mean girls started, endless swarms of them followed.

"I'll bet Little Miss Prim and Proper does it every which way. Like a pet on some diamond-studded leash. You know, a girl-friend of mine dated him."

Unimpressed, Mean Girl Number Two responded with another slap in the face. "Who hasn't?"

The third chimed in. "Yeah, he's had more women spread eagle than the American Society of Obstetrics. And does that man have a dark side. Kink to the core. Only one way she's marriage material."

Madison's frustration and anger slid to the back seat as her curiosity called shotgun, with a flutter of hope that the next words spoken would be *true love*.

The third girl snickered. "Ménage."

"Not *à trois*, if that's where you're going."

Madison let out a silent exhale of relief.

"More like *à cinq*."

Her eyes popped open wide. *Five? Really? Oh, come on. Do I walk like I've been done every which way to Sunday?*

"Now we know why there are so many chairs in the boardroom," one of them said, which drew a titter of cruel laughter from the others.

Madison rolled her eyes. This was too much. With the air ripe with premium roast and vicious gossip, she was losing her cool. It didn't help that these women were taking the longest coffee break ever, lazily drawing out their time—and Madison's as well.

All I wanted was some freaking water.

Her options were dwindling, but she could always confront them. Jump out and defend her honor, slaying them with an accusatory "gotcha" finger pointing straight at their shocked faces as she exclaimed, "Aha! I heard every word."

So what if it lost its impact because she'd been listening way too long?

Jump up and confront them? At this point, standing might be its own challenge. Hiding had been a bad idea from the start, one that grew worse with each minute she stayed put.

No amount of yoga or deep breathing would prevent her cramped legs from falling asleep. And, of course, the women were taking their sweet damn time finishing up, because God forbid they actually get back to work.

Madison said one silent prayer after another that the women would leave before her legs completely gave out. Impatiently, she squatted, waiting out the swarms of prickles running up and down her calves and thighs, willing herself not to fall flat on her ass when her muscles finally gave out.

After about a million years, the gossips collected their coffee cups overflowing with freshly slung mud before inching their way into the hall, continuing their obnoxiously loud chatter and giving Madison a reprieve.

A much-needed reprieve that would have to wait even longer. It would seem that with all her patience and silent fuming, her wedged-in body was now hopelessly stuck.

Huffing, or semi-hyperventilating, she sucked in a long breath and gripped the watercooler with one hand while resting her other palm on the wall.

Madison's first heave to push herself up seemed promising. At halfway through heave number two, she stopped short to avoid the sloshing tank from tipping completely over. And when another set of footsteps casually strolled into the break room, she did what any self-respecting junior analyst marrying the boss would do in her place. She froze.

"Hello?" the sultry voice called out, undoubtedly noticing the still sloshing tank gurgling, complete with big, blaring bubbles and all.

Shyly, Madison peered around the tank as subtly as she could, watching the slow sashay of a five-foot-ten-inch supermodel with ass-length hair heading straight toward her.

Crap.

The woman who certainly didn't need the five-inch stilettos rocked them like the world was her runway. She moved like magical fairy dust had touched one of *Charlie's Angels*, endowing her with a crazy blend of beauty, boobs, and even maybe the softest touch of badass that Madison admired.

This woman set Madison's nerves on edge as she stooped before her, eyeing her up and down with a grin. "Everything okay?"

"Oh. Yes." Madison nodded, struggling to appear casual and nonchalant. "I just, um, dropped something."

The ruby-red lips of the strange woman widened with intrigue as she barely glanced around the floor. "And then sat on it? Is it an egg? If you're a golden goose, I'm claiming you."

The stranger stood and extended her hand. Madison graciously accepted the hoist of her remarkably strong and effortless pull.

The relief of standing pushed an uncontrollable sigh from Madison's throat. "*Ah*, thank you." She rubbed at the pins and needles in her thighs, pointedly glancing down. "See? No golden egg."

Her rescuer smirked. "Well, I guess I won't be your captor, then."

"Good thing too, as I'm already spoken for."

"So I hear," the woman teased, arching a perfectly shaped brow.

When Madison's face fell and she ducked her head, the stranger tipped her head back up with a couple of soft fingers beneath her chin.

"Yeah, the trio in the hall weren't exactly curbing their enthusiasm." Confidently, she stroked Madison's arm. "Don't let them get to you. Jealousy is *très déclassé*."

Soothed, Madison wasn't sure what to say in response. "Thanks. I appreciate that. Can I treat you to a coffee?" she asked, offering up the selection of coffees displayed next to a dozen Keurig machines.

"Actually, I don't do coffee. I just came to recycle my water bottle." Giving the clear plastic enough of a squeeze to make it crackle, the woman placed the empty Evian in the recycling bin. "And I should really get back."

"Well, thanks again for helping me up." Extending a hand, she introduced herself. "I'm Madison."

The woman clasped it in both of hers, smoothing a thumb

against her skin. "I know," she said, leaning close and flashing a knowing grin. "Pretty sure everyone knows."

A short silence hung between them while their eye contact teetered to awkward.

Finally, the woman released Madison's hand, offering her own cryptic introduction. "Just call me *J*."

"Jay?"

"Mm-hmm. You know . . . like J-Lo."

Madison smiled, finding the name fitting, considering the woman carried herself with the confidence and poise of a known triple threat. "Well, *J*, it was nice to meet you."

"You too."

J began a very catwalk departure, pausing only for a moment as Madison called out, "See you around."

With a slow turn and a suggestive grin, *J* gave her a solemn but friendly reassurance. "Definitely."

She then disappeared down the hall, leaving Madison with an unsettled knot in her chest.

Without a doubt, the underbelly of the DGI grapevine would be buzzing with everyone's take on *Junior Analyst Beds the Boss*. Yup, this was the perfect way to grow a budding career built with hard work and integrity, taken seriously at every step for the smart, savvy, growing businesswoman she was.

Riiight, her inner voice said before another thought hit her. *I could leave*.

Leave? For how long . . . a day? A week? It didn't matter. Everyone knew. *Everyone*. And the few people who didn't—like the preppers avoiding the news or the castaways on deserted islands—offered little solace that this would all blow over.

Desperate to shake off her plummet into the freefall of anxiety, Madison weighed her options. Fresh air was always a good call.

Tempted by the bright outdoors peeking through from the lobby exit door, Madison took a determined detour to a street vendor on the corner. Hurried and trying not to make eye contact with anyone, she bought a pre-wrapped salad and a glass bottle of Coke—the kind with real sugar—because it was that kind of a day.

Armed with lunch, Madison slunk back to her office for a little alone time to focus on two side-by-side oversize computer monitors filled with lots and lots and lots of data.

Because data didn't gossip, and data didn't judge. And the mountain of glorious data at her disposal was enough to hide behind for the rest of the day. Alone. Diligently working and not obsessing over the ticking time bomb of an expiration date for this very precious and amazing job.

CHAPTER 2

ALEX

"FIVE HUNDRED MILLION?" Alex Drake asked, staring at his computer monitor while barely paying attention to the conversation from the speakerphone.

Preoccupied, he wasn't exactly on top of the discussion, but like the CEO he was, responded decisively. "Sounds fine," he muttered, approving who the hell knew what. For all he knew, he'd agreed to bribes, sex toys, and a year's worth of hookers for the Senate.

The email that had snagged his attention sat unopened for several moments, his finger hovering with uncertainty, because approving whatever half a billion dollars was buying was an easier decision than opening that email.

Labeled PRIVATE, it had been sent by a ghost he hadn't heard from in ten years, the only person he'd thought about all that time with the same interest as he'd wondered about his close friend's little sister. Madison had become his fixation. But *J. Stone* had been an unclosed chapter of his past.

With the shame of idiocy settling in and the insistence that there was no fear in reading an email, he finally clicked it open.

Within the email was a video clip taken from the DGI headquarters lobby not ten minutes ago. The *J* from the email was front and center, strolling through the lobby of the headquarters of his multibillion-dollar empire as if she owned the place.

Is there some corner of her misguided mind that thinks she owns me as well?

With thoughtful intensity, Alex studied the footage frame by frame, desperate to analyze the three-minute clip. The statuesque woman made long, stately strides to the security desk. Fife, DGI's chief of security, stood to greet her and pointed to the lobby restroom. She thanked him and stepped away.

In her natural sashay, she made her way to the ladies' room, waving her arm back to the camera and holding up three fingers. She disappeared behind the door.

A sound of gruff irritation left his lips, followed by, "Shit," as he jumped to his feet. The video was done.

"No to the orphanage donation?" his vice president of corporate charities asked, shy surprise in her tone.

"What?" Briefly, Alex focused, mentally flipping through the slides he'd scanned a few hours earlier. Recalling the line in question, he rushed to agree.

"No, no. We're good. Approved for the orphanage, and I've gone through your analysis. Well done. Approved for all charity requests for the next six months, but let's keep a close eye on the burn rate for the food banks. I'd like to revisit in thirty days in case we need to send them more."

Rising to his feet with a finger ready, he said, "I need to cut this short." He blurted out a *thank you* before killing the call and taking his private elevator downstairs to the lobby.

With a quick glance around as he tried to appear nonchalant, Alex swiftly stepped into the ladies' room.

An observant glance at the orthopedic shoes revealed beneath the door of stall one urged him to rush past the closed door, eager to avoid any face-to-face meetings. He ignored the usual sounds commonplace in bathrooms.

At stall three, the closed door he was sure was vacant gave with the slightest push of his fingers. Having said a silent *thank God*, he entered.

Empty.

He took a doubtful look into the pristinely clean bowl, certain no further exploration was necessary, but made a mental note to give bonuses to the cleaning staff.

When the toilet from two stalls over flushed, Alex shut the door. Behind it, he found a note, recognizing the ornate penmanship.

Alex

Tamping down the faintest trace of a sentimental thought or emotion, he snatched down the taped note and flipped it open. One word was carefully scrawled, with a heart over the *i*.

Congratulations

Alex flipped it over, diligent in making sure he hadn't missed more.

J wasn't his past. She was ancient fucking history, returning to taunt him in his own lobby while leaving behind no trace except an email and a cryptic note about his impending nuptials. It didn't make sense.

Dumbfounded, Alex couldn't make heads or tails of it, but was certain this wouldn't be her last word. Slipping the note in his pocket, he stepped out of the stall without checking to be sure he was now alone.

"Oh!" the elegant older woman said in shock. She wore a smart blue suit that matched her wide eyes, and the orthopedic shoes he'd glimpsed beneath the stall door.

Grateful that he didn't recognize her, Alex gave her a shy smile. Clinging to a hope, a prayer, and blind faith that her thick glasses made him indistinguishable in a lineup, he apologized and excused himself, briskly moving past her.

"Ahem." Her expression stern, she cleared her throat and glanced pointedly at his hands, then at the sink.

He took a begrudging step to the sink, not bothering to explain he hadn't actually used the toilet in the women's restroom. He wrapped up as soon as he'd mentally finished his ABCs and headed back to his office, pretending, as Fife did, that he hadn't been spotted.

Between the mysterious note and the uneasy feeling that, as CEO of the company, he might be adding another idiosyncrasy to the growing list of rumored ones he knew of, he welcomed an incoming call from Mark Donovan.

The man might be his evil arch nemesis in public as CEO of Excelsior/Centurion, but to Alex, he was one of only a handful of very close friends.

"Hey, Mark. I see you're calling from your cell, so may I assume bail money isn't required?"

"Not this time." Mark's tone was far from easygoing as he blew out a heavy breath. "Listen, we need to talk. It's a guy thing."

It's a guy thing wasn't a guy thing. It was code. Mark needed Alex's ear, and it had to be somewhere secure and away from both of their offices. In these situations, they met at an off-the-grid secure facility both of them knew the route to by heart.

Frowning, Alex kept his voice even and light as he said, "Sure."

Tonight, they were supposed to be heading out for a weekend getaway. Alex and Madison would be meeting Mark and his wife, Jess, at their luxury cabin hidden deep in the Adirondacks. This would change the plans.

"How about you ask Jess to grab Madison?" Alex said. "I know she would love a girls' drive up." Caution prevented him from saying anything else.

"Perfect," Mark said quickly. "You let Madison know, and I'll tell Jess."

"When do you want to get together?"

"You know. See ya."

From the *see ya*, Alex did know. Those two words translated to a time. *Five thirty*.

CHAPTER 3

MADISON

Lightly moving the bits of lettuce and chicken of her barely touched Caesar salad around in its plastic container, Madison couldn't bring herself to eat. The spreadsheets she tried to analyze were blurring together, one nonsensical cell at a time, while the computer's clock seemed to be going painfully in reverse.

She ignored the cream-colored corporate walls as they closed in on her, but couldn't push away the agony of the incessant itch creeping up her arm. A few scratches to ease the small patch of hives was enough for the time being.

How bad will it get? How do I prepare? Can I prepare?

Prepare for what? Whatever *this* was, it wasn't like a Twitter swarm, where people she didn't know trolled her from behind the anonymity of a computer screen.

No, the people letting their voices be heard weren't anonymous. And though she couldn't pick any of them out of a lineup, or even a corporate directory, they were people she'd continue to see, day in and day out. Bump into in the hall. Hide from in the break room. And avoid like the plague.

And what about Alex? Was she his Achilles heel? A DGI

liability where corporate gossip became the catalyst for a sharp drop in stock price? If the world at large wanted to look down on her, so be it. But Alex didn't deserve this.

The scrutiny of cavorting with a junior analyst—because obviously, she and Alex had cavorted—should be a non-starter. The truth was that Alex had nearly died trying to save Madison's brother years ago, but it was none of anyone's business. And that type of news wouldn't matter, because stories like that didn't sell. At least, not like a bogus, tantalizingly lurid and horrendously salacious office scandal.

Ménage à cinq, my ass. Wait! That came out wrong.

Defeated, she dropped her head back against the soft leather of the headrest as she closed her eyes and pushed out a heavy breath, wishing she'd stayed in bed.

"Sleeping on the job?" a cheerful Latino voice called out.

Relieved to see the man who was always a friendly face, she lifted her head and gave him a huge grin. Leaning against her door frame was Paco Robles, Alex Drake's right-hand man. An invisible mastermind behind the scenes. And the only man in the world who could earn his way to becoming her brother.

Madison gave him a wry smile. "Just reminiscing about how nice life was yesterday."

Paco took a seat and wheeled his chair next to hers. Making himself comfortable, he leaned back into it, clasping his hands across his Tom Ford-clad abs as he said casually, "Ignore it."

Without a word, Madison handed over her phone, showing him that the notifications and messages were well past a thousand so far.

Completely unconcerned, he waved a manicured hand. "It's just a blip. A little sensationalism. I promise you on all the couture I cherish more than bacon, it will pass. And no matter how beautiful yesterday's sunset seems today, we have to focus on the sunrise ahead."

How can I argue with this man? Seriously, he loves couture and bacon. He's obviously brilliant beyond his years, and it would serve me well to listen to him.

Without asking, he gently gripped her wrist, stretching out her arm and delicately sliding up her sleeve. Clinically, he scrutinized the reddening splotches wrapping her forearm.

Dismayed, he let out a long breath, his expression filling with concern. "That's pretty bad. Want me to take you home? Or at least out of here to get some fresh air for a bit? I know all the people-free secret passages."

"I'll bet you do," she said, hesitant and shrugging away his concern.

Surprising her, he pushed her executive chair aside, letting it wheel away from behind her desk as he took ownership of her keyboard, clicking away as he accessed her calendar. Like any nosy big brother would.

"Wow," he said as he let out a whistle. "An exciting afternoon of South American market analysis." After typing a few keystrokes at lightning speed, he hit ENTER with exaggerated satisfaction. "There."

She pulled herself closer to examine his work. With a playful glare, she asked, "My entire afternoon is now blocked for a last-minute Latin-relations meeting?"

"*With* the ambassador to Puerto Rico. Get your stuff. *Vámanos.* There's nothing the ambassador hates more than waiting."

Heading out of her office and down a hall, they made their way through a door Madison hadn't noticed before. "Puerto Rico is a US territory. There is no ambassador."

With comfortable authority, Paco challenged her. "That just means the title's up for grabs. Called it."

"Yes, Your Excellency," she said, laughing.

They arrived at yet another private elevator, because apparently this place had more of them than floors, bathrooms, or parking spaces combined. Entering, he swiped his access card across the panel, which brightened the blue backlight of all the stainless-steel buttons. He pressed G.

During their descent, Paco focused on texting, and it suddenly dawned on her that she was probably encroaching on his own agenda for the day.

She covered his hand with hers, giving it a gentle squeeze and stopping him mid-text. "Seriously, I appreciate everything you're doing for me, but I can't tear you from your schedule."

The elevator opened. "You're not. This *is* actually a business trip."

Madison smirked. "Oh, I'm sure it is, Ambassador Robles."

Once they arrived at the private garage, Madison's thrill level kicked up a notch as Paco opened the driver's door of his very new and droolworthy Rosso Mars red Aventador and beckoned her to climb in. The man changed Lamborghinis as frequently as he changed boyfriends, and this would be Madison's first time behind the wheel of his new beast.

"What's her name?" Madison asked as she started the engine.

"Hot Cherry."

"Could be sexy. Could need antibiotics."

"Hush your mouth. She'll hear you." Reassuring the car with several long caresses to his side of the dash, Paco said, "Don't listen to her. You're sex on wheels. Easily making men hard from your curves and your purr."

"True."

As Paco was the bossiest navigator ever, Madison drove well beyond the comforts of the speed limit as soon as traffic let up.

"I'm not an old lady," she said with a giggle.

"Seriously, my grandmother would kick your ass from her walker. In a few minutes, we'll have an open stretch. Gun it, girlie."

Nothing weighed on her mind in that moment. Just the roar of the engine, the rumble beneath her seat, and the exhilaration of pushing Paco's Hot Cherry to the point of nearly popping.

In no time, Paco gave her the signal that they were nearing their destination and she could slow down. A few turns later, they arrived at what Madison recognized to be a government building. It was a VA medical center, but one with a satellite building attached. The letters DGI were on the side.

"What is this?" Madison asked as she pulled into the reserved spot he directed her to and parked.

"Drake Robotics works closely with this VA medical center. I thought you'd like a tour."

Madison beamed. This wasn't your run-of-the-mill distraction from a hard day at the office by heading to a mall or a bar. It was an opportunity. A gateway to work closely with cutting-edge science and veterans.

As she and Paco began their tour, the vets they met with were unique, each battling their own mental and physical challenges and conditions.

One man, John, had been the sole survivor from his team. She didn't know why she opened up about the loss of her brother. And she didn't know why he opened up about his guilt. But both were raw and honest, with no expectation to fix or be fixed. Just to listen. And understand. And be. It was a deep, tear-filled connection, and it felt good.

Also, John reminded her of Alex, what he might have been like a month after Jack's death. An Alex she never knew, but somehow connected with now.

Over the course of her visit, she moved on to others. Others who were missing pieces of their bodies, or their minds, or their hearts, or their souls. People who were shadows of the people they once were. And people who might never again be complete, or fulfilled, or happy, or whole.

But being around them gave Madison a glimmer of hope that she could take her own incompleteness, and unfillable emptiness, and never-ending sadness, and use it for something that might be good, even if only in the smallest way.

What each of the veterans she met wanted was as much of a surprise as what they didn't. No one wanted accolades, and they definitely didn't want pity. Madison could relate.

On the want list were ordinary, everyday things. Food items like Girl Scout cookies and a real goddamn drink were popular. Their favorite brand of toiletries and books ranked on the achievable scale, and Madison promised to return with all of them.

On the other end of the spectrum? They wanted their lives back. Their friends alive. Their sanity. Answers. Why?

These were all the things Madison wished for them because that was where they connected with the strongest. She'd wanted all those things too, and to this day, she still did.

Paco had given up his pocket square for her near the beginning of their tour, but it was apparent early on that the big, bad Mr. Robles needed it just as much as she did throughout the day. Though there were tissues at every bedside, sharing the single handkerchief seemed to soothe them both.

Before rejoining the others, Madison stopped Paco to ask, "Does Alex come here?"

Paco shook his head slowly, giving his lips a tight, disconcerting crimp. "It's not for lack of trying. The flashbacks kick in the hardest here. And it's not the men or women. He works with plenty of vets. Something about the smell of a hospital, I suspect. And," he said carefully, "it was the last place he saw Jack."

With a weak shrug, he sucked in a slow breath, cautious before letting her in on more about the man she'd be marrying.

"It knocks him off his game, and not for hours or days, but for months. We all have our triggers, and let's just say Alex Drake has more than his fair share. It took some convincing, but we assured him he was doing enough. More than enough. With Alex, it's like watching him snuff out a raging fire to a smoldering flame, only to douse it with kerosene. We all have our limits, *hermanita*. This isn't for Alex. But perhaps it's the chicken soup tailor-made for your soul."

Smiling, Madison pulled Paco into a tight squeeze, with his strong hug back rocking her gently.

"It's all perspective, Madison. A few hours ago, you were wishing today away." He pulled back, dabbing away her tears while beaming at her through his own glistening eyes. "And now?"

"Now?" She inhaled, not needing to think it through. "Now I think this is one of the most amazing afternoons of my life. And I can't let it be the last. There have to be ways I can help."

He kissed her cheek. "I'm sure there are." A series of short buzzes erupted from his pocket, and he pulled out his phone. "Fife's getting antsy. Must be the new access cards. Ready?"

Madison nodded, naturally wrapping her hands around his arm as he led her back. Heading outside, she couldn't quell the butterflies fluttering in her stomach. Or pinpoint what exactly her future held.

She sensed the winds of change storming about, like a tornado raging across the Oklahoma plains.

Apprehensive yet resolute, she knew she needed to share this with Alex.

But when?

CHAPTER 4

MADISON

Although with a little less tread on Paco's tires, Madison returned both the car and them safe and sound—and scratch-free—to DGI headquarters. There was no hiding his small, relieved breath when she eased Hot Cherry into her assigned space in the garage.

Although she was ready to make a beeline straight to Alex's fifty-second-floor office, Paco yanked her back, directing her to the security desk.

New access cards were ready for beta testing—a highly customizable form created to give unfettered entry to anything and everything in the building. Only a short list of people could perform the test. A very short list.

Other than Alex and Fife, just Paco and Madison, actually.

Fife seemed ready to take their prints and retina scans, modifying the data in the beta cards. But once they arrived, he hopped to his feet, standing at attention as he struggled to stutter out, "G-good afternoon, Ms. Taylor," without an ounce of love for Paco.

Coughing through a laugh, Paco drew her attention to the *New York Times* on the desk, splayed open to the prominent engagement announcement several font sizes larger than the rest.

"Not you too," she said, exasperated as she cringed. Her stern words softened his expression to the helpless look of a scolded puppy, which was ridiculous for the hardened ex-SEAL. It sent her over the edge.

Grabbing his giant shoulders, she pushed the two-hundred-eighty-pound behemoth of pure muscle effortlessly to his seat.

"Fife, I need you to pay very close attention to every word I'm about to say. I. Am. Madison. Your pal Madison. The girl who tosses you chocolate-covered espresso beans when your lunch slump hits. The girl who challenges you on a daily basis for who will come in first and leave last. The same girl you picked up like a rag doll right in the center of that very floor."

He followed the path of her finger as she pointed for effect.

"So, do not—and I repeat—do *not* even begin to look at me and see the CEO of DGI, Mr. Alex Drake, because you and I both know he couldn't carry off these heels to save his life."

Cracking an amused grin, she was relieved to finally see Fife give her one back, at which point she playfully poked his chest. "Is that clear?"

"Yes, ma'am." He saluted sharply, then leaned in. Even from a seated position and with Madison in four-inch-heels, the two were nearly eye-to-eye. "So, which of you decides if we press charges?"

Confused, Madison turned to Paco, then back to Fife. "Press charges?"

Nodding, he explained. "I sent you both an encrypted email."

Paco checked his phone. Frowning, he hesitantly passed the phone to Madison, highlighting the email Fife was referring to.

Urgent and Confidential. We caught a woman with items on her computer that violate her terms of employment. Images of Ms. Madison Taylor in unflattering poses. Doctored images had Ms. Taylor's face superimposed on various women's bodies. All in compromising positions. All retrieved. All recipients identified. Termination procedures in progress. Press charges?

With a loose hold on her skyrocketing anxiety, Madison found herself right back in the mess she'd left before lunch.

Great. And by great, I mean everything about this sucks big fat donkey nads. When, for the love of God, is this day going to end already?

Paco pointed to the center monitor of Fife's computer. "Pull up her badge credentials, and what we've got on her right now."

Fife brought up the DGI-issued ID of one Margaret Cunningham on one screen, while loading several documents across the other screens. Madison let out a gasp of recognition, stealing Paco's attention.

"You know her?"

"Yes. I mean, no. I mean . . . I—I've seen her around," she said with a meek shrug.

Yanking her elbow gently but firmly, Paco pulled her out of earshot of Fife, then unbuttoned his suit and pocketed his hands. "What? Who is she?"

Madison swallowed her embarrassment as best she could, unable to quell the heat rising up her cheeks. In a hushed voice, she explained. "I saw her this morning. Her and a couple of others. I overheard them talking trash about me, but it was just, um, watercooler gossip. Hurtful. Hateful. But nothing to get fired over."

"Well, Fife didn't put everything in the email. The stuff he pulled up is a lot more incriminating than that, and not just about you. Looks like she offered confidential corporate intel to a competitor." He cleared his throat. "Our best competitor."

And by best competitor, Paco had to mean Excelsior/Centurion and its CEO, Mark Donovan. To the outside world, he and Alex were hard-charging, fight-to-the-death competitors. But to those in the know, he was Alex's brotherly BFF.

"So, that's how they caught her?" Madison asked.

"No, actually. Security was tipped off earlier today and called me. Hang on." Paco gestured to Fife waving at them, motioning for their attention. "They're escorting her out now. Here, let's move out of sight."

From their observation point, they watched as Mean Girl Number Two was led away by security, carrying a big box of her belongings. Her eyes were swollen and red-rimmed.

But before she could exit the building, another woman deliberately crossed her path. A woman with high heels, ass-length hair, and that familiar crimson smile.

It was J, pausing only momentarily during her casual stroll to find Madison across the room. Dropping her sunglasses, J touched the arm of them to her full, flirty lips and shot Madison a very deliberate, very direct wink. Returning her shades to their placement high on the bridge of her nose, she widened her smile as she watched the woman being escorted out.

Urgently, Madison patted Paco's arm. "See that woman?"

Paco looked in the direction Madison pointed with her chin. "The femme fatale? Who could miss her."

"Who is she? Or what department does she work in?"

Paco looked at Madison and spoke carefully. "No idea who she is. She doesn't work here. Why do you ask?"

Adoring the man beside her, Madison gave him a look of disbelief. "Maybe your walking encyclopedia mind of all twenty thousand employees is off, and she hasn't made your radar yet."

"Nobody's off my radar," he said with equal parts confidence and admonishment. "I might not recall random facts, and I'm no contender for *Jeopardy*, but images are my thing. Faces, maps, anything visual. Like a glistening, bare-chested Hemsworth after a long, breathy swim, what has been seen cannot be unseen. It's a blessing and a curse."

Straightening his tie, he added, "And it's twenty thousand, four hundred, and eight people, and that includes the nineteen onboarded this morning. Maybe Nikita was in the building for a meeting or something else. Like a leather convention."

That made Madison stifle a laugh.

"And I didn't vet her, so she wasn't meeting Alex. All I can say is she doesn't work here. Guaranteed."

Madison glanced back to find J, but it was too late. Both she and the now former employee Margaret were both gone.

"Come on," Paco said, ready to head back to Fife's desk.

Fife repeated his question. "Press charges?"

Paco examined the screen. "Let legal take care of it. They'll see if we have enough to press charges."

"Paco," Madison whispered with a pang of paranoia. "Could she have maybe been, oh, I don't know . . . set up?"

Instantly, Paco tugged her away from the desk, emphasizing the importance of his question with a firm hand on her shoulder. Lowering his voice, he asked, "Why would you think that?"

Hesitant, Madison only shrugged. Honestly, she had nothing. And it wasn't like she missed the middle mean girl. *Good riddance.* But she couldn't shake the niggling feeling.

Paco patted her hand reassuringly, giving her a comforting smile. "Look, the information she tried peddling was an attempt to seriously compromise DGI. Legal will investigate it, and TRex will verify all of it." He leaned in. "And we'll wipe whatever she had on you. No matter what, DGI will at least threaten her with criminal charges if she persists with a fake-news smear campaign. According to the law, doctored photos are libel. We can't just sweep it under the rug, Madison, or have it looming over your head like it's your fight alone. Our strongest position is to protect you, because protecting you *is* protecting DGI."

"But . . ." *Damn this nagging feeling.* "Are you sure she did it?"

"No, I'm not." His words were flat and direct. "But Fife is. If you saw her this morning, and she was just escorted out, I know what that timeline means." He lifted a confident eyebrow, holding it high for effect. "Your little gossip girl confessed. Totally cracked under the pressure. Sometimes, one cross look at a person, and they fold like a cheese quesadilla."

It was Madison's turn to check on a buzzing text. "Oh, Jess is almost here, and I wanted a quick chat with Alex before heading out."

With a warm hand pressed to her back, Paco led her to Alex's private elevator, one she knew well. Hidden from sight from any onlookers in the lobby, it would quickly whisk her directly to his office. But even that didn't ease her tension or unfurl her brow.

Paco grabbed both her hands and brushed his thumbs over her knuckles. "Relax, or I'm booking you with my Botox guy, stat."

As if on command, she relaxed and a giggle burst from her lips.

"It's under control, Madison. Don't worry about a thing. And for the love of all things Henry Cavill, and I do mean all things, have fun."

Paco pecked her cheek good-bye and reached in to hit the button for her. It seemed he'd developed an annoying new habit to keep her from doing anything at all for herself.

As the elevator zoomed upward, Madison shot a text to Alex before arriving at his floor.

MADISON: *Free? It'll just take a minute.*

CHAPTER 5

MADISON

A<small>NXIOUSLY</small>, Madison stared at her cell. With no response from Alex by the time she reached the fifty-second floor, uncertainty set in. It might be a bad time to interrupt his day. Meekly, she headed for his office. There, she checked her cell again.

Nothing.

Pacing slowly in front of Alex's closed office door, she stood there, hesitant to knock. Startling her, it flew open, revealing the hardened features of a damn good-looking man as his solid body filled the door frame.

Pretending to be taken aback, Alex gave her a stern look. "Free? Seriously? I'm afraid not."

Without another word, he whisked Madison into his strong arms, lifting her off her feet to his chest in a tight embrace. His lips crushed hers, melting her with a passionate kiss. In seconds, he'd swiftly moved her into his office and against the door as he closed and locked it. His cock was hard against her belly, making her ready for him in that instant.

Whatever she had to get off her chest could wait. Not that she could remember what it was.

Pulling away just enough to lean a hand against the door, Alex drank her in with dark eyes, just a glint of boyish charm behind his devilish gaze.

Alex Drake, CEO of Drake Global Industries, was a corporate hard-ass and a fighting badass. But to her, he was the man who nearly died trying to save her brother from the RPG that took Jack's life.

Alex's magnetic eyes and suggestive smile were permanently laced with naughtiness and sin, but he was her safe place. Her hero. And at some point in the near future, her husband.

Amused, he cupped her cheek, tracing his thumb along her full bottom lip. "I'm not free, Ms. Taylor. I'm engaged. I thought we had an understanding."

She welcomed another kiss and smoothed her hands along his chest. The muscles of his sculpted body were barely a mystery beneath his well-fitted suit, much like his insistent and exceptionally large hard-on.

This man was lust personified, and she'd forever be at his mercy with his lips. His heat. His closeness. His touch. And that deep rumble from his throat that lit a wildfire across her core.

As his tender kisses made their way down her neck, he took a breath, releasing its warmth with his sincere words. "Sorry I didn't text you right away. I needed to cancel my meeting."

His thumb brushed her nipple, gently gliding across it as it peaked beneath her bra and blouse.

Her breath hitched. "You . . . canceled a meeting?"

His hand slid over the curve of her breast, down her waist, until he palmed her ass and pulled her in. "That's what happens when something comes up." He rocked his erection against her. "Change of plans, beautiful. Jess will be here in twenty minutes to pick you up, which doesn't leave much time. And you know how I like to take my time."

Do I.

His words were insistent and demanding as he growled, "Undo my pants," leaving no room for negotiation.

Lowering her hand, she lightly traced his abs beneath his shirt before moving to his slacks. She unfastened his belt, undid his zipper, and let the weight of his cock jut free and fall into her caressing hands.

His deep rumble of approval made her wet, and the bead on his tip begged for her tongue. Before she could lower herself, he said, "Take off your panties. I have to see your pussy."

Madison obeyed, sliding down the soaked panties from beneath her skirt and placing them in his hand. He pocketed them.

"Now, take off your skirt."

Biting her lip, she did, inching it slowly enough to bring a moan to his lips. She slid the soft fabric down her legs, then stepped out of it, bare from the waist down except for her peekaboo-toe heels.

"You're so wet," he said, brushing his hot mouth against hers. "Stroke yourself and give me a taste."

Madison moved two fingers down, slipping them in and out across her folds. His large hand wrapped her wrist, pulling those soaked fingers to his lips. He sucked them in and pinned her with a hungry, desperate gaze.

"I need you," she said, barely able to breathe.

"And I need you. Against the window. Facing out."

She stifled a gasp. It was broad daylight, and Alex Drake was telling her to flash the world.

Taking in the floor-to-ceiling wall of windows, she then turned back to him with a questioning glance that was met with his nod. Madison's lips lifted into a shy smile as she did what he asked.

Slowly and unsure, she stepped to the window overlooking the panoramic views of Manhattan's Central Park. She scanned about. DGI was one of the taller buildings along the skyline, but not the tallest. Most buildings were a good enough distance away that anyone looking out their window shouldn't be able to see what was going on.

Hopefully.

His hands gripped her waist, and his lips warmed her neck. "Give me another taste of you."

In the spotlight of a bright day, Madison slid her finger between the lips of her pussy, coating them with the sweetness of her dew. She tensed as he slid his hands higher to release the buttons of her blouse.

"*Shh*," he whispered, and even with her heart thundering, she relaxed. "Let me have this. Have you."

Closing her eyes, Madison moved her soaked fingers over her shoulder and waited. Button after button, he undid her blouse, exposing her to the world as he sucked those glazed fingers into his mouth.

The front clasp of her bra released with a snap. Her nervous body jolted, calming as his hands took their time caressing the weight of her breasts. Feeling her. Freeing her. Keeping her body on unforgiving display.

Alex released her, letting her stand for a long minute as he removed a condom and sheathed himself. The tip of his cock barely touched her aching entrance.

Her body bucked back, a reflex of raw desire and need. He took her hips, holding them tightly to control everything. What she received. How she received it. Her pulse. Her breathing. Her wetness. Her want.

"Rub yourself," he said, the low rumble of his voice cascading from his chest down her spine. "That's it. Fuck yourself for me, Madison."

And she did, over and over, showing the world her dirtiest desires. Peeling back her private, most secret needs.

His powerful hands moved up again, gentle as he took her nipples into a pinch, guiding her to lean her body flush against the glass. The heat of his body pressed hard against her back. She cried out, the icy sensation flashing across her body in a wave of heat.

"I'm going to fuck you, Madison. Fuck you hard and make you mine for all the world to see. Would you like that?"

God, yes.

His lips sizzled against the nape of her neck, and she shivered. Her lips trembled as she admitted it, as much to herself as to him.

"Yes," she said softly.

"Yes," he growled against her temple.

In one full thrust, he pinned her against the glass, pumping her hard. It was frightening. And exhilarating. She shuddered, feeling herself start to tumble under his merciless pounding, forcing her climax before the world.

"Alex..."

She panted out his name, growing dizzy and delirious as he buried himself with each hardened thrust. Over and over, Alex Drake staked his claim on Madison and Manhattan at the same time.

God, that's hot.

"Come for me," he said, picking up speed until his thighs tightened, riding her to his own peak. His low words were at her ear, their tenderness a contrast to his raw, carnal plunder. "Now, Madison. *Now*."

She did, falling hard and free, giving herself over effortlessly and completely. She was his. All his.

∼

Madison smiled, feeling weightless and light as Alex reluctantly replaced her clothes before seating her on his lap. He held her, leaving kiss after kiss along her lips and cheeks.

Checking his watch, he blew out a breath of resignation. "You two will have a head start, but Mark and I will catch up as soon as we can."

Madison's cell pinged with an incoming text, and she checked it. "Jess is here."

Her pout was met with his smiling kiss. "Come on. I'll head down with you and say hi to Jess. Fife sent someone to your office to pick up your bag and purse and take them downstairs."

Their short walk to the elevator was quiet, and Madison grew more unsettled as they entered the car that would carry them down. Uncertain if this was the best time to spoil the mood, she stayed silent and still. Like there was any way that would fly in the face of Alex Drake.

Cupping both her cheeks in his warm hands, he took a long look into her eyes before asking, "What?"

It was no use denying it. "Alex, I'm . . ." She tried looking away, but his thumbs gave the gentlest nudge, softly stroking her cheek.

"You're what?"

He smiled, inviting more of whatever she had to say. He could see right through her and melt her with his gaze. Denial wouldn't work.

She clasped his hands tightly to her cheeks, nuzzling her face in the warmth of his palm. Stalling for a second, she took a breath and let it out slowly. "I'm leaving DGI."

Contemplative, he took in her words before strengthening his smile and softening his response. "You know I want you to stay. But I want something more than that. I want to talk about whatever's on your beautiful mind. Because no matter what, I want you to be happy. I *need* you to be happy."

His lips pressed hers, then again. And again. "Your happiness is about to be part of my legal obligation," he said, dropping his forehead to hers. "And I take my obligations very seriously."

She let her body mold to his, secure in his hold. It was always easy losing herself in the heat of his touch, the rise and fall of his chest and the pounding beats of his tender heart.

Another lasting kiss burned deeper between them, locking them in a moment undisturbed by the ping of their arriving floor, or the opening of elevator doors to the hidden entrance off the side of the building.

"Hey, if y'all want to head back up for a quickie, I can wait."

The sweet mountain twang of a mischievous voice rang out from the curb. Jess was a definite New Yorker, completely uninhibited in letting the passing pedestrians know what she was thinking.

Alex pulled away from the kiss but placed a loving peck on Madison's head as she waved to Jess.

As Madison took several steps to the Land Rover, Alex scooped her back against his chest. "Just where do you think you're going? You heard the lady. Jess said she can wait."

With a stern lift of her brow, Madison gave the man she loved an adoring scowl, tapping his watch as a reminder. Sinking his shoulders in response, he let out a frustrated grunt, giving in to the demands of his unrelenting schedule.

Hand in hand, they made their way to the SUV.

"Fine," he grumbled, "but you'd better make it up to me. Speaking of up . . ."

Alex tilted her chin, encouraging her to take in the full view of the sweeping building behind them. DGI was a solid wall of reflective glass, holding every secret tight within. Her shocked smile was met with his words.

"You're mine, Madison. And mine alone."

"Yours," she said softly, beaming.

Before she could move, he opened the car door with enough reluctance, she soothed his pout with another peck, then hopped in.

"Drive safe, Jess," he said before giving Madison a last kiss good-bye. He shut her door, giving the roof two taps, then stood back as he sent them off.

Madison thrust her arm out the open window, letting her hand slide across his sleeve to his fingertips as Jess pulled away.

CHAPTER 6

MADISON

As Jess drove away from the city, Madison took a relaxed breath, ready to be done with the drama of the day. A long, winding drive with Jess was just what the doctor ordered.

Jess Bishop wasn't just a friend. She understood in ways no one could, having married her own tycoon despite her repeated attempts to push him off.

Feeling free at last, Madison kicked off her shoes and told Jess about what had happened that day, purging her pent-up emotions, knowing she could count on Jess for something no one else could give her on the topic. Perspective.

"So, the way I see it, you've got three options," Jess said matter-of-factly once Madison was done. "Option number one, you can stay at DGI and ignore the gossip girls until the rumors die down. Even if that never happens."

Unimpressed, Madison folded her arms over her chest with a frown.

"Or two," Jess said pragmatically, "you ditch that whole work bullshit and become Alex Drake's little woman, never to lift a finger again in the service of others. Well, except for Alex, of course."

"Of course," Madison said. "But I like working."

"You don't have to convince me." Jess gave her a chagrined smile. "I drove hours to come to the city for a one-hour meeting with a select group of donors. Trust me, I feel you on this. I'm not here to make up your mind for you, missy. I'm doing my duty as your friend and pointing out your options."

"Fair enough. It's an interesting suggestion. But I'm not sure I could convincingly pull off a life of leisure."

Jess gave her a side glance. "From one working girl to another —and not in the lady-of-the-evening sort of way—neither do I."

Their kindred connection was just the boost Madison needed. It was wonderful not to be judged for wanting to be comfortable in her own skin.

And with Jess, explanations were never necessary. She understood Madison's need to contribute to something bigger than herself. Jess got it because she'd made her own career a priority long before her marriage.

From what Madison could glean, marrying Mark Donovan hadn't changed Jess. From everything Mark said, Jess was still the same small-town mountain girl who held her own and stood her ground. Something Madison suspected she did long before any man appeared. Not that Mark Donovan was any man. He was, after all, a billionaire.

"So, what's behind door number three?" Madison asked.

With a mischievous grin, Jess exhaled a long breath. "Three? Three would be where your give-a-fuck factor flies out the window, and you do whatever the hell you really want. Whatever makes you happy."

Madison smiled. "Alex sort of said the same thing."

"Well, I've known Alex a good long time. If anyone's a fan of the zero-fucks-given strategy, it's him. He and Mark definitely have that in common."

Madison let her gaze float out the window, following the thick evergreen tree line as Jess continued.

"You and I are cut from the same cloth, Madison. Our paths will always be paved by passion, regardless of what we do. Or where we go. Or how many men we're reputed to pleasure at once in a corporate conference room. Four, was it?"

A burst of giggles filled the SUV, and any remaining frustration Madison held on the topic evaporated. Laughing over the same situation that only a few hours ago had her backed into a corner between a watercooler and a panic attack was a welcome relief.

"Five is the word on the street," she said proudly with a shake of the head. "Yup, Madison's my name, and passion's my game. I'm gonna need a website, and I'll have to check to see if one-eight-hundred-P-A-S-S-I-O-N is available. Let the Kickstarter campaign commence!"

Madison's laughter rang out, then faded, replaced by curiosity and possibilities. "Jess, what did it take for you to start your charity? I mean, other than your passion?"

"Let's see." Jess drummed her fingers on the steering wheel. "Well, there was—and is—a whole lotta begging for money. Donations, both in financial backing and for things like supplies and office space."

"Really? Office space?"

"Sure. People who might pass on donating cash will be all in on surplus items, including unused real estate. It's a tax write-off for them and the foundation of a nonprofit for us."

Jess paused, swerving just enough to avoid the squirrel on a suicide mission, before casually proceeding.

"And that kind of door-to-door soliciting meant I had to get over my awkward shyness. Never hold back. Ask donors for exactly what I want. I put the needs of the nonprofit over my own comfort zone, and I had to recruit an army of volunteers. But at the end of the day, I'm driven, believing that if I didn't do it, no one else would."

"Do you love it?"

"Madison, I live for helping others. It's incredibly rewarding. Not a week goes by that I don't hear how I've made a difference in someone's life, straight from the mouth of the person whose life I helped change. It's not about money. I'm making a difference. And it's all I've ever wanted to do."

The road stretched on, leaving behind the noises of the city and high-rise buildings, unspooling to reveal thick dark green pines, fresh air, and the blue skies of a brightly lit, late summer's afternoon.

Jess meandered along memory lane, sharing the origins of her nonprofit work and the stories of the people her charity impacted. Tucking a leg beneath her, Madison relaxed into her seat, attentively hanging on to every one of Jess's heartwarming words for the duration of the ride.

CHAPTER 7

ALEX

Half an hour behind Jess and Madison, a black diamond Rolls Royce Phantom made its way into a different area of the countryside north of New York City. Alex was pushing the speed and agility of the vehicle well beyond that of a leisurely drive.

Usually, the car provided a luxurious yet carefree escape, an indulgent respite while moving from point A to point B. But now, its use was much more utilitarian. And frankly, would far exceed the preferences of anyone riding with him, except perhaps Paco.

It couldn't be helped. Adrenaline was slamming the gas, and Alex could only hold on for the ride. Maybe his past was catching up to him, the remnants of the former civilian operative who often lurked just below his polished surface, materializing whenever needed.

Most days, Alex was a work-hard, play-hard multibillionaire in a $12,000 suit. But not today. Now he was back into trained operative mode, observing a myriad of subtle signs that triggered his intuition to levels long ago suppressed, but never fully abandoned.

The excessive speed only spiked his pulse and heightened his instincts, but some level of solace would await him at his destination. He was needed, and whatever wisdom he could impart would be well received by Mark. Perhaps in return, the man could reciprocate with some sage advice on Alex's own perplexing issues at hand.

Not quite two hours outside of Manhattan and closing in on the Hudson, Alex veered off onto a nondescript wooded country road with no street signs and no asphalt.

The road slowly narrowed to a rugged dirt trail, intentionally giving the *you must be fucking lost* vibe to anyone who happened upon it.

But Alex was far from lost. On the contrary, he was safe and sound, and in a strange way felt as if he were heading home.

The road came to a dead end at a cinder-block wall twelve feet high with an intimidating towering metal gate. A DGI swipe panel greeted him, and Alex was ready, hovering his access card across it.

The gate opened, letting his car proceed through before closing behind. A short distance away was a plain building in the middle of a field. At the side of the building, another panel awaited him, and his swipe opened a steel garage door easily two cars wide.

The garage was empty at the moment, but the high shine of Mark's familiar dark-sapphire Bentley would be there soon. Alex parked and then headed inside, unconcerned at leaving his cell phone behind in his car.

The highly customized Sensitive Compartmented Information Facility, or SCIF, would block all cell phone service and any other radio frequencies. The only phone or internet access was completely reliant on a web of long-line communication cables buried deep within the ground below.

With the building impenetrable to electronic surveillance and data leaks, bringing his phone inside would be pointless unless he wanted to snap a selfie.

Again, Alex swiped his access card along a panel in the wall, and the heavy military-grade security door gave a loud clank as it unbolted, then swung open to the interior of the building. A smile formed as he stepped through. Once he reached the main control room, he made the necessary preparations—turning on the lights, setting up controls for the ready, and unpacking a well-used deck of cards.

He took a seat, and within minutes, the door opened again.

Lounging comfortably in a luxurious chair at a small round executive table as Mark walked in, Alex said, "Good to know your memory isn't slipping. Or did you have to make a few U-turns?"

Expertly, he shuffled, then flipped a few cards in succession. Mark took his own seat as Alex silently lipped the face value of each card before revealing it—a parlor trick they shared in common. Playing cards helped pass the time during extended surveillance missions or while stuck in a no-cell zone.

Mark scooted his executive leather chair closer. "No U-turns. I might occasionally misplace my key fob, but I could drive here blindfolded."

Mark had called this meeting, but without words, Alex understood. Something was weighing on his friend's mind. Something heavy. Something that required a secure facility away from the office and couldn't be discussed by phone.

Conclusion? Cards would be needed.

The game was perfect. They could talk through anything while playing, letting their right-brain thinking work effortlessly in the background and in tandem with their left-brain rationale.

Blackjack was out. They were both so adept at counting cards, a game of twenty-one might as well be played with the cards facing up.

Alex dealt, skillfully flicking two cards to each of them before laying several between them, face up, to commence the game. Each had small stacks of chips ready and waiting, and the men scooped up their hands, wearing their game faces with knowing grins.

"And don't forget about the pantry," Alex said. "The prepper stash has plenty of Jefferson's Ocean and those wasabi almonds you love."

Without warning, Mark slapped his cards on the table. "I can't possibly play on an empty stomach."

Grinning, both men abandoned their cards to free up their hands for whatever booty they would bring back with them. Briskly, they made their way down the hall.

Both walls were lined with handguns, rifles, an occasional semi-automatic, and an assortment of knives, all neatly held in place with custom-fitted fasteners that not only kept the items secured, but managed to provide an elegant display of the lethal weapons.

The hall ended at an expansive walk-in pantry, filled with chrome shelves stocked with a balanced assortment of fine and junk foods, sodas, liquor, and glass tanks of water.

Looting through the pretzels and chips, Alex checked his watch. "Madison and Jess should be at your cabin in about two and a half hours. We won't be far behind with the baby out back."

The *baby* referred to Alex's Sikorsky S76-D executive helicopter, whose custody he and Mark enthusiastically shared.

With his stash pocketed, Alex poured two bourbons, then handed a lowball to Mark.

"To marriage," Mark said, holding his own glass high.

"To marriage." Alex gave the waiting glass a clink and took a sip from his, breathing out the warmth of the smooth spirits in a long *ahh* of a breath.

Once Mark crammed wasabi almonds in one pocket and M&Ms in another, they were set. Nearly set. Both men snagged a Snickers, and Alex grabbed the bottle of Jefferson's before they headed back to the cards. At the table, they settled again into their chairs and refocused on the game.

"What's on your mind?" Alex asked, peering over the cards he held.

Mark tossed a few chips to the center of the table before answering. "I've landed this deal. A hundred-million-dollar deal."

Alex let out a long, impressed whistle but didn't say a word.

"They even wired me a million bucks up front just to sit down and chat."

"Well, we're sitting and chatting. Where the hell's my cool mil?"

Even with Alex's smartass remark, Mark would only return an unenthusiastic smirk. Staring blankly, he folded, giving up that round to free up his hands to grip the half-filled glass. Mark studied it but didn't sip. Instead, he swirled the glass, coating the amber liquid up its walls, watching the lazy legs trail down the sides.

"It's the perfect deal. Perfect," he said with a frown. Huffing, he took a sip. "Too perfect. And I feel crazy questioning it, but my hackles are up. I'm right back in full-on operative mode, and I have no idea why."

With a slow shake of his head, Mark seemed to be wrestling for the right words. He sipped again as if it was his only option. Or possibly because it couldn't hurt.

Alex reshuffled the deck but didn't deal another hand. Patiently, he bided his time.

Finally, Mark met his eyes. "Just to satisfy my own curiosity, I tried tracing that million-dollar direct deposit. And . . ." He paused with an unsettled look. "I couldn't. And this is me saying that." The man who built a global empire by tracing the untraceable.

"How's that possible?" Alex asked aloud but almost to himself.

It was impossible. Mark's company wasn't one of the best. It was *the* best at tracking money movements for a range of government agencies and private corporations. And when they were sure no one would else would ever know it, they tracked money at DGI's request as well.

Excelsior/Centurion didn't stop there. They could discover the real sponsors behind suspicious activities of any funds movements imaginable. And yet, here sat a genius, thrown off by a million dollars that had materialized out of thin air.

Alex set the cards aside, opting to wrap his hand around his own bourbon. "Sounds like someone knows how to cover their tracks. Let's start at the beginning. What do they want?"

"That's just it. All they want is to meet. One-on-one. And when I say one-on-one, I don't mean company to company. I mean just me and one of them—whoever *them* is."

"I see why you're nervous. It feels like—"

"A setup. Or an execution. God knows, I've got just as many enemies as friends."

"Don't be ridiculous." Alex scoffed. "We all know I'm your only friend."

Mark ignored Alex's grin and pressed on. "On a deal this big, I'd expect a small entourage on both sides, with lawyers and accountants up the ying-yang. Nondisclosure agreements as thick as the Bible."

"So would I."

"The money was wired specifically for a meeting with me. Just me. Anywhere I want. Literally anywhere in the world. They just need a location before midnight, and the meeting will happen at two p.m. local time wherever I select, the next day."

Alex lifted an intrigued brow. "So you're skeptical, yet interested."

Mark nodded. "Skeptical? Yes. And idiotically interested? Of course. How could I not be? A hundred million dollars is a big fucking carrot. What do I say . . . a date sounds fun but I'm washing my hair?"

Alex speculated aloud. "You told them you'd think about it?"

Mark lowered his gaze.

"Ah. You agreed to meet."

Mark pointed an accusatory finger his way. "You would too!"

Nodding, Alex agreed. "I would."

"On top of everything else, they only send emails. No calls."

"Smart. Phones are too easy to trace."

"Exactly. With email, each transmission is hitting false nodes, and not just a few. Literally hundreds upon hundreds. The emails could be coming from anywhere. From anyone. I don't know if I'm dealing with a head of state, someone on the dark web, or a crazy-genius twelve-year-old in his mama's basement." Mark popped a few almonds into his mouth, deep in thought as he chewed. "I know I'm being played, but with that much money on the table, I'd be insane to turn down a meeting."

"Look, your paranoia might be wrapped up in a conspiracy deep-fried in insanity, but your instincts are solid. They've saved your ass and the asses of your teammates too many times to discount them. They're always spot-on, like a sixth fucking sense." Unwrapping his chocolate bar, Alex pointed it at Mark. "Got anything else?"

"Yeah, their name. But a name that's absolutely clean of any cyber footprint. Not even the pretense of a backstory. A ghost."

Mark downed the rest of his drink and helped himself to another pour as Alex sat up, giving Mark a curious look as he ripped open his bag of M&Ms.

With a sufficient amount of suspense between them, Alex asked, "So . . . what's the name?"

"Jordan Stone." Mark tossed out the name and refreshed both drinks. It wasn't until he looked up that he found Alex's expression had dropped. "What? You know this guy?"

Suddenly cold, Alex felt the blood drain from his face. "Maybe," he muttered, clenching his jaw.

He didn't sip this time. He tossed back the contents of his glass and stared off. Mark let him go for a minute.

When warmth returned to his cheeks, Alex filled with a spark, springing back from his thoughts with a vengeance.

"You're taking the meeting," he said firmly.

Mark sat up straighter. "I am?"

"You are. Send them an email." Pointing to the console at the other end of the room, Alex nudged Mark to grab a computer where communications were enabled through a deeply buried land line. "They want to see an untraceable email, they've come to the right fucking spot."

Both men stood and moved to their own systems, each set up at either side of the room, logging on with an insert of their access cards.

Mark opened an email, posturing his fingers, ready to type. "Okay, what do I say?"

Smiling, but not looking at him, Alex began his own feverish typing. "Tell them you're ready to meet. Right here. Give them our coordinates. Tell them they've got one hour, or you're gone. Let's see just how close this ghost is."

But Mark didn't type a word. Waiting for an explanation, he did nothing but sit quietly and level Alex with a heavy stare. His reticence wasn't surprising.

Alex knew that what he was saying was madness. Giving up the position of a secured facility that had for the better part of a decade remained off the grid? Absolute fucking madness.

Without otherwise acknowledging his friend, Alex began to speak. "You know my history. My loss."

Mark nodded as he sat back in his chair. "Yes," he said solemnly, his voice soft. "Madison's brother, Jack."

Instantly, Alex stopped typing. "It wasn't about the mission. There was something about it that was . . . different. Strange."

"Strange how?"

Struggling for the right words, Alex finally blew out a frustrated breath. "I don't know. The way I was . . . recruited. And the way you're being lured. It's familiar. Has the same look and feel as . . ."

"As what?"

"As the person who recruited me. The same one who vanished without a fucking trace. The person at the bottom of everything." Alex resumed typing as he let out a huff. "Jordan Stone."

PART II
THE PAST

CHAPTER 8

JORDAN

Over ten years earlier – Southern California

Jordan Stone pulled her brand-new Mercedes convertible to the curb in front of a run-down two-story house. The custom red paint of her car bore a striking resemblance to her favorite shade of lipstick, making her car stand out like a sore thumb in the neighborhood that wished with all its might it could be considered middle class.

The dilapidated home looked like a frat house in the middle of an otherwise quaint street in the suburban neighborhood. Blinking through her disbelief, Jordan flipped open her moleskin notepad to double-check the address, disappointed to find the street name and number were indeed correct.

Drake Cable and Comm had all the sophistication and grandeur of a heaping pile of horseshit. At least most garage startups could mow their lawns.

Fuck me.

Once again, Jordan had managed to draw the shortest goddamn straw, though she never actually held the power to pull the straws herself. But at the end of the day, it didn't matter. She had one job to do, and just like FedEx, she'd deliver.

Her assignments were strategic and precise. The recruiters, much like the recruits, were never random. If Jordan had been selected, she knew what it meant.

The targeted recruit had to be male, under thirty, hardworking, unattached, and with enough *fuck authority* in him to make waves but never attract the wrong kind of attention.

Bribes were easy, but they were out. MICE incentives would go nowhere with a man like this because *money*, *ideology*, *coercion*, and *ego* couldn't lure this man. The only way her handlers could know that for sure was if they'd already tried.

But with her ass parked on his street, she had enough presence of mind to know the man met the two must-haves warranting a visit from Jordan Stone.

First, he was critical. An essential cog in some game-changing mission's wheel, and nobody else would do.

And second, he had a hard-core vice—sex—which just happened to be Jordan's specialty. She could set a honey trap like no other, with an impressive and disturbingly high track record for sealing the deal by tapping into a man's filthy desires and giving him everything he craved. For a price.

With a quick flip of the visor, she examined her reflection, taking in her dark hair and big, dark eyes that could come from anywhere. Men loved an exotic look they couldn't exactly pin down.

Jordan's fluency spanned seven languages, with enough of an understanding of a dozen others that she could blend into the woodwork wherever she went.

Time and time again, men called her striking, and she could pass for any range of ethnicities. Latin or Middle Eastern. With the right makeup, some blend of Asian or Indian. And all too frequently, Eastern Bloc.

With all that goodness wrapped up in a body that wouldn't quit and a nonexistent gag reflex, she'd managed to find her perfect line of work, commanding an under-the-table salary that kept her deliriously comfortable in the lifestyle she'd very much become accustomed to.

On days like this without knowing exactly what to expect, she kept her hair pulled back, protectively secured in a bun at her nape. Today, her eye makeup was smoky, but not overdone, but her lips needed refreshing.

From the center console, she reached past the subcompact Glock to grab her signature dark-cherry lip gloss, smearing the line just a smidge over the rim of her DSLs. The look exaggerated their fullness, like she'd just sucked a man dry and was hungry for more. Admiring her *fuck me at will* glamour shot, she flipped the visor closed and sighed before she climbed out of the car.

The cobblestone path to the front door was a bitch on her thousand-dollar heels, but she donned a smile, nonetheless. With her hand postured to knock, she lowered it, hearing loud voices and high-pitched giggling coming from somewhere around the side of the house.

After picking her way through the unkempt grass around the house, she found her day was looking up. The apparent sorority kegger by the pool was abundant with beer, string-bikini butts, and too many bouncing breasts to accurately count. Some were covered but most were not, with the gorgeous women opting to go *au naturel* in the glowing California sun.

Always a fan of the water, Jordan found herself perking up at the idea of a party by the pool.

When someone slapped a cold beer in her hand, she accepted graciously, enjoying a long, slow sip. Her semi-sheer white blouse and skin-tight black pencil skirt didn't exactly help her blend in, but it wasn't like anyone was enforcing a dress code.

She took her time heading into the house through the open

sliding glass door. Whatever douchebag she needed to recruit could wait. Jordan was too busy soaking in the semi-nude bodies of every woman around her.

Eventually, and only after letting a topless woman lead the way, she finally entered the home of what had to be the hero of frat houses across America. His round-the-clock partying explained the empty bottles of booze, candy dishes of condoms, and strategically placed dildos. Apparently, dinner around here came with a floor show.

An attractive blonde, adjusting her string bikini top, teased Jordan with a smile. It was enough of an invitation for Jordan to slide a hand along the woman's shoulder. And the loud music gave Jordan the perfect excuse to lean close to the buxom blonde's ear.

"I'm looking for Jack."

Blankly, the woman stared back, so Jordan smoothed her hand to a more attentive caress.

"The guy who lives here."

"Upstairs," the blonde replied, disappointment dragging down her smile. "But if you change your mind about him, I'll be right here."

Softly, Jordan's lips brushed the woman's ear. "I'll be back," she said, giving her earlobe a seductive suck before leaving it with a terse bite.

Satisfied at her new playmate's peaked nipples, she brushed the nearest breast with the cold bottle of beer, then handed it to her before heading upstairs.

Jordan found most of the bedrooms wide open, despite the sleeping or debauchery going on inside. But it was the double doors of what had to be the master bedroom down the hall that caught her interest.

Target acquired.

Trying the handle, she found the door was locked. She examined the builder-grade hardware, recognizing the miniscule hole in the center of the knob.

Whisking a thin bobby pin from her bun, she shoved it in, easily releasing the lock. Silently, she slipped inside, enjoying what had to be the matinee.

Two women, easily mistaken for twins, had apparently flipped a coin to decide which end of the man each would be riding.

The first—the one Jordan mentally nicknamed Reverse Cowgirl—got tails and was thrusting vigorously across the naked man's cock. The other—not doing anything particularly worthy of a nickname—held a steady pace grinding across the man's mouth.

With her eyes wide and her panties soaked, Jordan leaned against the now closed door. Joining the ménage was enticing. And the surest way to lose a new recruit.

Putting out before the ink was dry was the fastest way to tank a deal. When men couldn't get what they wanted, they were attentive. Obsessive. Willing.

Appetizers were totally on the table. But a full meal of Jordan Stone? That would remain a promise for the future, and the surest way to keep her marks so very hungry for more.

With Cowgirl picking up her pace, things seemed to be wrapping up. Or so Jordan thought. Not missing a beat, the woman stretched toward the nightstand, reaching for the leather wallet resting there.

Seems a bit late for a condom.

Amused, Jordan watched as the woman tugged out a thick wad of cash. Sweetly, Jordan spoke. "I'm not sure that belongs to you."

Both women jumped from their respective positions, quickly slipping on their ridiculously small bikinis in a misguided effort to escape with a modicum of decency. But just barely.

The man, still rock hard, wiped his face before propping up on his elbow.

"I'm not sure what's going on, but looks like a seat just opened up." His voice was groggy and deep, and he looked Jordan up and down with a decidedly diabolical grin. The kind that had *sucker* written all over it.

Jordan opened the door wide, letting the uninteresting one escape. But as Cowgirl tried following, Jordan slammed it shut, slinking back to lean against it.

"Bitch, get out of my way."

Jordan took a moment, looking the girl up and down. "Like I said, I'm not sure that belongs to you."

They both eyed the wad of twenties held tight in her hand.

Snarling, the blonde fisted the money in front of her. "Yeah? Well, it's mine now."

Her feeble swing at Jordan backfired, giving her the opportunity to grab the girl's arm and flip her around, pinning her hand high against her back.

"Fucking bitch, get off me!"

Impressed, Jordan smiled to find her still clinging to the wad of cash. In an unchallenged move, she forced Cowgirl forward onto the bed.

With her target enjoying the action, Jordan took center stage in the girl-on-girl show. As she pouted her plump lips, she dragged the girl's fist down to the top of her ass, taking a second to imagine sliding her tongue through the crevice encasing the thong.

Captured in Jordan's grip, Cowgirl tried to struggle as Jordan skimmed her fingernail down her spine. At the base of her butt, Jordan playfully snapped the thong, causing her captive to squeal. A few moves later, she'd lassoed the stretchy bikini bottom around the woman's wrists like a scrunchy, immobilizing her on the spot.

"Goddammit, let me out of this!"

It took a small amount of effort for Jordan to wiggle the cash free. With it, she took a seat on the opposite side of the bed, setting the cash on her thigh.

"I believe this is yours." She took his hand and placed it on the small stack of twenties, pressing his grip firmly to her thigh. Directing his eyes, she glanced at the open wallet discarded on the floor.

He inched his fingers around the money, slowly pulling his hand from her leg. "Thanks," he said, hopping off the bed but not bothering to get dressed. He took a look at the woman hogtied in place.

Jordan smiled. "The trick is in the knot. If the little thief moves too much, she'll feel the excruciating sting of one hell of a stem-to-stern wedgie."

Straining to turn her head, Cowgirl sweetened her tone from minutes ago, doing her piss-poor best at being persuasive. "Look, you had a great time. I didn't think you'd miss it. J-just let me outta here, okay?"

"Jesus," the muscular man said, blowing out a breath. He couldn't take his eyes off the knot. "How the fuck do I undo this?" In an innocent move for such a sexy man, he scratched his head, with an inquisitive helplessness to his almost boyish gaze.

He's sweet.

Taunting him, Jordan handed him a challenge. "Well, if you must. You'll probably have to cut it." Then more deviously, she said, "Or tear it . . . if you can."

Her dare was enough. Smacking the jiggliest part of Cowgirl's ass, he scolded her.

"Now, I'm going to let you go, but only so you can get on the straight and narrow. Hmm . . ." Looking down at his wilting shaft, he smiled. "Well, at least get on the straight, because I'm far from narrow."

Leaning down, he softly suggested, "Hold still."

It was good advice, and she sucked in a breath. With the

bikini bottom in both hands, he ripped it apart and tossed it away.

Free, Cowgirl jumped up and scurried out of the room, slamming the door as hard as possible behind her. Alex moved his attention back to Jordan, now splayed across his bed.

Grinning seductively, Jordan said, "She seems nice."

CHAPTER 9

ALEX

Without a way of knowing who this woman was or why she was making herself comfortable on his bed, the man stood, his willy flying free as he smiled, patiently waiting for an explanation.

"You must be Jack."

Fuck me.

And just like that, the party was over. It didn't matter that her giggle was spellbinding, and her lips were everything his cock ever wanted. Whoever she was, he wasn't interested.

He huffed out an irritated laugh. "And you must not know me at all if you're calling me that. What are you, some sort of banker or site inspector or something? Did I miss dotting an *i* on the three-hundred-page document where I signed away my house, car, and firstborn to the bank?"

Pulling on his jeans, he instantly regretted his tone as she shifted just enough to give him a glimpse of something enticingly red beneath her skirt.

His irritation wasn't about his name. Sure, he hated it. His easy-breezy middle name was convenient, often the focus of telemarketers, a few members of his deliberately distant family, and a revolving door of apathetic attorneys.

The name had also been his dad's, which was the extent he knew about the man, other than the guy's credit was good. It served its purpose, giving him enough of a start in the absence of an actual father.

The name was good enough for business documents and legal representation, but being called it was never preferred. Ever. For all the pomp and circumstance of his given name, Alexander Jackson Drake went by a simple moniker.

"My apologies, Mr. Drake," she said, diplomatically backpedaling as she licked her lips. "From the looks of this place, perhaps you prefer Big Daddy Plumber."

He couldn't hold back a small grin.

"What do you prefer I call you?" she asked, her tone alluring and hypnotic.

Everything in his body said he was being played. Well, everything but his cock. As much as he wanted to tell her to fuck off, his dick had other plans.

"AJ." He turned away, scanning the mirror to check his appearance. Clean shaven but disheveled, he figured it would do. Catching her eye in the reflection, he asked, "And you are?"

"Jordan. Jordan Stone. And I'll only take an hour of your time."

Sales talk. Best dick deflater ever.

"Well, Jordan, Jordan Stone, did we have an appointment? If so, we'll have to reschedule because I'm fully committed today."

Impatient, he headed for the door, opening it wide and waiting. Yet, there she sat, far from deterred. Unconcerned, she slipped off her shoes, letting the stilettos fall to the floor.

"No, you're not. They left." Stretching across the bed, she looked up at him through the thick lashes of a smoking-hot woman in heat. "You're all mine."

He stayed close to the door, not entirely trusting himself with the woman eyeing him like a juicy steak. "Look, whatever it is you're selling, I'm not interested."

With effortless ease, she removed the remaining pins from her hair, letting the lush locks cascade freely down her shoulder and across her breast. "Oh, I'm not selling, AJ. I'm buying. Your products. Your services. You."

"Me?" he asked, covering his curiosity with a weak attempt at indignity.

"Only in the dirtiest way possible," she said with a promising tone that charged straight to his dick. "Why don't you close the door and see if my lips can . . . convince you?"

Not needing any more convincing, Alex was sure and decisive as he slammed the door shut.

CHAPTER 10

JACK

The same day – Newburgh, New York

As approaching footsteps echoed from every wall of the vast room, Jack Taylor heard the voice that went with them booming with a confident authority that was warm and friendly as he chatted with his escort. A lowly cadet, Jack remained locked in place, used to the perpetual state of standing at attention. It had become second nature over the past four years.

His West Point training ensured his eyes didn't move, remaining fixed on an imagined point far away. It was tempting to take in the view overlooking the blue Hudson River, or the vintage military paintings that lined the walls. Or to glance at whomever happened to be commanding his attention. But he waited, not meeting the man's gaze, whoever he might be.

"You must be Jack." A tall man with salt-and-pepper hair came to a halt in front of the first-class cadet, a senior by civilian university standards.

"Yes, sir. Jack Taylor. Nice to meet you, sir."

Remaining at attention, he waited for an *at ease* before

relaxing his lifted chest or locked arms. After all this time, old habits would die hard.

Apparently knowing this, the gentleman went ahead and gave him permission to relax. "At ease, young man."

"Thank you, sir."

Jack understood the visitor to be retired, but a lieutenant general, nonetheless. And once such upper-echelon titles are achieved, retired or not, they're never willingly relinquished, even after retirement from the military.

Why a man of his stature would be meeting with him, Jack didn't know. But the reason had to be good. Visits like this were unheard of unless the parties happened to be related. With his father being a retired gunnery sergeant, Jack knew his own relations were definitely on the opposite end of the social spectrum.

"Great to meet you, Jack. My name is Jordan Stone, and I've heard a hell of a lot about you."

Though the statement took Jack by surprise, he didn't ask any of the many questions running through his mind. What he was meant to know, Mr. Stone would undoubtedly get to.

Jordan Stone took a chair at a round table kitty-corner from where Jack stood and offered him a seat. The table that normally seated six instantly became cozy and comfortable. Somehow, Jack suspected this man harnessed that power naturally, making everyone he met feel vital and appreciated.

"I'm glad we could make this meeting happen, since I'll be returning to the Pentagon this evening."

Attentive, Jack found himself admiring the man. His well-fitted dark gray suit was perfectly rounded out with a red, blue, and silver regimental tie. The pin on his lapel featured a compass rose, adding a handsome elegance to his outfit.

The man could be a congressman. Or a multimillionaire. The strength and power emanating from him was enough to make or break people, armies, or whole countries, yet he kept it wrapped tightly in a quiet commanding presence and easy smile.

"Yes, sir. I appreciate that you have a very busy schedule. The commandant said you needed to speak with me about my future." Jack's questioning tone was deliberate, as he was dying to know what an important man like this might want.

"Jack, I'm gonna cut to the chase. We've been watching you since you arrived at the academy. Top scores in every subject. Impressive performance with weapons and hand-to-hand combat. But what really got our attention is the paper you presented."

"My paper? The one on securing a tactical advantage on the war front?" It wasn't rocket science. To Jack, his conclusions were simple and obvious.

"What can I say? Your idea has a fan base, and we'd like to put it to the test."

Surprised, Jack lifted a brow. "A live mission? With my strategy?"

"Well, there's a little more to it than that. But everything we're going to discuss will be strictly *need to know*. We can discuss the details once we've upgraded your security clearance, but nothing about this can be disclosed. Not to family or friends. And by your looks, I'm sure you're popular with the ladies, but no pillow talk to impress. Can we count on you?"

Despite a pitch that felt a little too "ask not what your country can do for you," it tugged at every sense of military loyalty and patriotism in Jack's soul.

Not needing to think it over, he simply said, "Yes, sir."

The hand Mr. Stone laid on his shoulder felt proud. Paternal. "I'm not just asking if we can use your idea or if you'd like to play along, Jack. I'm talking about a covert mission with you leading the charge. American lives are depending on this. Depending on you. If you have any reservations, you can turn me down. But we have a mission that can't wait, and I need your answer now. Jack, are you in?"

There was no hesitation. No need for a second thought. Nothing would keep him from this once-in-a-lifetime opportunity. It would forever change the course of his life—Jack could feel it.

"Absolutely, sir. I'm all in."

CHAPTER 11

PACO

The same day – US Territory of Puerto Rico

STAFF SERGEANT PACO ROBLES strolled out of the Fort Buchanan Education Center into a wall of hot, humid air that always took a second to adjust to after the comfort of an air-conditioned room.

Having grown up on the sun-drenched island, Paco was used to the conditions. With the exception of boot camp, he'd spent every day enjoying an ocean-front life close to the equator.

One step out the door and intense sunlight flooded his face, causing him to squint as he adjusted to the brightness of the day. And despite his thick battle-dress uniform smothering his skin, his two-percent body fat prevented him from ever breaking a sweat. To him, ninety-eight degrees was nothing. Just another day in the life on an island.

Today, he'd taken his second crack at the Defense Language Aptitude Battery, or DLAB, but he didn't consider it a second chance.

The ninety-minute assessment gauged one's aptitude for picking up languages. In theory, with a higher score came greater potential for the test taker to master increasingly complex languages. For a man seeking action and adventure away from his island home, only the highest of scores would do.

The Department of Defense's home-grown test was a web of complete insanity, comprised entirely of made-up words, nonexistent phrases, and strings of noises that made no sense at all. Arrogant as ever, Paco considered the challenge a piece of cake.

He wasn't discounting the importance of the results. Quite the opposite. This test would be the determining factor for coveted opportunities in a high-paced linguistic training program, and Paco wanted in.

He understood the expectations. Training in romance languages like the Spanish he grew up with required the lowest marks. Russian, Punjabi, and Croatian needed scores in the mid-level range. For three types of Arabic, as well as Chinese and Korean, the assignments were a golden ticket to a new life and would require the highest of grades.

When Paco completed his first test, he knew his results would be high, but a perfect score was unexpected. Prideful and arrogant, he accepted the news without a lick of modesty. His superiors rejected the score and demanded a retake.

Ecstatic at another chance to show off his instant mastery of nonexistent languages, Paco welcomed the challenge. That wasn't just his ego leading the charge. He knew what they all knew. He was getting all the right sorts of attention to change the trajectory of his life.

Today was the retest. He'd bet his last ten dollars before payday, his well-earned stripes, and his left nut, that he'd aced it once again.

Knowing round two was in the bag should have eased him into a leisurely rest of the day. His future was shaping up. Promise was in the air. But so was something else. An unnerving feeling. A sense he couldn't shake. A tension in the air.

Street-fighter instincts that shaped him in his youth had molded him into a deft predator. As such, he was rarely the target. So, why the fuck were his hackles up and his heart pounding out of his chest, like some goddamned bunny about to be snatched up by a hawk?

He knew why.

He was the prey. Or, at least, he was being watched like one.

Surrounded by several buildings, he scanned the perimeter, but no one was keeping an eye on him from any of the industrial windows.

Several cars were parked close by, all without occupants. At this time of day, the lunch-goers were already back in their offices, and the early birds would start heading out in another two hours or so. So, why in the ninety-eight-degree heat with ninety percent humidity was there a man standing on the sidewalk, wearing a bright linen suit?

The man wasn't doing anything particularly suspicious. Just standing there wearing some expensive-looking glasses and a baby-blue tie knotted at his neck. As he was, holding a casual pose with his hands pocketed, anyone walking by might think he wasn't doing anything at all.

But that was just it. On a military installation in this unforgiving heat, who just stands? Stands and stares?

Not one to run from his shadow, Paco took a keen interest in testing his theory.

The staff sergeant secured his government-issued cap and straightened his battle-dress uniform, then headed a few buildings over. In a move that felt strange even to him, he walked around a corner, then ducked behind it, crouching down.

Slowly, he moved his head enough to peek past the corner at where he'd just come from, but there was no one in sight. Wondering how the man had disappeared so quickly, Paco remained where he was, waiting.

With nothing happening and the guy gone, why did he need to keep his position? Hell, even if no one was watching him before, anyone who saw him now would sure as hell be watching him.

He set aside his doubt. *I'm never wrong.*

Eager to enjoy the few remaining hours of the rest of his day to hit the beach before sunset for once, he glanced about.

Nada. Not a fucking thing going on other than him getting dangerously close to failing to report for duty because he needed to waste more time playing chase with a goddamned ghost.

Lamest game of hide and seek ever.

Finally fed up with skulking about and feeling like the village idiot, Paco stood up, dusted off his uniform, and took several steps out in the open, ready to get back to work.

"Staff Sergeant Robles?"

The man's voice wasn't exactly booming. More like blithe and playful.

Paco whipped to the right, now facing the suited man, who seemed to have made himself comfortable leaning against the wall. Just around the corner from where Paco had been crouching. Had he peeked his head around the corner just a bit more, he would have seen him.

Eyeing the guy, Paco had the unsettling suspicion that this man, whoever he was, had known Paco was there the entire time. Hiding behind the corner. In all his idiotic glory.

Shit.

Despite the wave of irritation that nearly forced a *fuck* from his lips, he kept his mouth buttoned up, not knowing exactly who he was dealing with.

With a second and much closer glance at the man, Paco took him all in. From the bright white of his cocky smile to the sunglasses Paco imagined would cost two months' of his salary, the man was everything Paco wanted to be when he grew up. *This* was his vision of the future.

Hopefully, this wasn't some guy about to snuff out his dreams, relaying some trumped-up bullshit message like *we don't care how high you score or how many times you test, you're not getting in.*

Arguing with the voices in his head, Paco stood nearly at attention. "Yes, sir, that's me." *As if he couldn't read my nametag now that he's three feet away.* "And you're following me, so what do you want?"

"I wasn't following you." The man dropped the facade and chuckled. "Well, not at first. I was waiting to speak to you, but when you raced around this building, you piqued my curiosity."

The man's smile was absolutely perfect. Too perfect.

That did it. Whatever extra money Paco managed to scrounge together was now earmarked for a set of bright white and perfectly straight veneers.

The man slid the impressive glasses off his nose, then twirled them with casual indifference by one hand. "And it's not about what I want. It's what I want to give you. A career proposition. Come on, I've got a car waiting, and the garrison commander has already approved your indefinite leave so long as you're with me."

It was Paco's turn to laugh, breaking form and folding his arms tightly over his chest. "Indefinite leave? Sure, because that's a thing. Is that why they slapped these stripes on my arm? To let me leisurely stroll away from my duties on a whim?"

Whatever his game was, Paco was done buying this guy's bullshit. Breezing past him and walking away, Paco felt the man's deceptively strong hand yank him back.

Paco's instinct was to fight, but when he whipped back, punch pulled, the man merely held up an envelope.

Paco's name was typed across the front, with the base commander's return address in the top left corner. He ripped through the sealed flap, unfolding the letter inside to read it.

Was his linguistic mastery suddenly deceiving him?

Not completely sure, he had to read the letter again. On the commander's letterhead, and with his barely dry signature, the message confirmed everything this stylish, albeit mysterious man had said.

Before Paco could respond, the man was briskly walking away. "Hey! Wait up." He hurried after the guy who moved remarkably fast, yet gave every appearance of maintaining the pace of a casual stroll.

"Come on, Robles. Move your ass." Again, the man flaunted the sunglasses Paco lusted after, sliding them down just enough to give him a scandalous wink.

When Paco caught up, he slowed his pace, mimicking the man's mannerisms by standing taller as he stepped. "Are you gonna tell me what this is about?"

"Eventually."

Paco's pout must have caught the man's eye, moving him to nudge his elbow lightly at Paco's side.

"Hey, I promise, I'm about to put a whole new life at your fingertips. It'll be up to you if you take it."

"So, you grant wishes?"

"Not exactly. You only get one wish out of me."

Confident, Paco said, "One's all I need."

They arrived at a Jaguar convertible far too upscale for most workers at the base. It had been left running, assuring Paco of a sweet, air-conditioned ride to wherever the hell they were going.

The man removed his glasses. "Here," he said, handing them over. "I saw the way you looked at them. I've got another pair in the car."

Whatever hesitation Paco had about accepting the lavish gift was fully ignored as he snatched them up. He put them on, posing just enough to get a few claps on the back from his new best friend. "Thanks."

"You got it."

"Since you know me and my commander, and I have no idea who you are, what should I call you?"

"You can call me Stone. Jordan Stone."

CHAPTER 12

ALEX

Three days later – Denver, Colorado

BETWEEN HIS FLAT tire on the way to the airport and then a flight delay, AJ still managed to arrive at the two-bedroom penthouse suite of the Four Seasons Denver a little ahead of the requested time. Hopefully, that was fine.

From his first-class flight to the awaiting chauffeured town car, his travels since leaving California had been extremely comfortable, despite his uneasiness. First flight. First real trip away from home. First deep-throat blow job that landed him here today.

Fuck, that was amazing. His jeans tightened at the thought of it.

As he walked through the expensive hotel, he assumed yanking at the front of his pants would be a no-no. Letting out a frustrated huff, he refrained from publicly adjusting himself.

His throbbing cock wasn't his fault. It's one thing for a man to press into a woman's mouth and come down her throat. It's a whole other thing to push past her tonsils while her tongue tickles your balls.

The furthest thing from AJ's mind was a business deal, no

matter what he might have said in the throes of her sword-swallowing trick. No, AJ was here for one reason and one reason alone—to get to know this woman's God-given talents better.

But had it not been for her attempt at a Guinness world record, he'd have passed, and not so politely. And that went for whatever she wanted, because it was a little vague.

Or maybe she'd laid out everything in extraordinary detail that he just hadn't heard in the afterglow of being balls deep in her mouth.

What he did hear was Four Seasons, Denver, today at six thirty p.m. And *all expenses paid*. What he didn't hear was *dress code*, realizing way too late—as in now—that he might be under-dressed.

Wearing well-worn jeans, a Gap pullover, beat-up loafers, and carrying a cheap overnight bag with a few moth holes, everything about him screamed *does not belong*. AJ half expected hotel security to escort him out.

But they didn't. Hell, they even called him *sir*. Because they obviously mistook him for the sort of man who would frequent an upscale joint like this.

The sort who wore suits from William Hunt on Saville Row and custom Antonio Meccariello shoes made in Italy, and wrote big fat fucking checks to charities, and tipped well. Bummer for them that they didn't get the memo, because it sure as hell wasn't him.

AJ was, however, a fast learner. And Jordan had seemed sure that she could teach him everything she knew in a few hours, so here he was.

Cautious, he checked and rechecked the number on the wall, ensuring he had the right room before he let himself in. He pulled the keycard from the overnight envelope. It had been sent to him with instructions on accessing his airline ticket, and a note on how to get to the hotel, as well as the room.

He swiped the keycard, surprised when the door unlocked. Still, he knocked as he slowly opened it.

"Hello?" he called out, taking a slow step inside, but there was no response. He set his bag down near the entrance, gaining the confidence to walk further in.

The lavish suite was unlike anything he'd ever seen, staged with contemporary furnishings and dozens of fresh roses the color of buttercream frosting. For reasons he couldn't fathom, he leaned in and took a long sniff, appreciating their sweet perfume. They brightened the room and made him feel cozy and at home. Not at *his* home, but at home, nonetheless.

For a few minutes, he took in the view, then headed toward what he presumed was the master bedroom, practically tiptoeing across the suite wherever he moved. In the center of the biggest bed he'd ever seen was a note, weighed down by a black leather riding crop.

A wide smile spread across his face. *Fuck, she's sexy.* He unfolded it.

> *Take a shower.*
> *I'll be back.*

As she instructed, he made his way to the master bath, stripped, and showered, washing away the grime of the day as well as the life he'd known.

The luxurious bathroom was aglow with the natural light of early evening in Colorado, casting the walls in crisp golds and rich oranges. Glass and stone fixtures gave way to the Rocky Mountain sunset flooding through the floor-to-ceiling windows on the sixteenth-floor.

The experience was alluring and exquisite, as much as it had to be temporary and fleeting. This sure as hell hadn't been his life —where bathrooms came with nicer toiletries than he'd ever seen, plush robes, and fuzzy slippers, where hot water somehow managed to feel and taste soothing and soft . . . and expensive—but it was the life AJ wanted. And in the deepest part of his soul, this was the life he vowed to have.

AJ lost himself in the view. If the sun never set, he'd probably stare at it forever.

I could get used to this.

He soaked it all in, ignoring the Debbie Downer voice in his head that told him none of this was real. Once-in-a-lifetime deals didn't exist, and even if they did, they wouldn't for a guy like him.

Shower done and feeling refreshed, he grabbed a towel, bringing its fluffiness to his nose for a whiff. It was then that he realized his pile of clothes seemed to have vanished.

What the . . .

Still wet with water dripping from his hair and chest, he wrapped the oversize towel around his waist and opened the door.

There lay Jordan, lusciously long-legged Jordan, sprawled in the center of the bed. Which seemed to be her natural habitat.

No complaints.

Her lacy black bra left absolutely nothing to the imagination, and her matching G-string was barely there. But what stood out for AJ was her bright red stilettos. They were the hottest shoes he'd ever seen, and he'd be damned if those weren't staying on the entire time.

"AJ. So good to see you again."

Her raspy voice was like a vise grip to his cock, which tented the soft cotton bath sheet as he stood before her.

"Hi," he said like an adolescent idiot, unable to think of another thing to say to this goddess before him. His attempt at a predatory stroll toward her was juvenile and awkward. When he neared, he bent a knee, ready to set it on the side of the bed.

"No." Her voice was commanding, stopping him in his tracks. "You're not ready."

Uncomfortable and uncertain, he paused. Her gaze washed

over his body, as if memorizing every line. No woman had ever studied him like that. Like she was measuring him up. Taking a tally. Making decisions.

Opting to follow the instincts of a man in his early twenties, he flexed a muscle or two. It spurred her smile . . . maybe in approval. Maybe not. He smiled warmly in return.

Did he need her approval? The longer she looked, the more he did. In the long moments filled with the distance between them, he became consumed. He had to please her—give in to anything and everything she desired.

"We have a deal, AJ, and I plan to deliver."

Fuck yeah, they had a deal. A truck filled with cash. Being his own boss. A clothing allowance. Topped by the delectable Jordan Stone promising him the lesson of a lifetime.

In one night, she'd guaranteed to teach him how to never be manipulated by a woman again.

Jordan Stone had managed to nail his Achilles heel. He'd nearly been taken for three hundred bucks a few days ago. It was a weakness, one he intended to shield in chain mail.

And it was important to him. How she knew that, he didn't know, but she did. And he was game. Having his cake and eating her too? It was a win-fucking-win.

So, here he stood, right next to the bed. Waiting. Eager. And ten seconds from humping the bedpost if she didn't get on with it.

"Remove your towel and hand me my crop."

He took a moment before complying. The crop was seductive in her hand. She licked her lips, then let the tip of the crop barely touch his sensitive balls.

His head dropped back as he let out a breathy, "*Ahhhh*."

A low moan erupted from deep within his chest as the crop continued upward, tracing a lazy line around his shaft. When it reached the tip, it moved away. Without warning, she struck his outer thigh.

"Ow, fuck," he said, scowling as he jumped back out of reach.

"Now that I have your attention, here's how this works. You're going to listen to me and do exactly as I ask. If you don't, I'll—" She lifted the crop to her lips, tugging it with her teeth before releasing it. "Redirect you."

AJ looked down at the bright red welt forming, then noticed his rigid cock was throbbing too. It was another surprise.

The tip of the crop found his chin, drawing his eyes to the intensity of her gaze.

"If you can't follow simple directions, you'll have a few more of those little love taps, and neither of us will be satisfied. But . . ." Her smile ticked up, and she bit her pouty lower lip. "If you're a quick learner, and I have faith you are, then we'll both enjoy your lesson. Oh, and just so we're crystal clear, you have just under two hours to learn all you can."

Pointing the crop toward the door, she said, "You'll notice we're in a two-room suite. When we're done, I'll need my privacy."

She tapped the crop to his shoulder, and he sucked in a flinch.

"Ready for your lesson, Mr. Drake?"

He tried maintaining eye contact, but the leather circling his shaft again made his eyes slam shut. "Y-yes."

His dick stiffened like granite. Opening his heavy eyes, he watched as she wiped the bead of precum that had formed, giving the leather a glossy coat, before laying the crop at her side.

"Look at my breasts." She plucked her nipples, then caressed the weight of her breasts in each hand. "Don't be fooled by headlights. High beams don't mean I'm into you. Maybe they're always like this. Or maybe it's cold. Maybe I'm fantasizing about all the money I'm stealing from you."

Instantly, he frowned, and she continued.

"My point is even if I'm not into you, you can get me into you." She scooted away from the center of the bed to make room. "Now, sit."

As was becoming their custom, he obeyed, taking a seat next to her. As soon as he rested back, she straddled him. Every part of him paid attention.

"For the next few minutes, I'm going to enjoy myself, and you're not going to move a muscle. Understand?"

"Y-y-yes," he stuttered, barely able to speak as she rested her weight on his rod.

He could feel her dampness, and wetness like that couldn't be faked. She was into him. She had to be. Didn't she? As her hips swayed, he moved his hands, palming her perfectly round ass.

Crack!

"Fuck!"

Her smile widened with diabolical delight. "I'll repeat myself, so you don't make this mistake again. You're. Not. Going. To. Move. To ensure we're clear, I'm going to ask you again." Her cleavage spilled against his chest as she spoke into his ear. "Do you understand?"

"Yes," he muttered through clenched teeth, accepting that his hardened dick couldn't deny that he enjoyed the pain.

With two fingers, she pulled her panties to the side and slid her weeping pussy up and down him. "Feel me gliding against you?" she asked, nipping his ear with her teeth. "Do you want me?"

Must not move. "Yes."

"Right now? Can you think of anything other than pounding me senseless?"

"God, no. I can't. Jordan, please, I need you." He squirmed through her excruciatingly slow, torturous rhythm.

Must not move. Must not move.

Must. Not. Move.

Holding his breath, he fisted the comforter in frustration, not minding another lash necessarily, but holding out for whatever he should be learning. Because he was, after all, a fast learner.

"So, tell me something, AJ." Her mouth brushed his wanting

lips, and for the first time in his life, they trembled. "In this condition, could you possibly steal from me?"

His body stiffened, snapping his mind back to the game.

"No," he huffed out, realizing what she'd been doing. Luring him. It was just a distraction. A sweet, hot, soaking-wet distraction that coated his dick in her heavenly juices, and one he now understood.

With barely a kiss on the lips, she lifted off him, rolling onto her back. "Now, my turn."

God, yes. Her turn.

She slid two fingers through the string of her panties, releasing a breathy gasp as she pushed in, pumped a few times, then pulled out her coated fingers. He could feel an orgasm just out of reach, and all he could do was watch.

Touching his lips, she rubbed her fingers back and forth, glazing them before pushing through. Once he'd sucked them clean, she said, "Remove my panties."

The second he made a grab for them, she raised the crop. He froze, staying very still, anticipating the sting. But it didn't come.

"With your teeth," she said.

Headfirst, he dove down. As soon as his breath hit her skin, she fisted his hair, forcing his uncertain eyes to lock with hers.

"Do it slowly. So much so, you're sure you're going too slow. Your primitive little caveman mind will be in a perpetual state of feeding impulses. Fight that. It's not about you. It's about stoking the flames. Mine. Teasing and tantalizing my pussy so it aches for your touch."

She let go. "Do it, AJ . . . make me desperate for you."

Nodding but not taking in a word of what she said, he moved too quickly.

Crack!

Fuck, I can't believe how much I like that.

Still, he got the point. Slowly, he nibbled, kissed, and licked her soft skin as he traveled from one side of her hips to the other.

Though her body wasn't much more than a foot wide, it may as well have been the George Washington Bridge for how long it was taking him to cross from one side of her to the other. At one point, her breathing became so still, he wondered if his snail's pace had actually lulled her to sleep.

But then, like a light at the end of the tunnel, her body shifted. Her moan was the siren's song he'd been waiting for. Daring a look at her face, he noted her heavy eyes sparkled with a hint of lust.

Finally.

This well-earned victory almost got the better of him, but he was patient as a greater conquest lay ahead. He considered a brazen reposition, then inched his way down until his mouth was directly over her center. Gingerly, his teeth tugged the stretchy scrap of lace down, bit by itsy-bitsy bit.

He let his lips graze her clit but didn't lick it like he wanted. Half expecting the crack of the crop, he enjoyed her hips rocking against his mouth. She was moving to let him pull the panties out from under her ass.

"*Mmm.*" She moaned, but he ignored it.

Not yet. Focus. He forged onward and downward.

Continuing his path, he brushed his lips down the length of her legs, breathing, kissing, and nibbling throughout his passage. When he reached her strappy shoes, his teeth took care, delicately taking the dainty lace past her cherry-red stilettos.

She spread her legs, inviting him. The clear shot of her soaked pussy nearly reeled him in, stopped only by the slice of her six-inch heel digging into the center of his chest.

"No." Her tone was commanding and unapologetic.

He felt a crack, but it wasn't the whip. It was his spirit breaking beneath the weight of sexual frustration.

"Remove my shoes," she softly commanded, "and massage my feet."

Massage your feet? Now? What the—

His nearly begrudging pout was stopped. Somehow, between his devastating disappointment and her sly vixen smile, the rules of the game revealed themselves. He understood.

Instant gratification was the root of all evil. Predictable. Anticlimactic. All the power he coveted was in the delay itself, obliterating every calculated brain wave with a heavy dose of lust.

This was the promised land. The holy grail. The ultimate power of the *P*, and his priceless prize on the merry mount to orgasm.

He might have been at the brink of insanity, but so was she. Plump lips. Bedroom eyes. Heavy breaths. Nipples that could cut glass, and a river running through her pussy. How long could she deny herself?

Game on, baby. Game fucking on!

Unhurried, he uncinched the thin leather strap on her shoe with its bright red sole, and pressed soft, tender kisses along every inch of her ankle and lower leg.

Devoting the power of his strong hands to the arch of her foot, he was pleased to hear her pleasurable moan. Attentively, he caressed her ankle and kneaded her calf. Only after an *ahh* escaped her lips did he remove her other shoe.

"I knew you were a fast learner."

"Mm-hmm." Tamping down his ego, he accepted the compliment without getting arrogant. But she was changing, and it was undeniable.

Her muscles relaxed. Her body responded. And fuck if her pussy wasn't getting wetter by the second.

With a single finger, he stroked the inside of her thighs, and she spread her knees, blooming like a naughty little flower. A taste was tempting, but he'd give anything to hear this woman beg.

Moving up her body, he teased her, laying tender kisses in a solid perimeter around her weeping folds, but not getting near them. Her body writhed, and he smiled.

It would barely test his strength to rip off her bra, and probably result in a whip-worthy offense. He staved off that temptation by tracing a single finger down one bra strap at a time, tugging it low enough to set her weighty girls free. He teased her nipples, coming close, but staying just far enough away to avoid them.

Like the temptress she was, Jordan breathed hard, her breaths raising and lowering her chest, closing the distance between her nipple and his mouth.

His eyes met hers, as if to ask permission before a featherlight lick. It was enough that she arched her back. His hungry lips took her in his mouth as her core found his staff. He pulled away, and this woman who held so much control released a whimper.

That's it, baby. Let's hear you beg.

Her expression transformed, swinging from seduction to desire. No longer the lion tamer, she wanted to be taken. Tamed. Maybe it was his turn to take the whip.

When he reached for it, she shoved it away. As her sex chased his rod, he held it just out of reach.

"No," he said with gruff insistence. "Not yet." It was his turn to fist her hair, sear her skin with his touch, and take control.

He moved two fingers across her clit. Her legs fell open as her eyes fluttered shut. But he wasn't crossing the River Jordan until her pretty pouty lips actually begged.

"Lick me," she said on a sigh that sounded like a beg.

Her two little words were pure caffeine, and his tongue surged in for the taste he'd waited for. Jordan Stone, this mouthwatering rush of a woman, had all the makings of his new favorite meal. He ignored the nagging suspicion that his first taste would be his last.

He nearly came when her hand unexpectedly groped for his cock. With a growl, he stopped mid-thrust and steadied his breathing, but it took every bit of trembling willpower he could muster.

"What's the matter, baby?" Her question was torture. "Are you coming in my hand instead of deep inside the hungry walls of my tight, wet cunt?"

She was playing dirty. Dirty words. Dirty ways. It nearly sent him over the edge. His mantra shifted to *must not come*.

"Don't you want to fuck me?" she asked, adding sweetness to her tease.

He froze, so ready to flip her like a coin toss, not caring which hole he sank his desperate cock into.

I've got to calm down. Think of anything. Paying bills. Closing sales. Haven't been to church in a while. Catholic school. Itchy uniforms. God, and girl-gone-bad Jordan bent over the desk. Skirt hiked up. Ready for the ruler.

Shit! This isn't working.

"I give," she said, and he didn't care that it was a lie. "Make me come. Then shove every inch of that monster dick inside and ride me until you blow so hard, you forget your fucking name."

After several long licks across her swollen folds, he found her clit, nibbling the little nub before sucking hard.

Certain his tutor was far from a delicate flower, he shoved three fingers inside and gave her several deep thrusts. Instantly, she came, clamping his hand to a stop as she screamed several instances of *fuck, oh God,* and of all things, his name.

Hearing it come from her devilish red lips was everything. Sweet. Satisfying. Intoxicating. Something deep inside told him he'd never forget it. And for a woman who reeked of manipulation and a fake name, he couldn't help wondering if he could ever live without it.

"Don't stop."

AJ came up for air. "So demanding," he said, cocky and certain that in the afterglow of a jarringly strong orgasm, the last thing she'd want is to lift a finger toward the crop.

"Not just yet." Her tone was breathy as she struggled to lift her heavy lids. Still, that demand for compliance was very much present behind her dark eyes.

Nestling his face back between her legs, he nibbled and licked, eager to give her anything and everything she needed.

The condom she laid on her thigh gave him enough permission to slip it on. *About fucking time.* He sheathed himself and returned his eager body over her sweat-drenched one.

Panting, Jordan shared one last lesson. "After an orgasm, every square inch of my skin is hypersensitive. Any touch will only enhance the already exploded sensation. Use that little tidbit for all it's worth. But keep in mind your time's almost up." She chided him through panting breaths. "Not that you'll need all that much."

The base of his cock rubbed up and down. He savored the feel of her as he dipped in. Like tiptoeing into uncertain waters, he'd barely breached her slick entry before Jordan pulled him into the deep end. Both of her deceptively strong legs wrapped around him, heaving him hard and driving him to the hilt in one fell swoop.

It was pure ecstasy. "Fuck, that's good."

"I thought you'd like it."

"Demanding and impatient. A lethal combination."

"You have no idea."

Whatever she said next was lost. Reclaiming his thrusts, he slowed his achingly painful pace, but it couldn't end. Not yet.

It was his turn. To take his time. To tear down her walls. To top her.

He licked her nipple, letting his teeth graze it. Again, she tightened her legs around him, driving his ass forward. But despite what must be five hours a day in the gym, her slender frame was no match for his blockade of brute strength.

Easily, he held off, deciding to take a thumb to her clit. "What's the matter, baby? I've still got a few minutes on the clock."

"That's what you think."

Without warning, she gripped his hair, drawing his face to hers. Her fist tightened, enticing his lips apart. Her licks were that of a kitten, luring his tongue, enticing his mouth. Taking him one controlled suck at a time. His rhythm wasn't his own. Much like his mind. Or his cock. Or maybe, his heart.

Then he felt it.

Sliding slowly through the walls of his ass, the woven cane of the crop flossed through his cheeks, grazing his delicate hole. She rubbed away every one of his senses, until all that was left was a mindless thrusting machine.

Surrendering, he forgot himself in the depths of her body and the heat of her core. Erupting, he filled her until nothing was left. Just an empty, heaving, collapsing shell of a man who'd pretty much do anything for her.

Drained, their bodies stayed connected even after she rolled him back. She straddled him as every strained muscle in his body melted away and relaxed.

He looked up, seeing her body aglow with the sheen of satisfaction. Her smile was sweet and sexy and everything as she peered down at him through a thick cascade of tousled locks.

Captured in the moment, he lay there, content to live in the warmth of the moment and the softness of her gaze, not to mention the wet heat of her crotch.

Unguarded, he pinned her with a sentimental gaze that she seemed to return. Her fingers lowered to his ribs, lightly, almost lovingly, brushing his skin. When her nails unexpectedly raked up his sides, digging in mercilessly, his back snapped into an arch. Hissing, he buried his fists in the soft down comforter.

"AJ?" she said almost casually and to herself. "No. I don't care for the name at all. On you, AJ sounds like a handyman. Or a garbage collector."

"You're renaming me?" He forced out the words, still tightening his jaw.

"Let's call it branding." Her nails sliced his obliques, digging in until a moan shot from his lips. "And I know how you feel about the name Jack."

Her hands left him, but it was a temporary relief. His pulse spiked when again she handled the crop, swirling the leather tip to his sensitive balls. With an uncontrolled gasp, he stiffened.

"What does the *A* stand for?"

"Alexander," he huffed out with near certainty.

Slowly, she dismounted and stood at the side of the bed. "I'm going to call you Alex."

He felt the leather move from his balls and wilted shaft, up his abs and chest, then to his chin. Swallowing, he waited for round two.

"Rest for a few minutes, but head to your own room before I'm done showering." Her sumptuous curves made their way to the bathroom, not bothering to turn back. "This is good-bye, Alex. It's been a pleasure."

With that, she shut the door. The water turned on, alerting him that her shower was ready and the stopwatch had started.

∽

In his own bedroom of the suite, Alex lay in the darkness, sinking into the luxury of the king-size bed. It felt a million miles from hers, though her scent was everywhere.

With his eyes closed, he could see every peak and valley of her naked body. Every soft, velvety angle of her smooth skin. The endless darkness of her eyes. The poisonous pout of those full red lips.

Erotic. Mesmerizing. *Jordan*.

It couldn't be over. Not yet.

Aimlessly, he scanned the room, finally looking over at the digital clock on the nightstand. *Midnight*. Three hours since his time with her. Since she climbed off him and bid him an ominous and final farewell.

Whatever fleeting moment they'd shared, it was real. He had to see her. Now.

Unable to find a light switch, he made his way across the dark penthouse, only stubbing his toe once before finding her bedroom. Noticing the bright light beaming from beneath the bottom of the door, he prepared to knock.

The tightened skin of his fist aggravated the welt on it, making it sting again. *Fuck*. What sort of smack awaited him for disturbing her beauty rest? Freezing for only a moment, he braced himself for the whip ahead and gave the door a few light knocks.

"Jordan?" His voice was hoarse, and he cleared his throat. "Listen, I'm sorry to disturb you, but I, well, I—I have to talk to you."

Silence.

Slowly, he checked the handle, relieved when it moved freely. It was unlocked. He pushed the door open a crack before entering.

"Jordan?" Opening the door wide, he found the room bright, with every lamp on in the space, and he took a few steps inside.

Deflated, he understood. Everything was quiet. Bed made. Bathroom wiped. Closet emptied. All that remained was a large manila envelope in the center of the bed with *Alex* scrolled across it.

On the very bed that had changed so much in him, he plopped down, unbothered by his naked body making a fresh set of imprints in the fluffy down comforter.

Pulling in a deep breath, he picked up the envelope, checking the contents before spilling them out. Instead of a long, intimate note he'd briefly hoped for from the addictive Jordan Stone were several impersonal items . . . the makings of a new life.

The hotel bill showed the room was paid in full for the next five days. There was a pending offer on his home for way over market value. A first-class ticket for that fifth day would take him from Colorado to Dulles International Airport.

That's Washington, DC, I think.

An elegantly typed itinerary laid out locations and plans, including the town car service that would await him at the airport.

In a smaller envelope was an American Express Platinum Card and a letter granting him $20,000. Not a line of credit, but a pre-loaded amount he could spend recklessly and at will. And maybe use to tip well.

But to his dismay, there was nothing else. The mysterious Jordan Stone had vanished like a thief in the night.

CHAPTER 13

JACK

Five months later – Southern Italy

SIPPING A HOUSE RED, Second Lieutenant Jack Taylor was ready for some well-deserved R&R. The mission was taking its toll, dragging on endlessly for the three-man team. Permission had been granted for shore leave to nearby Italy. At least, that's what two of them assumed, but only Jack knew the truth.

The local cantina should have been laid-back and enjoyable as he and his teammates relaxed and forgot about the Middle East. Their work had been methodical and intense, without the luxuries of reliable electricity or running water. Or for that matter, actual beds.

Italy was a blissful world away, and with the money they'd all saved, it was easy to live it up. But their world-class, week-long getaway was taking an inconvenient turn for the worse, because, as usual, AJ was being his cocky self and stirring up shit.

A small but intimidating mob began circling AJ in the loud cantina while Jack and Paco kept their distance, remaining quiet but standing by. Unsure of his next move, Jack watched from the bar, thinking through the consequences of each possible reaction to the fight brewing. How would it impact their mission? Because any impact would risk too much.

Neither he nor Paco were in uniform, so nobody would suspect they were active-duty military, but the last thing their team needed was unwanted attention. As usual, AJ had missed the memo.

"*Scusami, signori.*" AJ held up his palms to the men as he fumbled through his pleas in broken Italian, not realizing he was being backed into a corner. "Um, the women, *le donne*, they approached me. Uh, *mi ha chiesto di uscire a cena* . . . they asked me to eat. To have dinner."

As if the angry mob gave a fuck. And the more he begged in his butchered Italian, the more irritated the already pissed-off men surrounding him became.

"He's gonna get his ass kicked," Paco quietly sang to Jack, not holding back a sexy smirk. "Perhaps we should just order another carafe and enjoy the show."

But Jack couldn't let that happen. Lowering his voice, he said, "We fucking need him."

"Fine."

They shared a knowing glance and an exaggerated eye roll before heading in to rescue their single biggest pain in the ass, but they were a minute too late.

When the first swing barely grazed AJ's jaw and the second landed solidly on his abs, fair play seemed to be drawing to a close. With AJ's arms wrestled behind his back, the tallest of the group was poised to punch. Jack managed to grab the man's arm in mid-swing.

Paco, who easily passed for a local, gave diplomacy a go in perfect Italian. "*Non è necessario. Porteremo questo turista a casa?*"

None of this is necessary, Jack translated in his head. *How about we take the tourist home?*

No one cared. And this show of testosterone was about to go from a few jabs to a full-throttle MMA match. AJ had broken the cardinal rule—*thou shalt not hit on the women other men called dibs on*—and an ass-kicking was in the cards.

A third man took a cheap shot at AJ, the blow to his gut sending him to his knees. It was enough to launch Jack and Paco into the line of fire.

Five against two. Jack wasn't sure about the odds. He hoped Paco's hand-to-hand combat moves would do better than his botched attempt at diplomatic relations.

Immediately, Paco held up his hands in surrender.

We're so fucked.

A towering man lurched at Paco but Jack couldn't help, caged inside his own cluster of three men. When the biggest threw a punch his way, Jack's adrenaline reinforced his training. The swing was hasty, and he ducked before sending his boot straight at the angry man's nuts.

One down. The two others were no match for him, and he easily subdued them.

Paco.

He whirled around, ready to rush to Paco's aid, but there was no need. Jack found his teammate smiling as he stood over both his opponents, rolling and moaning on the floor. Not only had Paco overpowered two massive attackers single-handedly, but he looked hot in the aftermath. *Damn hot.*

Jack refocused, scanning his surroundings for emerging threats. Everyone seemed to be settling down, with the latest commotion being the matronly owner, yelling at the instigators like hooligans and berating them for fighting with people who actually paid for their food.

For the moment, he could relax, but he didn't. Instead, he locked his body, avoided Paco's eyes, and desperately tried to ignore the tight throbbing in his jeans.

Just the thought of Paco taking on two goliaths alone—Jack couldn't get it out of his mind. The man was a lean, mean, fighting machine with the smile of a saint and a body made for ungodly sin.

"You all right?" Paco laid a hand on his shoulder. Without intending it, their eyes met and locked. For just a second. Maybe two.

Maybe—

AJ moaned, looking like hell. Jack and Paco each held out a hand, hoisting him back to his feet.

Holding his ribs, he mumbled, "Thanks. I really owe you both. I'll make it up to you someday, I swe—"

"Oh, you poor man," a buxom brunette purred in her native Italian. Nestling against him, she held him up, wrapping a hand around his waist.

"So courageous," a blonde said, also speaking Italian. Alex beamed at his understanding. The roll of her Rs was a universal mating call.

He was so brave?

AJ smiled, suddenly oblivious to how he got in this mess to begin with. The women moved to his sides, creating a lusty set of human crutches.

"Oh, uh, it was nothing," AJ said, playing it cool in an obnoxious and ridiculous sort of way.

Unnerved, Jack pinched the bridge of his nose, holding back his own urge to kick his teammate's ass. Without a doubt, Paco would be in.

Irritated, Paco shot AJ a glare and motioned him over.

"*Scusi*, ladies," AJ said, excusing himself while exaggerating the pain of moving away from them.

"Hey, Casanova, those two have just one thing on their minds," Paco said softly, and AJ waggled his brows. "No, dumbass. They're trying to steal your wallet."

AJ smiled with a nauseating degree of confidence. "God, I hope so," he said with a grin. He patted Paco's shoulder, then Jack's. "Thanks again, and don't wait up."

Jack watched as AJ welcomed the bodies of the women, exaggerating his stagger with every step. With a quick glance back, AJ winked. Jack looked blankly at him in disbelief while Paco simply shook his head.

"The fucker just won't learn," Jack said.

Paco nodded. "Buttheads never do."

CHAPTER 14

ALEX

THE WOMEN LED AJ to a quaint hotel a few blocks away.

Their room was rustic with amber-hued walls cracked and pitted from poor construction and age. The queen-size mattress seemed well worn, and he wondered if it would buckle under the weight of the three of them. A small floral scarf draped the only lamp in the room, giving AJ barely enough light to see the surroundings or the bed.

Smart choice.

The women wasted no time peeling off their clothes, down to their frilly undergarments. Eagerly, they began removing his.

"*Come ti chiami, caro?*" one asked as she looked him up and down, licking her lips.

"My name? AJ." With Jordan's voice echoing from the dirtiest crevices of his mind, he reconsidered and changed his response. "But, um, call me Alex."

"*Buono*, Alex."

He waited for their names. The brunette leaned in, speaking for them both. She introduced herself as Sofia and the other as Bianca. Bianca the blonde slipped her tongue into his mouth and her fingers into his pocket—a slick attempt to rid him of his wallet.

Perfect. Time for my field test.

With an excited grin, he tugged out the new leather wallet, holding the prize before them. Their wide smiles were just shy of a drool.

He gave the wallet a carefree toss to the seat of the only chair in the room, leaving it there for them to admire. As if hypnotized by it, the women needed a moment to remember he was even in the room.

Alex smiled wide. *Game on.*

Attentively, they massaged his arms and chest, steadily making their way to his cock. But Alex was ready to take his sweet time.

"Uh-uh-uh," he said softly, shaking his head playfully.

Pulling the brunette to his body, he laid a kiss on her pouting smile, while taking the other by the hand and caressing her skin. One kiss later, he moved his focus to the other and groaned out her name.

Bianca leaned in for a kiss, but he didn't give it to her. Instead, he lightly brushed his mouth to hers with barely a nibble of her ready lips.

"*Mmm.*" She moaned, enjoying the sensation of being gently tasted.

Maybe a man had never bothered taking his time with her. Hell, it was just as new to Alex too. He repeated the featherlight kiss with Sofia and elicited another moan.

A small step for Alex. A huge step for Neanderthals worldwide.

"Now, ladies," he said low, "I hope you're not in too much of a hurry, because I intend to take my time."

Ignoring him and ready to get things underway, they started removing their lacy bras.

"*Lentamente, mia preziosas,*" he demanded with a low grumble.

His request to go slower baffled them at first. Intrigued, they complied as he lined them up, one behind the other in his own sexy conga line. He began a very precise demonstration, making certain they understood there were rules to this game, and he was in charge.

Alex traced a figure eight on Sofia's shoulder, insisting she mimic his actions on the same spot on her friend. *"Fai come faccio io, capisci?"*

Sofia nodded, understanding they were to mirror everything he did, and transferred the sensation to Bianca.

He started with the smallest of tasks. Very slowly, his slipped off Sofia's bra strap. When she did it too quickly to Bianca, Alex corrected Sofia, taking her hand and showing that the move should be slower. Like Alex, she was a fast learner. He rewarded her with a peck on the neck, and she repeated the move on Bianca.

Damn fast learner.

He slid a finger down her spine, forcing her neck back with a shiver. *"Fallo, mia bella,"* he insisted, coaxing her to stimulate her friend likewise.

With the same softness, she complied. Bianca's response equaled Sofia's, though she added an uncontrolled whimper.

Satisfied they understood the rules, he mentally started the clock. "Now, let's have some fun."

For the first time in his life, there was power at his fingertips, and Alex relished it. Sure, it was sexual power, but as powers went, he'd take it.

His hard-on was like solid granite—partially fueled by that aforementioned surge of power—but it would have to wait. Stoking their desires was, it its own way, exciting. He hungered for more.

In the end, Jordan Stone had kept her word and then some. *She gave me a superpower.* With a single touch, he'd made not one, but two women writhe and moan.

Should I use this power for good or evil? he thought, then chuckled to himself.

Tonight? Fucking evil.

His lazy finger traced around Sofia's ass to the front of her upper thigh, then slipped into her panties and down her hot, wet center. Breathless, she gasped, dropping her hand. Succumbing to her own pleasure, she failed to repeat the move.

Gruffly, he murmured a tender instruction in her ear. "*Si, mia bella.* Go on."

She sucked in a breath, then did as he asked. Mimicking him, she pressed her finger past Bianca's panties and to the center of her core, forcing a gasp.

"*Mmm, molto buona.* Very, very good," he said on a groan.

In and out he moved, satisfying both women at once. The rush was euphoric.

Next, he unclasped Sofia's bra and discarded it to the floor. Pleased, he watched as his actions were willingly repeated. Moving through a series of activities his naughty mind made up on the fly, Alex pulled Sofia back to his chest, wrapping an arm around her and teasing the outer rim of her nipple. His other hand once again played with her pussy, which soaked the scrap of lace.

She was hot, but her responsive little friend was so much hotter, squealing from the lightest touch that cascaded across one desirable Italian woman to the other. Again, he kissed Sofia's shoulder, and she repeated the movement.

How far can I take them? How far will they go?

When he pushed two fingers inside, Sofia was in heaven, but there was no response from her friend. Sofia was hesitating.

Murmuring impatiently, he said, "Now, *bella*," maintaining a slow rhythm between her legs.

Finally, Sofia did it, and Bianca nearly burst his eardrum with her cry. Outwardly, he worried that their landlord might be heading up to their room. Inwardly, he ate up every decibel.

Best superpower ever.

He upped the ante, getting on his knees behind Sofia, enjoying her shiver as he dragged her soaked panties to the floor. As she was about to do the same, he halted her with a silent *shhh*. Pressing a finger to his lips, he motioned her to the bed, giving her enough unspoken commands that she tiptoed over and sat quietly on the side of it.

To Bianca, he tugged down her panties as well, relishing the tremble it gave her. Kneeling behind her, his warm, strong hands grabbed the front of both her thighs, yanking her back to the surprise of his ready tongue, penetrating her ripe pussy.

Her scream was twice as loud as the first, but he imagined if no one came rushing to her aid before, he was probably in the clear. Her raw cry was a wild mix of shock and joy, and she nearly came on his mouth as she fought to steady herself.

Delighted, Sofia laughed, grabbing her friend and pulling her to the bed. Standing before them, he motioned for them to scoot forward, just enough so their butts were at the edge. Eagerly, they did as he asked.

Alex retrieved a condom from the wallet they'd been so enthralled with, taking his time to flash it so they could see the cash inside. Instead of holding their attention, his dawdling seemed to irritate them.

"Hurry," Bianca said, for the first time giving any impression that she spoke English, and very well, he might add.

Casually, he stripped off his clothes, drawing their gazes, and hearing, of all things, Jordan Stone echoing in his ears. *In this condition, could you possibly steal from me?* He couldn't then, and they couldn't now.

Sex wasn't the superpower. Desire was, and it made him wonder.

What else do people desire?

Smiling, he stepped before them and tossed the condom to

the top of the bed. "Whichever of you gorgeous *donne* comes first will get a trophy. A big, hard trophy."

Longing painted their expressions, but they sat obediently, waiting for his next command.

He took the hand of each, overlapped one over the other, and delicately placed them suggestively at the source of each other's heat. Either from the lust he'd stoked in them, or genuine interest or instinct, their fingers began to sink in. Sink in and stroke, like two naughty little playmates exploring each other for the first time.

With the momentary loss of his damn mind, he watched as they closed their eyes and began exploring, rubbing each other as if rubbing themselves.

Fuck, that's hot.

If he let them keep going, they'd be done, and he couldn't have that. With their growing moans, they were seconds from simultaneous orgasms. He cut in. This was his time to shine.

When he moved their hands away from each other, an audible *aww* came from both women. They squirmed until he pumped two fingers inside each of them, sending them closer to that climax they so desperately desired.

It was a race for the history books. AJ Drake, two hot Italian women, and a neck-and-neck race to the *fucking* finish line. Nothing was more disappointing than a moment like this without a photo finish.

He couldn't predict it, but Bianca went over first, seconds from Sofia surrendering to her own wild orgasm. That Alex hadn't come just from watching was also, he presumed, another superpower.

Huffing and sweating, the ladies wove their hands together, connected in ecstasy as their breathing steadied and slowed.

"It was close," he said in a deep, rumbling tone. "But we do indeed have a winner."

He slid his fingers out of them and both whimpered from the loss, but Bianca spread her legs in anticipation.

Firmly, he said, "Put it on me."

Bianca grabbed the condom and tore the package open with her teeth. Before rolling it on, though, she took him in her mouth, sucking him hard until he felt the sensation clear to his toes.

"Yes," he said on a moan, checking his ego and realizing he might have lost this battle had they gone first.

He fisted her hair, pulling her away as he watched her bite her smiling lip. "Now, *bella*."

Obeying, she wrapped him and then returned to her comfortable recline, letting her knees drop wide with her wet pussy waiting.

"*Tsk, tsk, tsk*." Alex shook his head. "And what about poor Sofia?"

Obediently, Bianca moved her hand back to Sofia, pumping her fingers softly inside her swollen folds. He swiped the tip of his cock against Bianca's entrance, and she matched his pace with her friend.

In one, hard, forceful thrust, Alex was deep inside Bianca, and she was three fingers deep inside Sofia.

"That's right," he said, guiding her. "Fuck sweet Sofia just like I'm fucking you."

Again and again, he forced his way in to the hilt, keeping a rhythm Bianca easily matched, letting him please both of them at once. Letting him get lost in the moment. Having all the attention of two women at once.

A second later, he felt Bianca's walls crash around him, milking him hard. It sent the sensation through every square inch of him until his balls tightened, his thighs bore in deep, and every last inch of him was squeezed deep inside this beautiful blonde.

An uncontrollable shudder hit him, and he fell forward, deafened this time by his own rough screams. His arms braced, saving the beauty beneath him from being crushed. She let out a breathy giggle of relief, and he kissed each of her nipples before placing a gentle kiss on her lips.

He looked over at Sofia, her face glowing and radiant, and her heavy lids sleepy. They kissed as well before he lifted off the bed.

Catching his breath in the warm room, he watched as the two sweat-drenched women began to shiver. In a caring way he didn't understand, he moved each woman higher on the bed, covering their spent bodies with the tattered blanket. Looking down, he loved how beautiful they were—giving themselves so completely to him, and now cuddling with each other.

Sweetly, he kissed each on the forehead as he tucked them in. Heading to their bathroom, he passed the small chair still holding his unfolded wallet. Not meaning to, he'd left a lot of money in it—some of the spoils of his own breathless night not so long ago.

He moved past it, making his way to the tiny bathroom that seemed cramped by Western standards, but fared well compared to the accommodations of the desert home awaiting him.

Decidedly he shut the door, letting his performance determine the fate of his cash. AJ took his time, uncommon to his carefree nature, but at a pace that he seemed to enjoy.

Tending to his grooming, he cleaned up a bit, helping himself to their soap, comb, floral lotions, and something that might have been mouthwash. He couldn't be sure.

He took inventory of all their toiletries, uncapping them and taking intrigued sniffs of the local brands. He practiced his Italian, patiently sounding out each Italian word of the long list of ingredients on the label.

Through a small window, he breathed in some fresh air and admired a few passersby, talking, laughing, and eating whatever they must have picked up along the way.

After wasting as much time as he possibly could in the small space, unless he wanted to grab some spackle and start repairing and painting the cramped room, he'd exhausted all options for putting off his return.

Slowly, he opened the door. It brought a proud smile to his face that the two women were very much where he'd left them, curled up side by side, spent and asleep. The wallet seemed untouched, but that was just icing on the cake.

Silently, he dressed, taking in what had to be an A+ in his Jordan Stone lesson, and the vision of two women he'd never forget. And not for the women themselves as gorgeous as they were, but more for the bragging rights.

If only I had someone to brag to.

Finally, he snatched up his wallet and counted the bills inside, heaving out a satisfied sigh. Pleased, he flipped the wallet, pocketed it in the back of his pants, and slipped out of the room. With an amused grin, he headed back to the hotel.

Good-bye, AJ.
Hello, Alex.

CHAPTER 15

JACK

The shriek of sirens echoing off the stone-faced buildings on the narrow streets grew louder as they approached.

Out of habit, Jack barked out an order, immediately regretting his tone. "Let's go." He headed toward the cantina's front entrance, but was yanked back by Paco's strong grip.

"This way." Paco led him through the kitchen, and when they burst through the back door into an alley, Paco headed to the right. "Come on, I know a shortcut back to the hotel."

"How do you know that? I thought this was your first time in Italy."

"It is. But I looked over the maps you had."

Hurrying, they picked up the pace, falling into the comfortable stride of a military run.

"You only looked at them for a second," Jack said, remembering Paco had barely scanned them.

"Yeah, I've got this weird way with things like that. Languages. Images. Faces. Not everything, but those seem to stick in my brain."

"I guess you're stuck remembering my face." *Did I just say that?* Quickly, Jack added, "Mine and AJ's."

Paying more attention to the direction of their run, Paco said, "I guess so."

They maneuvered up and down the winding cobblestone streets until they reached the dim lighting of the back of their hotel. The door was unlocked, and they managed to get through the lobby and up the stairs without passing anyone.

Slowly, they approached the doors to their rooms, but Jack was still on a high from the events of the night. Looking over at Paco, he realized he didn't want the night, or vacation, to end.

"Hey, I'm still a little wired. Want a drink?"

"I've got plenty," Paco said, opening his door and gesturing inside with an easygoing grin that could melt a man from a mile away.

Jack took a few steps inside, feeling the heat of Paco's body follow him. With a gracious wave, he invited Jack to help himself to the small refrigerator, stocked with an assortment of minis, presumably identical to the one in Jack's own room.

"Help yourself."

"Thanks," Jack said, rummaging through the stash.

"I also bought some vodka. It's on the counter if you prefer something harder."

Harder? God, do I. Jack swallowed, unable to stop the heat rising in his cheeks.

"Perfect," he said, taking one for himself and tossing another to Paco's waiting hand. With the caps twisted off and each taking a sip, an unsettling silence fell between them.

They say people get close in combat. Well, Jack got close, all right. Too close, perhaps. With temptation sitting a few feet from him as they guzzled the booze, hiding his feelings was taking an exhausting toll. And hiding in plain sight seemed to be catching up with Jack Taylor. Another mini was in order.

"You okay?" Paco asked.

Jack took a deep breath. "I, um . . ." He turned to face Paco. "No, I'm not."

"Want to talk about it?"

Deflated, Jack shook his head and downed another drink. "Look, I'm about to say something . . . and it's something I don't *want* to say. It's something I *have* to say. It could . . . it could change everything."

"Could change everything?" Paco repeated each word deliberately.

"Actually, no. It *will* change everything. And I'll just leave once I've said it. I'm not trying to make things difficult. I just . . . I can't *not* tell you . . ."

Paco sat up straighter in his seat on the worn vintage sofa. "Shit, what is it?" he asked, concern growing in his tone. "Look, Lieutenant, whatever it is, I can take it."

Jack's wry smile faded. "Fuck, I don't even know how to say this. I mean, I've never said anything like this. I—"

"Just spit it out. It'll be fine. Things always seem worse in our heads. Just say it."

Jack's tortured glance met a flood of admiration from Paco's eyes. Respect. Honor. Suddenly, it all seemed so undeserved. It was a look Jack would never forget, knowing that any second now, it would vanish.

I can't keep living a lie.

Jack sucked in a breath, holding the air for a short eternity before letting it all spill out. "We've been working together for a few months now. And every day I get to know you better, but . . ." Again, he trailed off.

Despite the dangerous threats that were part of the daily lives of their mission, this moment was a thousand times scarier. But what if he let it pass and said nothing? What if they went back into the heart of enemy territory, and he never said a damn thing? What if something happened to him? To Paco?

It's now or never.

"I've never met anyone like you, Paco," he said, sinking into the truth of his words.

"Like me?" Paco gave Jack a squint that demanded he clarify. "What the hell is that supposed to mean—*like me?*"

"No, not like that. Not in a bad way. I mean . . . fuck." He huffed under his breath. "Look, it's just . . ." *Now. Or Never.* "You look, um, good. No, not good. You look great."

"Yeah?" Paco drew out the word, fully convinced of the truth in that statement, and seeming to wonder why that would be an issue.

Trying to ignore Paco's charm, Jack refocused. "I mean, *really* great."

"Still with you," Paco said proudly. "You look great too. But I'm totally lost on why this is an issue."

Stop smiling. Say it!

"It's not an issue. But it is an issue. I guess what I'm trying to say is . . . you're the sexiest man I've ever seen, and I . . ." He met Paco's gaze. "I'm in love with you."

His last words slipped out, quiet and soft. Unintentional. Apologetic.

As Paco stared at him, wide-eyed, his mouth agape, Jack found it unbearable. His gaze fell to the floor. "Like I said, I couldn't not say it. If you want to leave or be reassigned, I understand."

"You do?"

Jack paced the small room, suddenly cold and embarrassed, and uncomfortable in his own skin. "What the hell am I saying? *You* don't have to do anything. Not leave the team. Not be reassigned. I should be the one to be reassigned."

"Really, because isn't this your mission? Your play? But to avoid my discomfort, you'd be reassigned."

"Sorry, Paco. I should go. I just, I don't want to—"

His babbling was shut down by Paco's sudden closeness, his body blocking his path. Jack hadn't noticed the man silently stand and stalk over, but here he was. Meeting his gaze.

Caressing his cheek. Smothering Jack's lips with a blazing-hot kiss.

Holy fuck.

Jack couldn't think or move. The moment was everything. The decadent kiss was what he'd craved on a semi-daily basis. The sensation burned through his body, branding his soul while setting the rest of him on fire.

In moments, they'd ripped their clothes away. Jack dropped to his knees, wasting no time taking hold of exactly what he wanted.

"W-wait!" Paco panted out.

Jack looked up, releasing an exasperated breath but keeping a warm smile on his lips. "Look, I'm ready to take this at whatever pace you want, but I'm buck naked, kneeling before you with your gorgeous rock-hard dick in my hand. If you're having doubts, *now* is the time to say so."

Jack's chuckle quickly faded as Paco slowly shook his head.

"I'm not having doubts, Lieutena—I mean Jack. I just . . ."

Jack stood, not touching him but meeting his eyes. "Hey, we don't have to do anything. At all. That kiss was more than I could have ever dreamed of. Well, I mean I *did* dream of it."

Despite his smile, Paco's brow was creased, and he squeezed Jack's hand before lacing their fingers in a tender hold. "You could lose your commission. We're inches from fraternization."

Glancing down, Jack grinned. "Yeah, I'd say roughly eight inches. Hell, maybe nine." He reassured Paco with a kiss. "I wasn't bullshitting. I'm head over heels in love with you. You're kind, considerate, smart, brave, funny as hell, and hotter than fuck. I'd be crazy not to grab you and never let you go. If this is my last mission, I'm at peace with that. It is what it is. I want a shot with you—a real, wildly romantic, happily-ever-after shot with you. I've never felt anything even close to what I feel for you."

They kissed until Paco's warm lips relaxed.

Jack gave Paco's cheek a tender rub. "I've got another gig

already lined up after this mission. So, the only way this stops is if you want it to . . . because I know what I want."

"Are you sure?"

"Yes," Jack said firmly, "but this isn't all about me. What do you want?"

Paco didn't speak. He didn't need to. And there were no more words between them that night.

Words, or anything else.

CHAPTER 16

◈

PACO

The next day

Paco awoke and stretched in bed, quickly realizing his companion was MIA. The beams of sunlight peeking through the curtains meant he'd slept much later than normal, bringing a sly smile to his face.

His reminiscing about the amazing night before and his morning wood were interrupted by a strange noise from the hotel's hallway, drawing both his attention and suspicion. Maybe it was Jack.

Paco leaped up, cracking the door open enough to poke his head out, but keeping his nude body concealed.

He and his across-the-hall neighbor, AJ, opened their doors simultaneously. They questioned each other in silence, quizzically cocking their heads before realizing neither was the culprit.

Another set of noises drew their attention down the hall. A man wearing a hat was struggling to gain access to Jack's room.

"Hey!" Paco and Alex called out in unison, neither moving to catch him.

The man shoved something beneath the door before making a hasty escape.

Frustrated, Paco gave Alex a dirty look before instinctively understanding the reason Alex wasn't chasing the man down. Apparently, he, too, was buck naked.

They both shut their doors. Paco jumped into his pants and returned to the hall, practically racing AJ to Jack's room. They knocked.

"Jack?"

"Jack!"

"Yeah?" he answered from behind them.

They both turned. It seemed that Jack was up bright and early, and had returned bearing gifts not only for Paco but for AJ as well. In his hands were three small coffees on a rickety tray with an attractive assortment of local pastries.

Frowning, Jack narrowed his concerned eyes on Paco, transparent in wondering if the cat was now out of the bag. Paco returned a subtle shake of the head, noticing what might be relief pouring through Jack's silent exhale.

Oblivious as usual, AJ disregarded the silent conversation transpiring before him and crammed a pastry in his mouth. "Thanks," he mumbled, barely managing his mouthful as he grabbed a cup.

"We caught some guy trying to break into your room," Paco said low, keeping his alarm quiet from the neighbors. "He slid something under the door."

Jack handed Paco the tray. "Oh, uh, good. I was expecting a delivery. He left it. Great." He dug a tarnished brass key from his jeans pocket and unlocked his door before opening it.

Before Alex could make a grab at another pastry, Paco shoved the tray into his hands, giving himself the freedom to pop his freed hands staunchly to his hips.

"The guy was trying to get into your room," Paco said firmly to Jack, barely masking his concern.

Jack turned to Paco and gripped his shoulder. It felt condescending.

"I said he could if I wasn't here. Hey, um, why don't we all get together in about an hour to head back?" Jack snagged a coffee off the tray and slipped into his room, shutting the door behind him without another glance.

Dumbfounded, Paco stood, blinking in disbelief at the rustic wooden door. He glanced at AJ, still carrying the tray, who gave him a cheesy grin.

"Coffee?" AJ said, bringing yet another pastry to his lips. Paco's glare prompted him to add, "Sorry, it's just that I'm starving. I worked up quite the appetite with those girls las—"

Avoiding landing his fist on AJ's throat, Paco brushed by him and returned to his room. With the door shut, he leaned against it.

Well, fuck. Welcome to the morning after.

Hanging his head, he startled as a large envelope flew from beneath the door, knocking against his feet. As soon as he moved to pick it up, he noticed the shadow. Whoever pushed it through was still there. *The guy from Jack's room.*

Without the convenience of a peephole, Paco yanked open the door to check. But it wasn't the man in the hat at his door. It was Jack, carrying the tray with the last coffee and a single pastry left on it.

Grinning, he said, "I nearly lost a hand tearing these from AJ."

Unamused, Paco gave Jack a death glare harsh enough that it wiped the dimples right off his cheeks. *Curse those dimples.*

"Can I come in?" Jack asked. "I'll only stay a minute."

Reluctantly, Paco stepped back, letting Jack enter for the second time. And cursing the first.

Jack set down the tray and swooped the envelope from the floor. It had a slight bump in it that he fiddled with, thumbing it over and over again. "I know how that must have looked back there, but—"

"Don't worry, Lieutenant. Your secret's safe with me. If that's all, sir, I've got to get ready to leave."

The sadness in Jack's eyes made Paco turn away.

But Jack didn't leave. Softly, he said, "I see. We're back to *lieutenant* and *sir* again. I understand."

"Yes, sir, we are."

Undeterred, Jack tapped the corner of the envelope against the palm of his hand. "Well, speaking as your superior, Staff Sergeant Robles, I actually came here because I need you to hang on to this. For safekeeping."

With an air of gravity, Jack handed over the envelope, and Paco stood almost at attention as he accepted it.

"Open it," Jack said. "I need to confirm you're up for the task."

Carefully, Paco peeled open the flap of the brown envelope. He looked inside before tipping it to pour its contents into his hand. It was a ring. Golden, though it couldn't be gold. An embossed signet ring with a thick, plain band.

Paco held it to the light, studying it, not noticing anything but a cheap piece of jewelry whose value couldn't exceed five bucks.

Jack snatched it back from Paco, tossing it in the air and catching it again. "You can get a closer look later. But only if you're up for everything this task entails. And I hope you are. Just so you don't get the wrong idea, this isn't yours to keep. Think of it as a placeholder."

Paco set himself up for operative mode, remaining professional as he listened intently, ready to receive his orders. When Jack shifted, professional flew out the window, and all Paco could do was listen to the deafening beats of his own heart.

Before him, Jack lowered to one knee, lifting the ring high. Paco held his breath as Jack began to speak.

"I know we haven't known each other that long, and this might seem, I don't know, hasty. Impetuous. Fucking nuts. But I can't imagine the rest of my life without you, and I don't want to try. I love you, Paco." Jack filled his lungs with a nervous breath, then continued. "Will you do me the unbelievable honor of marrying me? I don't have much to offer, but I swear I'll spend every hour of every day of the rest of my life making you happy."

For one of the first times in Paco's life, he was speechless. He looked down on the man smiling up at him. A man who led with his heart and was too gorgeous for words. A man he'd laughed with until dawn and shared every last one of his secrets with. The man asking him to take a leap of faith.

Shutting his eyes, he nodded without a word. Jack stood, wiping the tear Paco hadn't noticed, and gave him several sweet, soft kisses that he eagerly returned.

Jack broke away with an unmistakable sigh of relief. "And if you keep calling me *lieutenant* when we're alone, it's gonna start to turn me on."

Paco let a wide smile burst out for the first time that morning. Slowly, and somewhat ceremoniously, Jack lifted Paco's hand and slid the ring onto his finger.

Small problem. It didn't fit.

Paco's raised brow met Jack's determined eyes. For a moment, Paco allowed his finger to be nervously twisted and turned, while the ring continued to ram his thick knuckle.

Clearing his throat, Paco took back his hand and slipped the band from his ring finger to his pinky, adoring it proudly. "As usual, officers give the orders, while we enlisted men execute the mission."

With a chuckle, Jack kissed him softly. "I'm too happy to argue." He clasped Paco's hand, then almost apologetically said, "It's just an IOU until we get back. But I had to get you something. So I know you're mine."

"I'm yours."

Jack pressed a long kiss to the back of Paco's hand, then wiggled the ring to ensure its fit. "Keep it safe. You'll get to exchange it for something perfect in a few weeks."

"You're perfect," Paco said, stepping into his embrace, but Jack pulled himself free.

"Hang on." He grabbed the corded phone from the desk and dialed a room extension. "Hey, AJ, I need a bit longer. How about we all circle back in two hours instead of one. Yeah, I just want to do some quick sightseeing before we go. Great, thanks."

Paco smirked as Jack replaced the receiver, then forcefully tugged his lover by the waistband. "Well, I'm happy to show you my Tower of Pisa, but I can assure you, it won't be leaning."

CHAPTER 17

ALEX

Three weeks later
An undisclosed location in the Middle East

"He's at it again," Alex heard an exasperated Paco exclaim.

It was well deserved. Alex couldn't help his pacing or muttering as he tested and retested the technology he'd created on the fly. So much was riding on this operation, and as the lone civilian on the team, his insecurities had set in hard. Nothing could go wrong.

"Well, I guess that's why he gets the big bucks," Jack said, trying to squelch Paco's irritation. The guy was a natural-born leader, always commanding, yet warm. "AJ," he called out.

Alex strolled over, fiddling with a small gadget in his hand. "I'm thinking of going by Alex. What do you think?" he asked, genuinely wanting Jack's perspective but feeling unusually vulnerable.

Jack studied him, thoughtful as he considered the question. "Alex Drake?" He nodded. "Hmm. Actually, I like it. Sounds like a name you could build a high-tech empire with," he said, teasing him with a smile.

"Good. Settled. I'm Alex from here on out." Decisive and confident, he stood taller, straightening his collar and returning Jack's nod.

"Okay, *Alex*, we're gonna take a quick picture before our mission officially comes to an end."

Alex pocketed his tools and reached for the camera, but Jack grabbed his arm. "All of us. I'll set the timer so we'll all be in the shot."

Jack was the things great men were made of. And Alex was a lone and often lonely wolf hiding behind his Mister Life-of-the-Party persona. As was often the case, Jack eased Alex's insecurities, determined to show him he was part of the team. And each time he did it, it was appreciated.

Deep down, Alex knew he was annoying as shit. Sometimes intentionally. Often, more precautionary than anything else. His OCD was unrelenting. Incessant. He might have already checked and rechecked absolutely every fucking thing, but he had to.

Okay, maybe he didn't have to. He was a perfectionist intent on covering for all that was imperfect in his life. A facade for all that was missing. And Alex could sense that Jack had his own mask on too.

Alex wasn't sure if Paco knew about Jack's feelings. The man was obviously in love. Certain he himself was too arrogant or vain for love—or jaded in the wake of Jordan Stone—but Alex enjoyed being a spectator. Deep down, he wished Jack all the luck in the world. A world he suspected would always be just out of his reach.

"You sure?" Alex asked.

Their orders had been unequivocal. There was to be no evidence of their time overseas. But Alex wasn't making waves. Far from it. Of all things, he had this strange polite streak he just couldn't shake.

There were more reasons than one not to intrude on the photo op. The unlikeliness of their blossoming relationship was just the start. Both Jack and Paco were military. Alex hadn't earned a part in that. If anything, Alex had been the *I don't work for you* guy a time too many and should have been permanently iced out.

Alex hoped his precision and tech savviness would guarantee his permanence as part of the team. His devices were an undeniable reflection of himself—tailor-made to hide in plain sight. He was as camouflaged as any of his products, and as closed off as they came. But Jack always managed to break through with his genuine caring and directness.

Jack punched his shoulder. "Don't be an asshole. Of course I'm sure. Robles, come on."

Once Jack set up the camera and timer, they all stood, nearly at attention, professional to a fault. As the timer counted down, Jack huffed out a breath as he shook his head.

"Oh, this isn't the shot we're taking. This isn't a mug shot . . . it's something we'll look back on for years. The beginning of our bond. Come on," he said, grabbing their waists and drawing them in.

Both men threw their arms around his shoulders, all laughing with smiles wide. That precious moment was captured with the countdown.

In three . . . two . . . one.

PART III
THE PRESENT

CHAPTER 18

ALEX

Upstate New York

LOST IN HIS MEMORIES, Alex stared at the photo from his wallet. The one of the three of them together the day before the attack. Before Jack's death.

Why did Jack have to die?

Unsettled, Alex shut his eyes, but a ping from his computer there in the bunker brought him back to the present, alerting him to an incoming email from an anonymous sender. Mark Donovan's one-hour ultimatum had worked.

Controlling his reaction, Alex calmly said, "Received," before making what he knew would be a fruitless attempt at tracing the transmission.

Jordan Stone was returning to his life, and he had to know why. Alex's gaze fell to his wrist, checking his watch to verify the rendezvous time.

A nervous energy filled the room as Alex read aloud the confirmation, which said nothing more than, "Give me ten."

"Ten hours?" Mark asked. "Is he negotiating?"

"No," Alex said, not bothering to correct Mark's continued

presumption on gender. "I'm pretty sure Jordan means ten minutes."

"That's impossible," Mark said, but Alex only gave him a knowing glance.

Cat and mouse just took on a whole new meaning.

Without a clue what to anticipate, they were ready for anything. The secured bunker was equipped with state-of-the-art surveillance equipment that should alert them to an approaching vehicle a full mile out, but no alerts were set off.

Five minutes.

"What are you doing?" Mark asked, sounding a little panicked as he watched Alex deactivate the audio alerts and ensure the surveillance was set to record.

"Trust me," he said, half wondering if he should trust himself.

The bunker also had a weakness—an area that could be penetrated. It was ingenious and barely discernable, but Alex had discovered and secured it years ago, wondering about it time and again. Early on, he'd chalked it up to a design flaw. But today, he suspected he was about to find out the purpose of its well-constructed design.

Electronically, he disabled the locks securing it. This wasn't about preparing for war as much as staging a welcome. Well, a welcome with weapons in hand.

Not overly concerned, but better safe than sorry, Alex and Mark geared up in the armory. Of course, Mark couldn't help but select the most outlandish weapon from the high-end arsenal, a Heckler and Koch MP7.

"Seriously?" Alex asked.

Mark embellished his ensemble by loosening his tie and slipping the silk to his forehead. He re-cinched it at the temple in an impromptu Rambo impersonation. "What?"

When Alex lifted an agreeable HK45 from the wall, a noticeable *aww* came from his BFF.

Grabbing an assault rifle, Mark said playfully, "How about I go with 'I'll give you a war you won't believe,' and you do, 'say hello to my little friend.'"

Returning the heavy weapon to its setting, Alex held up his moderate weapon. "I'm good."

Without warning, the lights died. The backup generator kicked on, flooding the corridor with the red hue of emergency system lights. Within seconds, the standard power returned.

"Showtime," he said to Mark.

Unsurprised, Alex added this incident to his running mental checklist of unexpected/expected events. And instinctively, he knew. They were no longer alone. His natural intuition was confirmed by a voice penetrating the air from within an impenetrable facility.

"I'm in your pantry." The voice was distinctly male, and a surprise.

They took hurried but deliberate steps down the corridor, Mark with a submachine gun, and Alex holding the familiar and comfortable grip of the reliable semiautomatic handgun.

Unthreatening, the man they came upon seemed to be preoccupied with pilfering liquor, leaning over to help himself to their bourbon. With his back to them, he stood.

The tall man's gray-white hair was neatly trimmed in trademark military fashion. Spreading his arms wide, he revealed that his only weapons were a bottle of Jefferson's in one hand and a lowball in the other. Still, he knew the drill, holding his arms out wide but not letting go.

It was a charming attempt to show he was unarmed, content to hold his stance. Calm and confident, he seemed to know they'd refrain from riddling him with bullets if only to prevent spilling a drop of some of their favorite booze.

"Relax, boys, I come in peace," he said evenly, chiding them as he slowly turned in a circle. "Sorry, I tend to have a flair for the dramatic." Completing his rotation, he took a long look at Mark. "Ah, I see I'm not the only one."

Alex darted a glance at his *First Blood* friend.

"Fuck," Mark huffed out as he yanked the tie from his head.

"An interesting trick," Alex said to their uninvited guest. "You mind telling us who you are and how the hell you got in here?"

Mark frisked the intruder, who kept his arms high, still firmly holding the bottle and glass. Deep in analysis, Alex gave him a once-over.

Considering the man's expensive slacks, pullover, and sedately casual demeanor, he had to be some form of senior operative, and of an age that suggested he might be retired. Possibly a free agent, which would always be a concern. But the intruder seemed to have no intention of reaching for a weapon, so on some level, Alex could relax.

"He's clean," Mark said, surprise returning as his statement sounded like more of a question. Unlike Alex, Mark was taking no chances, and when he stepped to Alex's side, he centered the semi-automatic straight on the man's chest.

"Who are you?" Alex asked.

"I'm Jordan Stone."

Squinting, Alex cocked his head as the answer lingered between them.

The man smiled. "Yes, I can tell by the look on your face that my name might have led you to expect someone else." When Alex didn't react, the man shrugged and continued. "True, I'm not *your* Jordan Stone. Let's just say I'm the senior Jordan Stone, both in age and hierarchy. You can just call me Stone."

But he does know Jordan.

"How about I call you Houdini? You wanna tell us how the fuck you got in here?" Alex maintained a calm tone with loosely masked comical inflections. He didn't exactly need answers, but he wanted them.

Never one to tip his cards, Alex preferred all would-be adversaries feel warm and secure in thinking they held the advantage. The subtle tactic always preserved the upper hand of knowing more than he ever disclosed. Unfortunately, he was sure the man before him was very much the same.

At a glance, Alex pieced together more about his opponent. With his thousand-dollar shoes and Mister Rogers sweater, before him stood a man who had no fear, least of all from the fashion police.

No amount of scare tactics would faze this guy. Threats and intimidation were out. Any attempts to retrieve his intel by force wouldn't go far and wouldn't be necessary. Alex didn't need to waste his time.

This man was here for a game. And on a completely instinctual level, Alex knew Stone would willingly bear it all. He was here to play.

"May I?" Stone asked, exaggerating his movements to set down the contents of his hands.

The show was slow and anticlimactic, but Alex noticed that Mark tightened the grip on the weapon anyway.

Once he set down the bottle and glass, Stone carefully pulled his wallet from his back pocket. He opened it, pulling out a business card, but didn't immediately hand it over.

"When this facility was built," he said, "you were given a phone number you could call for both rudimentary maintenance as well as emergencies. You were instructed to memorize that number, and to set up a password and access code that you'd need to give to any operator who answered, confirming your identity."

"Yes," Alex said slowly, skeptical.

Stone passed him the card, giving him a moment to review the information. The card simply said *Stone* for his name, followed by a phone number. It was the same number Alex had committed to memory years ago. Intrigued, he looked up from the card, permitting Stone to continue.

"Your password is Cristo, and your code is 1220," Stone said, and Alex lowered his weapon. "Jack Taylor's birthday, December twentieth."

No one could know that. It meant this man was probably knew more and was more threatening that Alex could have imagined. It also meant training a weapon on him was pointless. And perhaps a little rude.

Securing the safety, Alex stood down and pocketed his pistol. It was a noticeable contrast to Mark, who refused to drop his defenses, holding tight to his former sniper life. Hospitality be damned.

"Mr. Drake, I know all this because I was the contractor you hired to build this SCIF a decade ago. I've been in and out of your life for a very long time."

To that, Alex said nothing, preferring to listen.

Casually, Stone poured a healthy serving of bourbon into his glass. "I needed to keep tabs on you. Make sure you were, well, all right. I orchestrated this, just as I paved the way for your first few major defense contracts."

Alex let the words sink in before asking, "Why?" Unworried, he stepped over to Stone, studying his eyes as he thought back to the beginnings of his business. His life after Jack. "Why would you, or anyone, go to the trouble? I was a nobody."

Stone took a sip before blowing out a long breath of resignation. "Because I was also the mastermind behind Jack Taylor's last mission."

CHAPTER 19

ALEX

Alex led them back to the main control room, which was ideal for lengthy conversations. Stone's statement seemed to promise just that.

They offered Stone his choice of seat. He took the one Mark had used and picked up the cards lying on the table in front of it. Mark sat across from him, giving him the cleanest shot . . . just in case. Alex was sure that for Stone, distrust would only garner his respect.

With the comfortable club chairs and the conference table still set up for playing cards, the awkward circumstances seemed somehow laid-back and natural. Just a few guys hanging out, drinking, chatting it up, with near disregard for the locked and loaded weapons at the ready.

Stone slid two cards to the center, face down, inviting Alex to what just became his game. Alex gave in, abandoning his firearm to Mark, who set aside the machine gun and rested Alex's handgun on his lap. Alex had a clear view of it still trained on Stone, undoubtedly with the safety switched off.

Stone sized up his cards, then seemed to do the same thing with Alex. "You know, you've grown so much."

Alex engaged him, imagining for the moment that the older man was a long-lost uncle and not a potential evil mastermind. Skillfully, Stone walked a tightrope of sharing just enough to keep him intrigued, while not giving away his hand.

"You're not the same kid we found all those years ago, wet behind the ears and hungry for a deal. No, the man sitting before me has a penchant for finding the truth."

"Is that why you're here? To give me the truth?" Alex asked. Stone's words reeked of bullshit, and yet held to something sincere.

"I am. And not just because you've got the bottomless resources to bankroll what could be a costly mission, but that you aren't afraid of a little danger. For a man like you, it's less of a deterrent and more of an aphrodisiac."

"We all have our vices," Alex said, picking up his abandoned lowball and sipping in agreement.

Stone raised an eyebrow his way. "I'll give you two choices, Alex Drake. Call it an initiation. I want to see where your allegiance lies. And for the rest of your life and mine, you'll only ever get the answer to one. Ready?"

"Sure," Alex said without the faintest trace of concern.

"I have two different people I could tell you about. And I swear to tell you everything I know about one of them. No matter which path you choose, I'll still end this meeting by asking you for one favor. The same favor, no matter which way you go."

"Okay." Intrigued, Alex set down his glass and clasped his hands on the table in front of him.

"Tell me who you want to know about. Madison's brother, Jack Taylor, and his mission? Or your Jordan Stone and hers?"

Calmly, Alex said, " She's not my Jordan Stone."

And she never was.

For Alex, choosing between the two—the woman who gave him his name, and Madison's dead brother—didn't require any thought.

"Jack," he said firmly, then reminded Stone, "Everything you know."

Agreeing with an approving nod, Stone continued. "Jack wasn't just any recruit. He was my recruit." Averting his eyes, he said, "He was special. The whole reason I agreed to come in."

"Special how?" Alex pressed, annoyed by how Stone chose his words with caution. "Look, either you come clean or this meeting is over."

"Fold." Stone tossed in his hand, not bothering to acknowledge Alex's ready dismissal.

Coolly and without missing a beat, Alex dealt again.

After picking up his new cards, Stone pressed on. "Jack was special in the same way you were special, and Mr. Robles was special. In such a unique way, it's hard to nail it down in words. And Jack wasn't recruited for your mission. He was recruited for mine. Yours was his cover."

Alex snapped his gaze up from his cards. "Living in BFE for months on end was a cover?"

Stone nodded. "His real task was to get a list of names. Double agents. He was my hand-selected operative, and as soon as he'd finished the job, he would have been permanently assigned to my team—to me." He swirled his bourbon, watching the caramel-colored liquid glaze the inner walls of the crystal lowball. "I saw in Jack what someone saw in me a very long time ago. So much so, I planned to bring him up in the ranks."

"You made him a promise?" Alex asked, leery of a line.

"No. Just the hopes and dreams of an aging man with no children. Wanting to pass on my secrets and wisdom to an amazing young man who'd most likely succeed me."

Mark finally chimed in. "So, you were Merlin to Jack's King Arthur?"

With a sad grin, Stone looked suddenly older as he replied. "If you consider the tragedy of both endings, yes."

Alex noticed something unexpected about Stone in that

moment, that the loss of Jack was his loss too. Needing the rest of the story, he said softly, "Go on."

"Jack spent months grooming the informant, securing the intel, and assured us he had everything. We were about to pull the team back. Then, out of the blue, the contact had more. Something new. Something important. I didn't approve the continued mission, and yet Jack received word that he was cleared to proceed. But," Stone sighed, "he was burned. You all were."

Mark interjected. "Hang on. An elite team is sent in, one in deep cover, and you're saying their mission was compromised? Missions like that don't just get burned. Sounds like an inside job amongst you puppeteers."

Mark gripped the gun tighter, but Alex calmed him with a gentle tap on the arm.

Remorseful, Stone looked at Alex. And without the need for words, Alex understood. This was more than a mission mishap. Stone had been deeply affected by it, leaving him something that both he and Alex had in common.

Guilt.

"*We* weren't burned." Alex leaned in. "Jack was. And like Mark said, sounds like his mission—his real mission—was compromised by someone on the inside. Pretty high up. Even higher than you."

Stone slumped back, nodding as he tightened his jaw. "I've always felt the same, but never knew for sure. Above me or below me, whoever it was, they covered their tracks like a pro. Within a few months, I was so upset and pissed off, I couldn't think straight. In the midst of the blowback, I left. I wasn't to blame, but took the hit nonetheless."

Stone pointed a finger, then tapped it hard on the table. "I made every effort to unravel the truth, tugged every thread, grasped every straw, and spent the better part of a decade digging for any clue to what really happened. But a few weeks ago, a glimmer emerged, and I jumped on it."

"So, you're here for the big reveal?" Alex asked. "Like, why not just call if you wanted to talk?"

Adamant, Stone shook his head. "No one can know you and I have talked. We didn't have a middleman. We knew, with the right staging, that Mark would bring you in. Even after all these years, I never know who might be listening. Waiting. Meetings can't go through your admin support or be on your calendar."

Stone polished off the remainder of his bourbon and set the glass aside. "And I don't have a big reveal. Not yet. I'm here because, as I told you up front, I need a favor." He clasped his hands tightly on the table, returning his desperate eyes to Alex's. "I need your help."

CHAPTER 20

ALEX

For most of the helicopter ride to the Adirondacks after the meeting concluded, Alex remained silent, deep in thought. And Mark did what he always did when Alex needed to process things. He gave him the room to think.

The time passed quickly, and then Mark's lavish cabin emerged in the clearing past the green spikes of lush pines. The tension that had built in Alex's neck and shoulders released as he made out Madison, waving to them from below on her stroll along the lake. Deliberately, he lifted his mood, determined not to tear his fiancée from what was left of her lighthearted and carefree day.

After a soft landing on the grass, Alex hopped out to head in the direction she'd been walking. The heat and humidity gave him all the incentive he needed to shrug off his blazer and tug off his tie.

"Madison?" he called out, searching up and down the lakefront, unsure of which way she might have gone. When he nearly tripped over her pile of discarded clothing, he smiled.

Squinting, he looked across the brightly shimmering lake. The flickering sparkles masqueraded her, hiding her in a sea of glittering light. With a kidlike splash, she teased him, swimming out further.

"Hey, beautiful. Want some company?"

"You're a little overdressed for the occasion," she called out, the only woman who could pull him from his dark thoughts and entice him to come out and play.

And just like that, Alex began ripping off his clothes, certain his stripping would give him high marks in both technique and speed.

When there was little left to reveal, Madison shouted, "Alex, wait!"

"Wait? While a sea nymph skinny-dips before me? Like hell I'll wait." Defiant, Alex grabbed the waist of his pants, shoving the last of his clothes proudly to his feet.

A two-tone whistle broke through the air. It would have been welcome from Madison—not so much from Jess.

Fuck!

"Jeez," he said, hurrying to scoop up his clothes to cover himself. "Um, hi, Jess."

"Hey, hot stuff," Jess said with a wink, giggling as she laid down a fresh towel on the grass for Madison. Delighted but careful to maintain eye contact, she turned, meeting Alex face-to-face. "Just came down to bring Madison a towel. Oh, I didn't bring two. Shall I . . ."

As nonchalant as a man could be when mostly naked with his best friend's wife, Alex said, "No, I think Madison and I can make do."

Jess slowly sauntered away, stopping to whirl back around with juvenile enthusiasm. "Only if you're sure," she said, smiling as she waited out his response. Hearing Madison's giggles, Jess was no doubt enjoying his discomfort as much as his full moon.

Stoically, he faced Jess, replying under his huffed and embarrassed breath. "I'm sure, Jess." When she opened her mouth to reply, he shot back, "Positive!"

"Well, as long as you're sure." Jess gave Madison a very drawn-out wave and giggled her way back to the house, Madison's laughter echoing hers.

With the coast clear, Alex dropped the bundle and streaked into the water. "Time to take care of you, Ms. Taylor."

Squealing with delight, she swam out further but couldn't outpace him.

Stroke after stroke, his body pushed effortlessly through the water. Once he caught her, he paused, soaking in the amber shimmers and afternoon glow surrounding her. She was his angel.

As the sun began its descent, she floated, skimming her fingers along the surface, sending out soft ripples of the water with every pass.

Alex moved in, closing the distance between them, but stopped shy of a kiss. "Do you know one of the biggest advantages of meditation?"

Grinning, she gave him a quizzical look as she shook her head. "What?" The word whispered off her lips, daring him to kiss her.

He gazed at their fullness but pulled back. "It teaches the mastery of . . . certain things."

"Hmm, like what?" she asked, her eyes wide with interest as she treaded water before him, naked.

A foot taller than she, he was able to plant his feet firmly on the lake bottom. It took nothing to prowl up to her. He kept enough of a distance so there would be no touching. It was a small punishment for her sweet giggles, but it would do.

His gaze met hers before his mouth descended to her ear. "Like, breathing," he said low, then licked down her neck before submerging his head beneath the surface.

Her body was cool to the touch, and he enjoyed warming her with his hands, caressing her waist and hips beneath the water.

Her shiver was delicious, and he kissed her belly, feeling her soft panting as he worked his way down.

He placed the heat of his palms around the soft mounds of her ass, pulling her toward him and spearing her with his tongue. Hearing her muffled shriek above the surface, he lapped at her as her body went limp.

In the last few seconds of his held breath, he tickled her with a few bubbles, then stood.

Sliding a hand between her thighs, he laid her on her back, supporting her beautiful body as it floated on the surface. With his head between her legs and her thighs draped over his shoulders, Alex feasted on her, lapping her with his tongue as he enjoyed the scene. The sunset and her breasts. Her wet pussy against the surface of the lake. The two of them. Alone.

The water was cool and sweet as his tongue sliced delicately across her folds. Her own honey was decadent, and her swollen pussy was so soft and ready.

As he teased a finger to her entrance, his mouth found her clit and sucked. She moaned. Back and forth, he worked two fingers in, penetrating her deep, then deeper with each thrust.

When he found that sweet, precious spot, her walls clamped around him as she came hard, crying out in ecstasy. Waiting patiently as she came down, he removed his fingers and wrapped his arms around her, embracing her into his chest. She panted as he cradled her body close to his.

He gave her kiss after kiss as he carried her shivering body toward the bank.

"And where do you think you're taking me?" she asked, kissing his neck. Her fingers suggestively traced figure eights across the scars of his chest as she pressed delicate kisses here and there.

"The sun is setting and you're cold. I don't want you getting sick."

"Then warm me up," she said. The double dare behind her eyes was tempting, and it made Alex stall.

Indecisive, he paused in the shallower water as he weighed his options. Did he have the willpower to pull out when the time came? He considered it, taking in every inch of her voluptuous body as she lay in his arms.

Not a fucking chance in hell.

His angst made her giggle. "What's wrong? Can't whip out a condom from here?"

"Must you mock the misfortunes of others?"

"Alex, we're engaged, and I get my shot regularly. It's ninety-nine percent effective."

"I like those odds," he said, easily swayed to bareback it.

In one of her most persuasive moves yet, she nibbled his neck as she whispered, *"Please."*

God, she's good.

"So, are you just going to stand there all night, letting me freeze?"

"We are indeed engaged." He reached for her left hand, alarmed to find her ring finger bare. Concerned, he scanned the lake. *It would take a dozen divers to find it. Maybe two dozen.*

"I didn't lose it," she said to put him at ease. "I left it in my jacket pocket so it wouldn't slip off during my swim."

Relieved, he kissed the spot where her ring normally rested.

"Well, then, I won't let you freeze . . . but only because I'm a gentleman. And a gentleman would never let a luscious, wet, naked, breathtakingly gorgeous lady needlessly shiver."

"Thank God you're a gentleman," Madison said, either acknowledging his status or in relief, he wasn't sure which.

In waist-deep water, he released her body just enough to move himself between her legs, which instantly wrapped around him. "Especially for a water nymph who is so exceptionally . . ." He slid his fingers through her still plump, hot folds. "Aroused."

This would be a first. His bare skin inside her. He imagined it, fisting himself before moving his throbbing cock back and forth along her slick sex. Biting the fullness of her lower lip, she tightened her thighs around him.

"So impatient," he murmured.

"Yes," she said, pulling again.

It wasn't her strength that drew him into her, but the magnetic pull of her gorgeous cunt that readily swallowed every inch of his dick in a single, hard thrust. Her tight walls were heaven, encouraging his thrusts and drawing up his balls.

Too fast, he thought, and forced himself to slow down.

Trying, and failing, to take hold of his slick body, she whimpered as her nails clawed along the muscles of his arms.

"Yes," he said, urging her to dig into his skin harder.

All those practiced meditative breaths could help him hold out a few minutes, but not much more than that. "God, Madison, you feel so good."

As he steadied himself, looking down at this woman who was everything to him, his thrusts took on a new and different rhythm. It was beautiful. She was beautiful.

He memorized every curve and every movement. Every pleasure he could bring her. Then he stopped.

"What is it?" she asked, concern flashing across her flushed face as she panted.

As he breathed hard, he could feel his expression contorting. Her serious glance and wrinkled brow forced him to return a breathy laugh.

"I'm fine. I just need a moment." He was solemn, but sweet. "I've never been this close without reaching for a condom. Ever. And, God, you're squeezing me within an inch of my life. I never want it to end. I need to make it last."

Madison wrapped her arms around his neck, beginning her own slow thrusts. "You say that like it'll never happen again. And that might be a problem because I'm getting cold."

Wrapping both arms around her waist, he slid his thumb to her firm little clit.

"Then I'll warm you up," he said, circling his thumb and controlling the pace of their ride in the water. "But I *will* take my time."

Moving his mouth down to her breast, he sucked in her pert nipple, teasing it with his teeth before sucking it hard. She muffled her sounds.

"No." His command was dissatisfied and low. "No holding back. Not now. I need to hear you."

He felt the tiniest tremors building along the length of his dick. God, he wanted it too. Slamming himself deep inside, he forced those throaty screams out of her, satisfied as they echoed across the lake.

"Now, baby. Come for me, Madison."

His hoarse demand drove them over the edge together. The walls of her pussy clamped hard around his staff, milking him as he erupted. His legs buckled beneath the intensity of his own climax.

Alex tumbled backward, taking Madison with him as they dropped with a large splash into the water, letting their loud climaxes spill over into laughter.

∽

Sharing the plush bath sheet made way for more cuddling and less drying. Their hair stayed damp and dripping as they helped each other dress. Alex worried as the evening chill rolled in.

He snagged her jacket off the ground, anxious to retrieve the ring before sliding her jacket on her. His hand dove into the first pocket. Empty. In the second pocket, he could feel two items in his grip. When he withdrew and unclasped his hand, alarm set in.

"Shit!"

"What? Did it slip out?" Madison asked. But seeing his palm

spread wide, it was obvious the ring was there. Next to it was a small blinking bead. "What's that?"

"It's a tracker," a sultry voice said from behind them.

The woman's footsteps were slow as she took her time approaching them. The deepening darkness didn't help, but even as a silhouette, her tall legs and long hair were unmistakable. And deliberately walking toward them.

"Hello, Alex."

It was her. The seductive ghost from his past suddenly hell-bent on a haunting. An inferno's flame who never took *no* for an answer.

Sure, he might have hungered for her over the years. Even craved her touch in the best and worst ways. But he'd long ago abandoned the thought of it.

Alex held his ground between the angel of his future and the devil from his past. His step was deliberate toward the insistent intruder.

Now, faced with her smoldering gaze and bright red lips, the raw reality of his needs and wants stripped away every thought at all. All but one.

Madison.

CHAPTER 21

MADISON

Madison watched as Alex drew away from her in an obviously calculated move.

His full-body block was her fortress, and Madison's heart raced as she recognized it. He'd done it once before, in a street brawl right outside his office building. Three against one. But pitted against Alex, those thugs hadn't stood a chance.

Would she?

The woman who approached was unmistakable, despite blending into the twilight. The voluptuous, shadowy figure emerged in a body-hugging leather jacket and skintight jeans, every inch a predator on the prowl.

It was the woman who'd helped Madison collect herself in the break room. And, she suspected, might have done more. J, who'd given Madison no more than a letter for her name and a promise they would meet again.

Big surprise. She kept her word.

By the purr of her painted lips and the lust in her eyes, it was easy to see J and Alex had a past. No doubt an intimate one.

Well, you and a few hundred others, lady.

But why was she here, hunting them down like an alligator Birkin? A stalker?

What kind of deranged stalker hikes across twenty-five miles of wilderness in wedge boots?

Madison watched the standoff between this woman and Alex, anxious for him to make his move. By his hard eyes and ready stance, it was clear that whatever past he and J shared, they were far from cordial now.

"Hello, Jordan." His voice was cold and hard, slicing the air with a harsh tone that was unrecognizable to Madison.

Jordan. So that's what the J stands for.

With his finger and thumb, Alex crushed the blinking beacon, killing it before he hurled it into the lake. "What do you want?"

"I needed to see you. To talk with you. Alone."

Alex only chuckled, clearly unamused. Casually, he pocketed his hands and turned his face to the mansion behind Jordan. There, a red beam twinkled from the roof.

"Well, I'm not alone. And I don't just mean Madison. Turn around," he said.

Cutesy and spry, Jordan did a little dance as she turned in that direction. She gave no reaction to the sight except the lightest chirp from her lips. The bright red laser beam shot down the grassy slope from the mountaintop manor, disappearing into her chest.

Madison held her breath, realizing Jordan had just become a target.

"And now back," Alex said sternly.

Just as she did the first time, Jordan moved seductively to complete the turn, to find a new beam hitting her from across the lake.

Out of nowhere, two separate snipers were in position and ready, prepared to shoot a woman who apparently needed no introduction.

"As you can see, I'm not alone," Alex said, but if Jordan had a care in the world, she masked it well and simply smiled.

Pressing a hand to Alex's back, Madison softly said, "Alex." It was a worthless plea—not saying more to help a woman who seemed to have gone out of her way to help her.

"You misunderstand, Alex. I didn't mean you. I don't need to see *you*. I need to speak with your beautiful bride-to-be." Jordan raised her voice, hurling it past Alex to its intended recipient. "I need to talk with you, Madison. Alone."

"Me?" Curious, Madison tried to move forward, but Alex held her back with a protective hand, preventing her from stepping any further into the volatile area.

"That's not going to happen, Jordan." Alex's words were final, and perhaps not just to Jordan. "You want to talk, make an appointment."

"Stone already explained why we can't do that."

Before her eyes, Madison watched as the battle to gain the upper hand unfolded.

Alex crossed his arms over his chest. "Well, if you two are together, there's an appointment already set up. We'll see you then."

Without explanation, Alex whisked Madison to his side, keeping her from the gunmen's line of sight as he steered them both toward the house.

Jordan stayed in place, lifting her voice high. "Don't you want to know why Jack was killed?"

Madison stopped short, and Alex did too. She glanced at him, and based on his pensive expression, he knew more than he could share at that moment.

Dismissing his warning glance, Madison did what she knew she shouldn't do. Pulling from Alex's protective embrace, she stepped forward, stopping just shy of the potential line of fire. Cautiously, she closed in just enough to say what she needed to, knowing Jordan was an absolute temptress. A cunning wolf in skintight sheep's clothing.

For a moment, Madison stayed locked in Jordan's gaze, doing her best to shake off her power stare and intimidation. Still, Jordan's provocative allure and unmistakable badass vibe were harder to ignore.

The tension was obvious. Standing before some lethal supermodel from Alex's past, Madison was grateful to be cloaked in enough darkness that how wretched she must look after their swim might be missed.

Despite her makeup-free face and dripping hair, Madison spread her feet and crossed her arms over her chest, desperate to come off more as Cujo and less as a soaking-wet kitten. Because this woman, whoever she was, just brought up Jack as if he were bait.

Unsettled, Madison stayed calm and lifted a brow. "Our position is clear. See you at the appointment." With that said, she turned and hurried past Alex to head back to the house.

"I'm sure you can find your way back," Alex said to Jordan over his shoulder before catching up to Madison.

They walked quietly. Sedately. A few steps in, his arm wrapped around her. It would almost be romantic if not for the disturbing intrusion by a likely old flame of Alex, and a new stalker for Madison.

Lucky me.

Madison broke the uncomfortable silence as they traversed the grass. "Alex?"

He cleared his throat. "Yes?"

"So, that woman. Jordan. I met her today."

"What?" His voice was noticeably strained but remained low as his grip on her tightened.

"I thought it was just happenstance that she found me."

"Found you? Where?"

Oh, you know. Wedged between a watercooler and the wall, eaves-

dropping on my coworkers speculating that the conference room is where the reverse-harem magic happens.

Madison shrugged. "Around the office."

"She made it past the lobby of DGI?" Alex stopped, but her arm around his waist urged him on, keeping him moving.

"Yes. And now this woman has tracked me down to the middle of the Adirondacks. Where, come to find out, you hired two sharpshooters and had them at the ready."

"I didn't hire them," Alex said, adding to the mystery.

Sensing the tension in him, she said, "There's something I have to know," as they took the back patio steps to the house.

Alex leaned in to open the door, ushering her through. "Anything you want to know, I'll tell you," he said, assuring her as he secured the door and shut the curtains.

Once inside, she clung to him, letting his arms wrap around her. His comfort let her breathe.

Wide-eyed, she looked up at him. "Exactly how many people were watching us during our, um, wet-and-wild water sports?"

"My guess? At least three," he said with a shrug and an innocent smile. He stroked her hair, then tenderly cupped her cheek. "I swear, this wasn't as orchestrated as it seemed. I had no idea anyone was around until I saw the sniper laser. But it's probably a good idea to ratchet up the protection."

Holding her tightly, he smoothed his hands across her back and kissed her tenderly on the forehead. His words were soft. "Let's just say that from now on, I'll be treating you like royalty. Better, even. I'll have more security around you than a princess."

Madison's protest was weak. "Just for a while."

His mouth soothed her pouting lips with a kiss. "Promise."

She kissed him back before being hit by a wave of panic. "What about Jess and Mark?"

Alex glanced away, scrunching his face. "Well, the sniper on the roof was probably Mark."

Madison gasped as she sank against him, realizing Mark must

have gotten an eyeful. Mortified, she buried her face in Alex's solid chest.

"He wasn't alone," Jess called out, waltzing down the stairs with binoculars strapped around her neck and a large bowl in her hands. "Someone had to bring the popcorn."

Madison shook her head with an embarrassed whimper.

"Hey," Jess said, "I made sure Mark covered his eyes the whole time." Her chuckle was light as she laid a hand on Madison's shoulder. "Don't worry, you both were dressed by the time Mark got into position. Seriously, are you all right?"

Madison grabbed a few pieces of popcorn. "Yes. No. Maybe? Who's Jordan? Why was she tracking me? And who was the other sniper?"

"*Snipers*," Jess said, stressing the last *s*. "My brothers live on a few of the acres, tending the land. They're vets, and do everything from forestry to basic bodyguard work when needed. And if there's one thing Bishop men like, it's getting back in the action. The shorter the notice, the better. I texted them when Mark picked up your friend," she said to Alex.

Alex scoffed. "She's not my friend."

Worried, Madison asked, "Should we go somewhere safe?"

"Nowhere's safer than here," Mark said, double-stepping it down the stairs, one hell of a scoped rifle hanging from a strap over his shoulder. He pointed to the windows. "The glass isn't just bulletproof. It can withstand the blast from standard-issue grenades."

"For the record, you were right about our need for security upgrades," Jess said, tossing a kernel of popcorn into his mouth before giving him a peck on the lips.

Mark lifted a brow to Alex. "Whoever that was, she triggered the detectors a few miles back. That crazy cat woman moves fucking fast, and the proximity detectors lost her as she closed in on the lake. But I had your six. Friend of yours?"

Clearly exasperated, Alex shot back, "For the love of God, she's not my friend."

The three of them blinked at him in disbelief.

"Fine. But if she's my friend, she's just become yours too, Mark. *That* would be Jordan Stone."

"Another one?"

"And those are just the ones we know about."

Alex corralled them all to the oversized couches, promising to tell them everything.

But Madison guessed he would probably leave out a thing or two.

CHAPTER 22

MADISON

Later that evening, Madison watched from the bed as Alex sent a few quick texts. Once he finished, he painted on a smile as he slid in under the covers. His body moved to hers, and he pulled her back against his chest. Curled up in the solid arms of the man she loved, Madison could only think of him.

Despite quietly holding her, he was stiff, tension filling every muscle of his frame. He was preoccupied, which meant he must be strategizing.

"Mind if I interrupt?" she asked with a smile, tilting her head back toward his.

Alex let out a light laugh. "Was I thinking that loudly?" He kissed her lips.

She skated her fingers across his cradling arm. "Oh, I can feel every bit of your restless energy. I know when there's a disturbance in the force. And," she said carefully, tiptoeing into her next words, "it's obvious you and Jordan have a past."

"Madison—"

"*Shh*, let me finish," she said gently. "I know you two were more than casual acquaintances, but that doesn't matter. Not a bit."

With that, he moved back, turning Madison to face him. He studied her eyes, analyzing the truth in her words.

"Come on. I'm with the legendary Alex Drake. I'm far from the first woman you've bedded. Light years away, maybe." When an amused and exaggerated smile emerged from his lips, she added, "And it's not exactly like you were my first."

His proud grin soured to an instant sulk. Madison felt the vibration of his growl ripple through her, forcing a giggle as she nuzzled into him.

"Let's imagine I am," he said with a playful grin.

"And maybe we could imagine I'm friends with Jordan." Madison's fingers pressed against his lips, quieting him before he could speak. "I need to be ready to deal with her. It's obvious she wants to speak with me. *Alone*, as she put it in her ridiculously sultry way, and I have a sneaking suspicion she's the kind of girl who gets what she wants."

"So are you," he said matter-of-factly. "What do you need?"

"To know what to expect. Tell me about her."

His expression uneasy, Alex ran his fingers through her hair. "I don't know her as well as you might think. And even then, I don't know much. Our encounter was . . . brief." He swallowed hard at the last word, but Madison urged him on with a nod. "I know she'll use her sexuality when she can."

"Who could blame her? I would too, if I had it in spades the way she does."

Alex's lips descended on hers. "You do," he whispered, lightly rubbing his nose against her cheek.

Her head returned to his chest. "Okay, so she's sexy and she knows it. Anything else?"

"Yes." His hand trailed down her back, pulling her in. "She'll try to lure you. With something that, no matter how trivial it may seem to others, will be important to you." He blew out a long breath. "Dammit, Madison, I don't like it."

"Like what?" she asked, feigning innocence.

"That you're going to see her. But you are, aren't you?"

She stroked his chest. "Not exactly. I'm just not going to stop her from seeing me, but I can't make it seem too easy for her to get me alone. I'll have more of an advantage if she underestimates me. Gives me a chance to learn how she operates. Especially since she may have tipped off Fife's team about some corporate espionage."

"What?" Alex exclaimed, practically sitting up.

Patting his chest, Madison urged him to lie back down. "I'm not sure about it. It's just a hunch. But I can't figure out she would do that. Is she trying to sway me? Make me feel like I owe her? I need to let her closer, in a way that makes her think she holds all the cards."

Alex pulled her hand to his lips, kissing her knuckles sweetly, and softly wiggled the ring hugging her finger. He clasped her hand to his chest. "Well, those who underestimate you tend to get burned. And in this world of burn or be burned, my money's on you. Fortune favors a bold, brave beauty with fire in her soul."

"Might you be *fortune* in this scenario?" she whimsically mused.

"I am . . . and I'd love to feel the heat of your fire."

They kissed, and she welcomed his body between her legs, his hard cock firm against her core.

"Oh, one more thing," she whispered, adjusting her hips to the perfect position.

"And what would that be?" he murmured as his lips nibbled across her neck.

"Remember how we said no more secrets?"

Halting mid-kiss, he said warily, "Yeah?"

"Until this is all over, that's off the table. I don't want to risk inadvertently tipping your hand. Whatever it is you're planning, you can't let me know."

"What makes you think I'm planning anything?"

Sweetly, she brushed his lips with hers until they kissed.

Without questioning her further, he whispered, "I'll make you a deal, Ms. Taylor. After tonight, I promise to keep you in the dark, but only on one condition."

"What's that?" she said softly, enjoying the weight of his body on hers.

"Tonight, you have to keep me somewhere dark. And preferably deep."

The head of his cock slid to the entrance of her heat while he trailed hot, open-mouthed kisses delicately across her shoulder.

"Deal," she gasped, barely getting the word out before Alex forced upon her the firmness of his position.

CHAPTER 23

ALEX

Manhattan

BY LATE MONDAY AFTERNOON, Alex had taken every precaution, making the necessary arrangements to receive one—or more than one—Jordan Stone. As the CEO of a company specializing in next-generation surveillance and reconnaissance equipment, he used every technology available, all of which were at his fingertips.

The appointment booked in his calendar for him and Madison was simply marked PRIVATE. Jordan Stone would not be meeting them. Instead, the fake name of J. Slate would. Fife understood the VIP guest would arrive through a back entry of DGI's Manhattan headquarters, with him being the one and only gatekeeper.

Alex couldn't risk entry into his office, or any of his executive suites or conference rooms. Who knew what sorts of devious devices would be planted by these operatives?

Oh, that's right. He would.

Microscopic monitoring, retractable recording devices, and nano-tracking equipment the size of pinheads were par for the course. He'd grown a multibillion-dollar empire by developing and selling these covert gems to corporate giants and nation states. Today, he needed to ensure they weren't used against *him*.

With new cameras on every floor, he now had visuals on everyone who entered. Even the very persistent Jordan herself. And a sweeper crew, so that wherever any Jordan Stone went, the team would follow, ensuring a full scan and cleanup.

A few small conference rooms were scheduled for renovation on the second floor. The pre-demolition site was perfect for such a meeting. They only needed Stone and Jordan to arrive, and Operation Shadow would commence.

Alex sent a text.

ALEX: *Anything?*
PACO: *Already tracking. Shouldn't we warn Madison?*
ALEX: *No. Per her instructions.*
PACO: *Surveillance mode?*
ALEX: *Hell yes. And we'll interrupt if she looks distressed.*

With that, the ping of his cell phone alerted him that his visitor had arrived. Alex scrolled to the highest favorite on his phone and clicked it.

"Madison, Fife texted me. He's here, and he's alone."

"*He* this time?" Madison asked. "It's like we're dealing with a shape-shifter. Okay, I'll meet you down there."

"Love you."

"Love you too."

But before the call with Madison ended, he heard the words repeated again through the phone in a familiar sultry voice.

"Love you too," Jordan said.

The line disconnected.

CHAPTER 24

MADISON

Madison glanced up to find Jordan Stone standing in the doorway to her office. In her pencil skirt, high ponytail, and black-rimmed reading glasses, she looked like an executive. A very hot, strips-on-the-side-to-afford-her-Ferrari executive, but one, nonetheless.

"Mind if I have a seat?" Jordan entered the office, closing and then locking the door behind her.

"Please do. You must be tired after that hike." Madison hoped her tone came off less cocky and more campy. Based on Jordan's smirk, who could say?

Overall, she wasn't sure if Jordan was there to recruit her, seduce her, or skin her and make herself a Madison suit, perfect for walking down the aisle in the hopes of marrying Alex.

Seriously, it was hard to tell.

Jordan took several long strides into the office, rounding Madison's desk and making herself comfortable on the edge of it. She pulled something small from her cleavage, then slightly hiked up her skirt, allowing her butt to glide further back on the desk.

Relieved, Madison watched as Jordan crossed her toned, bare

legs, grateful for the lack of a money shot. The little device was pressed. When it clicked, Jordan explained.

"I just need to ensure we're really alone. This will jam any pesky listening devices."

Madison rested back in her chair. "You're sure determined to see me. What do you want?"

"It's not what I want, Madison. It's what *we* want. And when I say we, I'm not talking the royal *we*, like I'm tight with Queen Elizabeth or part of the mob. I'm talking about you and me."

Stretching her leg forward, Jordan slid the side of her six-inch stiletto against Madison's outer thigh. The move was playful. They could have been lounging at the pool, chatting about the cute guys at the bar.

Prepared, Madison didn't stop Jordan. Instead, she analyzed her. Her approach, her mannerisms, even her shade of lipstick. She understood why Alex changed when he briefly discussed her.

Jordan was different. For Alex, Madison imagined she'd have to be. But her mystique was so unusual. And disarming. Captivated, Madison listened attentively.

"At the end of the day," Jordan said, "you and I want the same thing, but this only works if you're in. If you're not, no skin off my nose. I'll be on my merry way, never to darken your door again."

Letting her intrigue lead the discussion, Madison leaned in, equally coquettish in her question. "And what exactly is it *we* want?"

Jordan's smile grew as she bent down, her nearly pitch-black eyes dancing with delight as she took a long peek down Madison's blouse. "For starters, a chance to work very closely together."

Holding out her hands, Jordan urged Madison to take them. She did. Jordan's thumbs brushed the top of Madison's knuckles, soothing in a femme Nikita sort of way.

"Your ring is stunning," Jordan said, admiring it. "Jewelry can be so personal. So intimate. Really sends a message. Now, Alex could have bought you anything . . . a rock as big as your face. But he kept it to a size and style that would suit you. It's undoubtedly flawless, unrivaled in its brilliance. But I have a sneaking suspicion the real statement isn't about the diamond at all. Right? It's inscribed, isn't it?"

Surprised, Madison nodded, trying not to look overly impressed under Jordan's observant eyes.

"Something small, obviously, and highly meaningful to the two of you. For sure, it's less than five words . . . maybe three."

Madison held her breath, wondering if Jordan could actually recite the inscription, *I'm all in*. But she quickly lost interest, moving on to the bracelet on Madison's other wrist. Slowly, Jordan turned it, letting the exquisite tennis bracelet catch the light. The diamonds twinkled like fire.

"Now, this one puzzles me. Granted, it's utterly amazing. But it doesn't seem to suit you like the ring. Like he got it before he really knew you. Or maybe he didn't buy it at all, letting some lackey do his bidding. Am I close?"

Madison said nothing.

"Hmm, you hardly strike me as someone who wears things for flash, and I'm not even sure you'd wear it just because Alex gave it to you. Knowing Alex Drake, he's given you a warehouse full of precious jewels. But deep down, your nouveau riche status doesn't hold your interest. Somehow, your personality seems a little, I don't know, meeker, perhaps. A bit less ball-busting and slightly more Stepford wife."

Jordan's eyes were bright with mischief as they met Madison's. "Why are you wearing it?"

As Madison looked down and stammered to speak, ready to make up something on the fly, Jordan squeezed her hands firmly.

"Oh, no need for that. Teeing up a deception? Don't bother. It won't work on me. You're too transparent. Keep me guessing, if you must, but don't lie. Much like the bracelet, it doesn't quite suit you."

With a brush of her fingers against a specific area of Madison's arm, Jordan reassured her with a grin. "No hives. Good. I won't worry I'm making you uncomfortable."

Madison had no idea how Jordan could know about that, but she did, and she was right. Madison wasn't nervous around her. The shock of that alone should have triggered a full-body breakout. There was a strange kinship between them that Madison prayed didn't remotely come close to romantic.

Jordan smiled. "Besides, your sweetly innocent inability to lie is exactly why I'm here."

CHAPTER 25

ALEX

ALEX KEPT STONE WAITING, preoccupied with watching the monitor and trying to figure out what the hell was going on between Jordan and Madison. By the looks of it, Jordan was making a move on his girl.

Which is bullshit, fucked up, and wrong.

Hot, but wrong.

The disrupter Jordan brought was anticipated. Its strength, however, was not, and seriously blew his tech out of the water. Attentive, he watched from the old-school coaxial-cable video feed. When high tech failed you, low tech was the ace in the hole. Every time.

A mic with any real range would be easily blocked. He tried anyway. Of course, it was jammed by Jordan's little toy.

Helplessly, he clenched his teeth and analyzed the feed. Per Madison's instructions, she had no idea about their surveillance. It prevented her from tipping their hand.

After an unusual amount of talking and touching, Jordan finally left. Madison also left her office. She was running late for their meeting with Stone and would likely rush to get there.

Alex sent a text as he raced after her.

ALEX: *She's on the move.*
PACO: *Got her. I'll keep you posted.*

Alex caught up with Madison as she arrived at the conference room door. Tightly, he pulled her close. "You all right?"

Frowning, she searched his eyes. "I don't know." She looked away. "Will she keep her word?"

His hands cupped her jaw, forcing her eyes back to his. "What did she offer you?"

"I . . . it's just . . . just tell me. Will she keep her word?"

Uncertain, Alex shrugged, shaking his head with a sigh. "I don't know. Probably. She did with me."

Opening her mouth, Madison seemed ready to share the details of Jordan's tempting offer when the door to the conference room flew open. Stone's impatience at their lateness melted before their eyes as his sincere gaze fell on Madison.

"Madison Taylor," he both asked and said at once, as if finding it hard to believe the woman was actually standing before him. Wrapping her hand in both of his, he smiled. "It's very nice to finally meet you. You're as beautiful as your brother always said."

Keeping her hand in his, he led her into the room, followed by Alex. "I'd always hoped we'd meet one day." His eyes still searching hers, he asked Alex, "Did you tell her who I am?"

Madison answered. "You're the handler that recruited my brother for his mission."

Reverently, Stone nodded. "I promised Jack I'd make it up to him someday."

"So, Jordan was telling the truth?"

There was no hiding his reaction. "Jordan? She was here?"

Alex chimed in. "That's why we're late."

Stone huffed before he smiled, turning sheepish between the two.

"I swear that woman has serious control issues. I told her I was meeting with you. Never mind. It doesn't matter." Straightening to his full height, he could easily pass for a senator or a diplomat. There was elegance in his plea as he asked, "Will you, Madison?"

Protective, Alex laid his hands softly on her shoulders as he gritted out, "Will she what?"

"Give us a minute, Mr. Stone," she said, taking Alex's arm and leading him out of the room. They crossed the hall, entering another conference room under renovation.

Seeing the construction crew, Alex made an announcement. "Gentlemen," he boomed above the noise, and the clamor quieted. "Why don't you take off for a bit. Enjoy the break room at the end of the hall. Come back in twenty."

The men filed through the door, leaving Alex and Madison to their privacy. Making her way past the pieces of metal, drywall, and debris, Madison crossed the room to stand at the large window overlooking the bustling street below. Alex let her wander, pocketing his hands. Though always protective, he remained patient.

"It's ironic, really. This room is in the swirl of a storm and looks exactly how I feel inside. And yet the outside world always goes on." A look of longing filled her face. "I love people watching. I get glimpses into what life could be like for me someday. If I could move on." Wiping away a tear, she glanced back. "But maybe if I had real closure. Maybe . . ."

Alex's patience was fleeting. In three steps, he had her in his arms.

"You were right," she said. "Jordan lured me with something important. Something meaningful, maybe to no one other than me. Even just the possibility . . . I have to do it."

"Do what?"

"Oh, not much. Just enter an ultra-secure intelligence agency with no cover to speak of, retrieve an item, or items, or documents, and possibly data, because they're not actually sure what I'm specifically looking for. After that, I hand over whatever we find to the Stone twins, and cross my fingers in the hope that they keep their word."

Alex sucked in a breath. "Is that all?"

"I have to do it."

"*You?*" Alex asked softly. "I think you mean *we*."

"No, me. It has to be *me*."

After a soft kiss, he lowered his forehead to hers. "Not happening. Not without me." When she shook her head, he opted to switch gears to avoid an argument. Brushing an errant strand of hair behind her ear, he asked softly, "And what would you get out of all this?"

Filled with hope, her eyes were pleading. "If Jordan keeps her word, and you said she probably would, somehow they'll reinstate Jack's record. He'll be honored for the military hero he was."

Madison held her breath as she stared at Alex, hoping that as they discussed it, he would come to the same conclusion she already had.

CHAPTER 26

MADISON

When Madison and Alex returned to the conference room where Stone waited, they found he was gone, leaving a small note behind. Alex read it aloud.

J said it's a go.
We'll be in touch.

"Why does Jordan think it's a go?" Alex asked.

Madison cradled the hard line of his stubbled jaw, soothing him with a kiss. "She needed an answer. I told her yes."

"It's not a go." When she looked up, puppy-dog eyes to the max, Alex sighed before tucking her into a reassuring embrace, muttering gruffly, "Fine. Maybe it's a go, but you're not going alone, and not without training."

"Training?" she asked. Not that it was a bad idea, but training —at least the type she imagined—would take a hell of a lot longer than they had. "Is there time?"

He picked up the note and slipped it into the pocket of his blazer. "Twenty-four hours is plenty. And I know just the right secret weapon to help us out. Someone else who's had a run-in or two with Jordan."

"So, you weren't the only man in her life?" Madison teased.

He laughed. "Not by a long shot, and it's not a man."

Madison let out a little huff. "Of course, another woman from your past. Another supermodel, no doubt."

Alex smiled and shrugged in shy agreement.

"And exactly how many more of your bed-post notches will be walking the halls of DGI before our wedding? At this rate, I'll have to get with the guys in PR to issue nametags and hand out swag bags. And we'll need to rush the ad for the yearbook committee. Hell, if every woman from your past shows up to the 'Alex Drake Bon Voyage' to puss-prowling, it'll be the social media event of the year."

"Hey, don't forget we're gonna need lots of velvet ropes and an extra-long red carpet," he threw out before sweeping her into a long kiss and a wonderfully tight embrace. "And for the record, Ms. Taylor, I never bedded Crystal. Let's just say I'm not her type. But Crystal is good, tough, and the only other person I know who has had any connection with Jordan. I've tried to get as much intel as possible about Jordan from her, but Crystal seemed a little tight-lipped."

A fresh grin appeared on Madison's face. *Alex couldn't pry open some tight lips? That's gotta be a first for him.* "So, anything useful?"

"Not much. From what I gather, Crystal wasn't a recruit. At least, not like I was. Sounds like their paths tended to cross. Perhaps still do."

"Cross how? Like, they're friends?"

"My gut tells me they're definitely not cozy BFFs. Maybe they just run in the same circles now and again. Seems like they both stay in their swim lanes and maintain boundaries."

"Well, that's reassuring," Madison drawled, paper-thin sarcasm at its finest.

"Don't worry about Crystal. She's been our best-of-the-best

for years. We bring her in when the situation calls for something unconventional. Where, frankly, we're not really sure what the hell we're up against. She always comes through. But..."

Alex checked his watch, reconsidering. "You won't get to meet her until tomorrow morning. We have to fly her in. In the meantime, you and I can work on some basic tactics and training."

He kissed Madison's hand and kept it in his, leading her out. She stopped, holding him back by the elbow.

"Alex, before we do any of that, I need to ask you something, and I need you to be completely honest with me."

"Always," he assured her.

With a sigh, she flung her arm at him. "Does this bracelet suit me?"

He glanced at the bracelet, then with confidence, back at her. "Don't diamonds suit everyone?"

"Just tell me, does it?"

"They're diamonds. Both Marilyn Monroe and Paco Robles swear by them. Why? Is something wrong?"

Avoiding the scrutiny of his gaze, she looked back at the bracelet she adored. Deflated, she agonized about what to say. Madison loved everything about the bracelet—from Alex offering it to her more than once, to Paco insistently wrapping it around her wrist.

It was precious beyond the jewels it held. But her sentiments were now tainted by the doubt Jordan had planted in her mind.

"Here, give it to me," Alex said, holding out his hand.

"Why?" she asked, holding her arm to her chest, suddenly protective of the bracelet at his suggestion.

"Well, if you don't want it, I'll take it. I've actually been eyeing it for something. By the size of it, I'd say it might actually be perfect."

"Perfect for..."

"A Tiffany and Co. ten-and-a-half-carat cock ring. Nothing says *my girl's getting it good all night long* like a blinged-out D, keeping me erect for hours on end by a band of brilliant square-cut diamonds encased in eighteen-karat white gold."

He took her wrist, gently turning it back and forth, studying the bracelet closely. "But by the way it's dangling, I just need to make sure it's not going to be too tight . . ."

He rushed to undo his pants.

"Alex!" Madison shouted with an innocent swat to his chest.

He whisked her into his embrace, kissing her growing smile.

Taking a breath, he dropped his lighthearted demeanor. "Look, there's something I need to tell you about Jordan. About how she's the best at what she does. Maybe the best in the world."

Madison frowned, not liking where this was going. *We went from his bedazzled shaft to scorching-hot Jordan? God, do I want to hear this?*

Cupping her face in both of his large hands, he softly stroked her cheeks with his thumbs. "Nobody, and I mean nobody, can top her at the mindfuck. She's messing with your head. Don't let her in," he whispered into Madison's mouth, soothing her with a warm kiss.

He scooped up her hand, adding more advice. "And no matter what anyone says, this ring is definitely you," he told her while pressing his loving lips to her fingers.

Madison smiled. Ring or no ring, cock ring or no cock ring, the one thing that suited her perfectly and without a doubt was Alex.

CHAPTER 27

CRYSTAL

Seattle, Washington

Taking in the views and the fresh air from her penthouse balcony atop Seattle's Loews Hotel, Crystal could finally breathe. Her assignments always took her far from home, placing her in the line of fire more often than not.

Here, high above Elliott Bay, the world faded away and she could relax. With a vodka lemon drop in her hand, she enjoyed her sip along with the sweeping views spanning from the Space Needle to the Seattle Great Wheel.

As her purring fur baby, George, twined between her legs, she reached down to pet him, looking forward to an evening of easing into her favorite pastime—her passion. Corey.

Corey was taking his time in the shower, washing away both the grime and tension from his day. He was often tense, and her role was to ensure he had a night of unadulterated stress relief—which would be her relief too.

The quiet was broken by a distinctive chime from her phone, a unique notification tone that meant an evening filled with pleasure and pain would be cut short.

Alex Drake?

Crystal took another sip before dealing with the message.

ALEX: *Jet picking you up tonight. Usual time. SeaTac.*

Shit. That meant she'd need to be at the Seattle–Tacoma International Airport in just a few hours.

At least she'd be flying in style. If there was one thing Alex Drake was good for, it was rolling out the red carpet. A luxury jet was just the beginning.

They'd talk money after the job was done. If anything, he'd be generous. Cash and cars were givens. This penthouse had her name on the deed as a bonus from her last DGI gig. Crystal could count on another big windfall. That is, if she delivered.

After another sip of her drink, Crystal slowly lowered her martini glass, revealing her soaking-wet and very built husband emerging from the bathroom. The towel wrapping his chiseled waist was disappointing, though the droplets of water still clinging to his damp hair, chiseled chest, and muscular arms weren't. Corey was a soaking-wet masterpiece.

His scowl drew her attention away from her ogling and would need to be dealt with. When he crossed those lickable arms tight across his rugged chest, she gave him her undivided attention.

"What?" she asked, but she knew what.

"Phone in your hand. Drink finished. I'm guessing our night together is off."

His terse tone was deserved. Despite the ring on her finger, he'd been without her and her attentive ways for nearly a month. She'd promised her time to him, but it was a promise she'd have to break.

After setting aside the glass, Crystal slinked over to him. Lightly, her fingers brushed his burly chest, tracing down its center to his ripped abs before nestling in the tight edge of the towel. "It is what it is, babe. But—"

Watching his eyes and testing his reaction, she slid her fingers deeper. Her body pressed against his, and despite his fevered breaths and pounding pulse, he held to his training and remained still.

"Good boy," she said, letting her raspy words heat his neck. She licked several drops of water along his collarbone, content that it lifted his scowl.

"But you're leaving."

His out-of-turn comment was barely excusable. She sliced her fingernail into the tight skin beneath his towel, signaling a beginning to the night. If he made that mistake again, he'd suffer the consequences, ten o'clock flight be damned.

"Mmm. I've got a few hours," she whispered, giving his neck a terse nip.

His moan released. His abs tensed. And his cock tented the thick plush towel.

Looking down, it was clear he'd missed her a lot. She'd need to take her time. A slow burn was required. Otherwise, he'd be climaxing in a few minutes.

Tightening her grip on the edge of the towel, she yanked it from him, exposing that hard, throbbing cock she could practically taste. Licking her lips, she worked her fingernails along the lines of his torso, down to the muscles of his upper thighs. Careful to avoid the eager hard-on demanding her touch, she painted featherlight strokes along his skin.

By the agony of his expression, she was doing it right. His eyes slammed shut as he fought to maintain control.

"What do you want?" she asked, allowing him to speak.

He struggled a little, formulating his words as her finger began a long spiral at the base of his cock, twirling around and up until it grazed the head. With the other hand, she gripped him hard, forcing a gasp as his hands remained in their locked position behind his back. He tried to stay still.

With a single finger, she wiped the bead of precum from the choked head of his cock. "Watch me, Corey."

He did, opening his eyes to catch her opening her mouth and tasting him as she moved her finger to the back of her throat.

"I asked you what you want. Don't make me ask again."

The dark gray of his eyes pinned her. "To . . . give you a massage."

Her lips curled up, then brushed his. "Are you sure?"

Several items awaited her on the table. She grabbed one of her favorite clamps, not only because the pinch was hard, but Corey was especially responsive to this one.

"I like a long massage."

The flash of self-control behind his eyes appeared as it often did. His low tone and direct answer sent lightning to her core. "I'm sure," he said insistently.

Corey was there for her pleasure too. Neither of them knew how long she'd be gone. It would be torture—rubbing his hands across her as she groped and licked at his dick. Each of them knowing that until she allowed it, he wouldn't come.

Skillfully, she clamped him, and he let out a hiss.

"Remove my clothes," she demanded sweetly.

"Yes, Mistress."

CHAPTER 28

PACO

Manhattan

Paco frowned at the twinkling lights of the approaching jet far in the distance. He looked down at his phone, rereading the untimely texts that had summoned him here to DGI's private landing strip.

> ALEX: *Jet picking you up tonight.*
> ALEX: *90 minutes. Need you back.*
> ALEX: *More to come.*

Never mind that Paco had been in the middle of a world-class charity event in Dallas. At Alex's summons, he'd dropped everything. It wasn't the abrupt words that caught his attention. Or that Alex was asking. It was the last line. *More to come.*

More to come meant it was both important and classified. *More to come* meant time was of the essence. But what really grabbed his attention was that *more to come* was often code for *you're not going to love it, Paco, so don't ask.*

Fucker.

There he was just a couple of hours later, still in his tux, in the heart of the Big Apple. Who cared that he was the master of ceremonies for the premier affair? Or that he had been moments away from his favorite role—playing Cupid to what promised to be another power couple of the century?

Nooo. Instead, he was once again at Alex Drake's beck and call. Hauling his ass back to New York, only to be the welcoming committee for some unnamed big deal arriving that night.

Dammit, Alex.

Paco didn't know exactly what was up, but something. Something big. Alex wouldn't have one of his top fleet jets landing now if it weren't carrying one of his biggest fucking guns.

To prepare for the landing, Paco opened both winged doors of his Lamborghini and popped the trunk. He stepped back, unsettled as he glanced up at the cockpit windows as the plane came to a stop nearby.

Alarmed, he took a closer look. With the pilot slumped over and clearly unconscious, it was clear Paco's night had just begun.

Fuck! I am so not dressed for this.

Peeling away his bespoke tuxedo jacket, he carefully set it inside the car, then rolled up his shirtsleeves. He narrowed his eyes on the jet's automatic door as it opened, cascading into steps.

Cautiously, he approached. "Let's get this over with, Crys—"

Flying at his head was a fifty-pound Louis Vuitton duffel, and it was flying fast.

"Shit!" He jumped back, catching it solidly in his chest. With an annoyed huff, he set it in the trunk.

Her silhouette seemed to appear out of nowhere, backlit by the lights of the jet.

"Miss me, boo?" Crystal said, her sweet and sassy voice a precursor to her attempt at a hellacious punch.

Paco weaved, avoiding the blow. "Hey, not around the car!"

When he stepped away, she followed suit.

"With all that worry, it must be new. Damn, you change cars more than most men change underwear." She spun, gaining a burst of momentum for the kick she aimed at his face. Once again, a miss.

"Oh, come on, Crystal. We both know the man in your life isn't permitted the indulgence of underwear." Attack mode high, Paco threw several hard punches toward her. "How is Corey?"

"Great," she said, effortless in deflecting his blows. "Besides, I make it up to him in other ways." She threw out three punches in rapid succession, but Paco avoided them all.

He was ready for her fourth punch, catching it in the power of his grip. "I'd hardly call getting my ass cracked with a bullwhip a luxury."

With unrivaled momentum, he yanked her in, spinning her around and thrusting her arm up into her back, a measure to thwart any further resistance. Just in case, he followed up with a chokehold. With Crystal, it was best to be safe.

Summoning her unusual strength, she bounced back against him, springing forward to run up the side of his car. Crystal propelled herself high into the air, clearing his entire body as she flipped. As expected, her landing was Olympic caliber, a testament to her years of devotion to parkour.

Cursing under his breath, Paco raced to his car, kneeling at its side. Carefully, he examined the paint, softly running his finger over the area in question. "Dammit, if you scratched her . . ."

Crystal pulled a penlight from her pocket and crouched beside him, flooding the tight area in several passes. "Looks fine," she said, patting his back. "Despite their sex appeal, all my shoes are reinforced with silicone skids. No marks. No noise. They let me sneak up on all my favorite peeps."

Appeased, he nodded, and they stood.

"Are we done?" he asked.

She dusted off her sleeves. "Not quite," she said, grabbing him around the neck. For the moment, they hugged, patting each other briskly on the back. "Okay, we're done. For now," she warned with a smile, pulling away.

"Should I ask what happened to the pilot?"

"Oh, him? Some bullshit about why I couldn't land the plane."

"Tell me you didn't leave a mark."

"No. The technique I used on him was much more subtle. And I barely knew the guy. To be branded by me means you're someone extra special," she said with a wink.

Paco strolled to the passenger side of his Lamborghini, the gentleman in him ready to help her in. That was a mistake.

Crystal seized the opportunity to plant her ass in the driver's seat. He leaned in, unamused and glaring. Before he could do anything, her door was closed, and she was already firing up Hot Cherry.

"Come on, live a little. Besides, who taught you to drive?"

Paco gave it half a thought, irritated that he was now beginning to perspire. Prying Crystal from his seat would lead to MMA round number two, and his chances of success were fifty-fifty at best. Stewing, he reluctantly took the passenger seat.

"Hey, that fancy sky cab didn't have much to eat," Crystal said. "I'm starving." Her words were just the straw to break the camel's back.

Shouting, Paco lost his cool. "Crystal, you are *not* taking my half-million-dollar Lambo to a drive-thru."

She sweetened her tone. "Now, I can see from your best Ken-doll getup that you were torn from a fancy-schmancy night with nothing but teaspoon-sized appetizers. You *nearly* worked up a sweat, and you've got a wicked case of the grumps. You and I both know nothing will hit the spot like a Big Mac meal."

"I'm not grumpy," he sulked under his breath.

She tapped a couple of buttons, closing the trunk and his door.

Lips crimped and scowl in full swing, Paco drummed his fingers in an irritated rhythm along his leg before he picked off an invisible piece of lint. "Fine," he said warily as he acquiesced. "Make it a number one. Large. With a Coke."

"That's more like it. Speaking of Coke, where the hell are the cup holders in this beast?" she teased.

Despite his glare, Paco enjoyed the moment she peeled out, looking forward to the sight of the nearest golden arches.

CHAPTER 29

MADISON

Madison's sleep the night before was restless, leaving her agitated for the day's training ahead.

Although Alex spent some time in the morning sharing what Madison now thought of as *Fundamentals of the Mindfuck*—that, along with a few basic moves did not an operative make. Madison was no more an agent than Alex was a showgirl or Paco was eight months pregnant.

From what Alex told her, the people she'd be dealing with—aka the two Jordan Stones and their ilk—weren't your garden-variety ex-spies. Those types were more like machines. Kill. Wipe for prints. Meet the next mark for a martini at Club Macanudo before a Broadway show.

Instead, she was working with an entirely different caliber of niche operative whose work was subtle and sophisticated. Their goal? Get what they needed and then vanish into thin air. No one would see them coming, and they wouldn't leave a trace.

Essentially, they were ghosts.

Alex seemed to have some insight into their standard operating procedure, an advantage he hoped to exploit. "We have to keep them from vanishing too soon," he said, reminding her of their usual disappearing act.

Correcting Jack's military record was purportedly their only objective. But Alex wanted to know more. Jordan hadn't emerged on the scene out of pure altruism. His goal was to find out why.

They, and Madison in particular, needed a tactical advantage.

Enter Crystal. Elegant. Strong. Smart. And most importantly, she had no prior sexual history with Madison's man.

In a private Defense and Tactical Training room at DGI headquarters, Madison greeted Crystal with open arms. Without tables or chairs in the space, they both stood. Crystal leaned along the wall of mirrors while Madison stood ready.

"I know a few moves," Madison said shyly, a little nervous. "But I'm worried if it really comes to a knock-down-drag-out girl fight, I'm gonna get my ass handed to me on a platter."

"Nah," Crystal said, her lips curled up in amusement. "Just to get some perspective, do you think I'm here to teach you to fight?"

Madison shrugged, giving her a timid "Uh-huh," and an uncertain nod.

"Well, you can relax. My reputation as a badass might precede me, but fighting is more of a hobby."

Crap. If this lesson required rote memory, Madison was screwed.

"Fighting is fun, but skills like that aren't learned overnight. We've got to find something you're good at and hone it. I promise you, whatever it is, we'll find it, and it's usually not what you think. Give me a little blind faith, and let's see where it goes. Okay?"

"Okay," Madison said, nodding firmly.

"Tell me what you're most worried about going into this."

Exasperated, Madison shrugged. "I feel like an average Jane at a superhero convention. I have nothing useful to add, and I'm terrified I'm going to let everyone down. I can't even lie with the least bit of conviction."

"Hmm," Crystal said, then moved the discussion along. "I hear you play poker?"

Cards, yes. Definitely. I'll bring a deck, and I can righteously spank Jordan with my wicked game of poker.

Weakly, Madison nodded.

Crystal took a step forward, stopping mere inches from Madison's face. "Your poker game is good, from what I hear."

Shy but proud, Madison agreed. "It's not terrible."

"So, there are two sides to Madison Taylor. On the one side, you dislike lying. If I strapped you to a lie detector, you'd fail. Your hands are probably sweating at just the thought of it."

"Yes," she said, hoping Crystal wasn't about to start an interrogation exercise. *Can I call a time out at waterboarding?*

"And on the other hand," Crystal said, "your deception game is on point so long as it's for sport and not for real. Not for keeps."

"If I tee up a lie," Madison blurted, "I'll let everyone down. Even Jordan knew."

"Jordan Stone?" Crystal raised a brow.

Madison nodded, not realizing Alex hadn't told Crystal about their meeting. "And I've probably just let the cat out of the bag. Alex didn't tell you?"

Crystal shook her head. "Probably slipped his mind."

She took a good, long look at Madison, studying her from head to toe. It was unnerving, but for some reason, Madison stood still despite the heat rising in her cheeks.

Finally, Crystal again met her eyes and smiled. "I've got it. Work with me. We're going to play a little trick on your mind. Everything's a game, and at the same time, everything's for keeps."

"I'm not sure I understand."

"Don't worry. You won't, but your body will. You're very

responsive, Madison. Your body is eager to express every thought and emotion."

Embarrassed, Madison tried to turn away, but Crystal spun her toward the mirror.

"It's a skill we can use," Crystal told her. "Allow your body to respond rather than react. You control what you share with the outside world. Give people only what you intend to. I'm going to give you a lesson, one I teach to very few people."

"Because it's remedial?" Madison joked.

"Because it requires a person who's highly responsive. That's something that can't be taught. You're the perfect candidate . . . and I'm sure Alex Drake thanks his lucky stars."

Flushed, Madison dropped her gaze.

"No." It was a command, not a request.

Instantly, Madison held her head high.

"Good. Look at yourself, Madison. You think your body betrays you with something as natural as a blush. You're worried it makes you vulnerable. But in your case, this vulnerability is pure gold. Exactly what we need."

Madison's breath hitched as Crystal stood behind her, moving her hands from the small of Madison's back, up to her shoulders, then down her arms.

"Breathe," she said low. "Relax."

Madison did her best as Crystal squeezed both of her wrists. The pressure wasn't painful, merely calming as it held her still.

Her breath tickled Madison's ear. "And you're going to learn to use that vulnerability because this is your strength. Your superpower. The most honest part of you. I'm going to take you through some exercises. No matter how uncomfortable you get, keep repeating these three words. Don't react. Respond."

Don't react.
Respond.

CHAPTER 30

ALEX

"What do you mean, she's gone?" he shouted.

It had been a long time since Alex Drake had flown into a rage. And by the looks on everyone's faces, it wasn't exactly unexpected.

Swallowing a mouthful of fries, Crystal shrugged. "You said teach her a skill, not hog-tie her to a chair. Which, for the record, I could have easily done."

Paco jumped on the Crystal-bashing bandwagon. "If his head explodes, you're cleaning it up."

Unconcerned, she gave him an eye roll.

Flipping the tails of his blazer behind him, Alex propped his hands on his hips. "Any idea where she went?"

After slurping the last of her Coke for an obnoxiously loud and drawn-out moment, Crystal said, "To meet Jordan."

Pacing, Alex flashed Paco a look, telepathically shouting *Save me before I kill her.* To his dismay, Paco simply nodded and grinned.

Crystal pointed a crisp fry his way. "All I know is she got a text from Jordan, and she was gone. But now you've got me all panicked about my Yelp rating, so how about I help you negotiate an arrangement with Stone?"

Alex froze mid-step. "You know Stone."

Chewing her fry, she answered. "Duh. I know everyone. Tell me you have his number. Because if you don't, I can't give it to you."

He knew Crystal wasn't being annoying. That would be a line she couldn't cross. Even for Alex Drake.

Fuck. Alex didn't have the number.

Wait. Maybe, he did.

From his wallet, he fished out the business card Stone had given him when they were in the bunker. Alex dialed the number listed on it, then pressed the button for speakerphone.

"Insurance Services," a man answered. It was Stone.

Crystal rolled her hand, mouthing the words *play along*.

"Yes, I need to check on my coverage for . . . stolen property," Alex said, keeping the conversation vague.

"Stolen property?" There was a momentary pause. "Of course, sir. I can have an adjustor at your place in an hour."

"He's got fifteen minutes," Alex said, insisting with the lethal calmness of a viper.

After a long silence that would have only been made worse with elevator music, Stone finally agreed. "Fifteen minutes."

"See you then." Alex disconnected the call.

∽

Alex was unsurprised that Stone had managed to find his own way into the DGI building, bypassing security, but was relieved to see Mark on the man's heels.

"Where's Madison," Alex snapped at Stone.

"Your guess is as good as mine. Probably playing with Jordan."

Obviously, Stone was saying it to get a rise out of Alex. Throw him off his game.

Letting it slide, Alex demanded, "Call them back."

Stone shook his head. "Out of the question. At this point, it could compromise them both."

"Mark?" Alex asked.

Mark had already moved to the console, pulling up information and maps. "They're driving. If you're sending them where I think you are, they're en route."

"I don't control Jordan," Stone protested.

Alex snorted. "And I love how you think you can bullshit me. If anyone's the captain of the *S.S. Jordan Stone*, you are. Leave Madison out of it. I'll go in."

"Fine," Stone said with a sigh. "May I?" He headed to the console Mark had fired up. "But you'll only delay it, not stop it. Jordan would never take Madison against her will. She agreed."

Mark jumped in. "What is she, the devil?"

"The devil isn't nearly this manipulative," Alex said with a growl.

Stone sent his message and turned back around. "This play doesn't work without Madison. She has to be in."

"Well, that's not fucking happening," Alex said, ready to grab his fiancée the second she stepped through the door and lock her away.

Maybe I'll take her to Paris. She'll be mad, but a chocolate croissant will settle her down.

Seeming to read his mind, Stone said softly, "You can't control her, Alex."

"I can try."

Stone gave him a wry smile. "Like I can control Jordan? As we speak, Jordan is no doubt whispering sweet nothings in Madison's ear, promising she's the only one who can discover the truth and save Jack's honor. And much to my chagrin, she isn't wrong."

"You all should work together," Crystal said nonchalantly as she sat back and filed her nails.

Before Alex could ring her neck and use her head as a bowling ball, the phone rang. It was an incoming call to the landline phone that might be a dinosaur, but it still had a speakerphone.

"I believe that's for you," Stone said to Alex.

With the press of a button, Alex activated the speaker, not knowing if he'd be speaking to Jordan or Madison. "Hello?"

"Alex, listen to me. We don't have much time." It was Madison. Her voice was rushed, but not alarmed.

"Yes, I'm here."

"I need you to let me do this. Let *us* do this. Remember how I said all bets were off? On us keeping secrets?" What Madison meant was that she'd consented to Alex keeping secrets during this op, a ploy so she wouldn't inadvertently tip his hand.

"Yes," he said slowly.

"Well, it's a two-way street. I trust you. Trust me."

What the hell is she saying. Trust her? "I do. I'm just a little distrustful about the company you keep."

The sultry voice shouting, "I heard that!" in the background was quickly followed by, "Trust me too."

Alex ignored Jordan.

"I told them they should work together," Crystal said because Alex had already missed his chance to wring her neck.

"I agree," Paco said, siding with Crystal for the first time in forever.

"Please," Madison said softly, and her sweet voice was his undoing.

After a long moment, Alex agreed. "But new rules. You'll be taken by helicopter, and Paco will join you. Once you arrive, Paco will drive you in a DC-Metro DGI van. We'll be monitoring you. All of us."

"Deal," Madison and Jordan said in unison.

"And I want the play-by-play," Alex said quickly, negotiating on the fly.

"No," came from the phone, this time from Jordan. "You'll just second-guess me. Me and Madison."

Holy fuck, he was going to bludgeon Jordan. Bludgeon her, bread her, deep-fry her, and feed her to the monkeys at the zoo.

"Fine," he forced out through gritted teeth.

"Excellent," Stone said, clapping his hands once, and Alex glared at him.

"Oh, and Alex," Jordan sang. "We won't be able to stay and chat. We're under a terrible time crunch."

Madison said, "I'm sorry, Alex, she's right. From the looks of the map Jordan has up, we'll be somewhere in the middle of nowhere in about fifteen minutes."

Alex pulled in a deep breath. "We'll be here. Paco will have the van ready to go. But I need you to listen to me very carefully, Madison. I have an idea where you're going. It could be dangerous. You're not just jumping in the van and taking off. At the very least, I deserve a kiss."

He could feel Madison's smile through the phone. "Yes, Alex Drake, you deserve a kiss."

"What about my kiss?" Jordan teased, dancing dangerously close to getting it from his ass.

"How about you focus on the road? And keeping my fiancée in one piece?"

"Anything for you, Alex."

The call disconnected on their end, most likely by Jordan.

CHAPTER 31

ALEX

Upstate New York

Via helicopter, Alex had moved their small team consisting of Mark, Crystal, and Stone to the secure bunker north of the city, as another helicopter had carried Paco to rendezvous with Madison and Jordan, and then drive them to Washington, DC.

As Alex's team gathered in the bunker's main control room, he heard Paco saying over the comm, "Just punching in the next directions. Taking off in a minute."

Alex and the others said nothing in acknowledgment. All communication was monitored, and the transmission was used to keep the signal steady.

In the driver's seat with the engine idling, Paco waited for the women to exit the DGI van as Alex, Mark, Crystal, and Stone watched the video of their every move projected by the discreet surveillance camera. There was no wiggle room. No forgiveness for a misstep. They were at entrance to the premier spy stronghold of the United States, about to flip the script on the puppeteers themselves. A clean entry was just the first in a long maze of obstacles ahead.

Alex's heart thundered and he could barely blink as he watched Madison step out of the van. He'd seen her for barely a moment as she got into the van before Paco had raced her and Jordan away.

But now it was different. He could drink in her image and take half a second to enjoy what he was seeing. Wonder if what he was watching wasn't Madison Taylor, but the soon-to-be Madison Drake.

Jordan barely drew his attention, blending in seamlessly with the crowd. Her nondescript pantsuit was the blah blue-gray preferred by too many women in the field. She kept her hair in a low braid that was too boring for words, and wore heels that were high, but not too high. She must have hit a thrift shop on her way in.

The lanyard she sported held her identification badge, no doubt one that was actually earned. Jordan Stone was a mystery. It came as no surprise that she might, on some level, still belong to the Company.

But it was Madison who captured his heart, eyes, and cock. The outfit she wore wasn't anything she'd normally select, making her look as if she'd stepped off the cover of *Vogue*.

The glossy black Louboutins showed off a peekaboo toe and a splash of red. His gaze traveled up her toned, bare calves to her thighs. The short black fitted skirt stretched in ways that were absolute sin as she moved, and the matching custom-tailored blazer hugged her breasts in a way that was the perfect blend of *nice to meet you* and naughty. Her hair was pulled back in a low, thick bun at the nape, and her black-rimmed glasses completed the sophisticated *sex on demand* look.

Madison turned back, waving good-bye to Paco and everyone else who watched the feed from the van, with her breasts spilling out and her pouty nude lips so ready for the taking.

Alex sucked in a breath and yanked Crystal aside. "Is there a reason my fiancée got the memo to wear *business scandalous?*"

"Mm-hmm." Despite his hard glare at her, Crystal kept her gaze fixed on the screen, watching the ladies as they headed away. "You said give her an advantage." Lightly, she laughed under her breath. "Trust me, she's got one."

Alex reined in his temper. *Suddenly, everyone wants me to trust them.*

With Stone turning toward them, Alex returned to the others, now wanting to discuss it.

"Paco, we've got her," Mark said into the mic.

With no more to see on Paco's end, and Madison's link confirmed, he would depart. Lingering would draw suspicion, and his access was restricted to a very short window of time relegated to drivers of VIPs. He drove the van out of the compound toward a satellite DGI stronghold a few miles away.

Alex flipped the monitors to a new channel, picking up the micro camera transmitting from Madison's glasses. Jordan held open the heavy glass doors, allowing Madison to enter.

From the console, Alex pressed a button. "We've got you. Clear your throat if you can hear me."

Madison did so just as she stepped through.

"What's the play?" Alex asked, realizing that never in a million years could Jordan manipulate Stone. This wasn't her idea, after all. It was his.

Not denying it, Stone said, "Madison was the key, the key to a coverup buried somewhere in that building. Her loss was genuine. And all good covers start with the truth."

CHAPTER 32

MADISON

Langley, Virginia

CLEARING HER THROAT, Madison anxiously eyed the larger-than-life seal inlaid in the floor. Along its border, it read CENTRAL INTELLIGENCE AGENCY. She stepped deliberately across the seal, determined not to be afraid, as she and Jordan walked through the large lobby.

Seeing the guard, she froze. Jordan had to brush her elbow, nudging her to move. She did, letting Jordan escort her to the security desk.

There, Jordan flashed the identification dangling from her neck. "I believe you have a badge for Ms. Taylor." She looked at him through her lashes, laying on the sultriness extra thick.

The young security guard thumbed through a set of folders standing in a desk organizer. Finding the correct envelope, he opened it and fished out the badge. Pointing to his clipboard, he didn't bother smiling as he said, "Yes. Sign here."

As instructed, Madison quickly scanned the entries. She found the skipped-over space on the sign-in sheet that Jordan was certain would be there. By signing there, rather than at the bottom, she avoided leaving any documentation that she'd been the last one to sign in.

Their end-of-the-day appointment was deliberate. It ensured the building would quickly empty as the civil servants left the office, either heading home or to happy hour. It also made her arrival time appear much earlier, and that by the end of the day, it would appear Madison Taylor should be long gone.

In the event of an overzealous end-of-day security check, they'd only follow up with the last entry or two to ensure all appointments were concluded and that security could lock up. As it was, Madison's sign-in placed her at the headquarters hours before.

To avoid the guard noticing, Jordan tossed out possibly the oldest distraction in the book. "So, you got big plans tonight, Officer?"

Predictably, her inviting tone snagged his attention. "Um, nothing special."

"Really?" she purred. "Well, if you need a hand doing nothing special, give me a call." Jordan slid him what Madison was sure was a real number—even if it was to a burner phone—and it did its job to draw his attention from Madison.

"I'll do that," he said, lowering his voice and palming the card discreetly.

From the corner of her eye, Madison noticed as Jordan swept her finger back and forth across his thumb. Madison's eye roll was uncontrollable.

Don't react, respond? I'm ready to respond, all right. Fingers crossed we get out of here before I throw up all over the security desk of the CIA.

Madison stalled for only a moment at PURPOSE OF THE VISIT, filling in that block with four letters: F-O-I-A.

FOIA, or the Freedom of Information Act, had been America's check-and-balance system since July 4, 1966, giving every citizen the right to access information from the United States government.

The government had always been cagey in complying with FOIA, which was why documents for Area 51 and Kennedy's assassination had never been fully released despite millions of FOIA requests.

If Madison's own request from years earlier had been received, it was left unacknowledged. The death of a no-name, average American citizen should have been inconsequential to the powers that be. But one of the Jordan Stones had worked a miracle.

All the right people had been convinced that Madison would need a face-to-face discussion about her brother's death, or she was going to the press. And no one wanted to risk a future billionaire's wife inadvertently digging up information that could compromise new and ongoing missions.

Distracted, the guard didn't even glance at the clipboard as he handed Madison a numbered ESCORT REQUIRED visitor badge. This was anticipated. Jordan's escort privileges, as remarkable as that sounded, remained intact.

"This way, Ms. Taylor," Jordan said, motioning her down the corridor. Each passage led to a maze of lookalike halls, cubicle farms, and walls lined with offices.

Scanning the wall plaques, they found who they were looking for. Mr. Jeff Lowell, a low-level analyst who would diligently give Madison some bullshit story about how the records were misplaced, or lost, or whatever he had to say to end the meeting and move her along.

Keeping him occupied for at least twenty minutes was their goal. It would take that long for Jordan to hack his computer and download the information they needed for the next step of their plan.

Anyone more senior to Jeff would immediately recognize Jordan's attempt. Someone junior to Jeff wouldn't have the accesses required. And the physical position of his office, optimally located a hall or two from their ultimate destination, made him a perfect match.

Madison had no idea how that was pulled off, but it was. And it would give Jordan enough time to pinpoint the exact location of the files they needed.

Jordan gave Jeff's door a brisk knock but opened it before he could. It was a quick way to check their security protocols. Apparently, its cypher lock was just for show.

Swinging the door open wide, Jordan breezed in. "Hi, Jeff. I'm Jordan, the escort for our visitor. I believe you were expecting us."

Fumbling to put away his late lunch, he swept the half-eaten sandwich and scattered potato chips into the top desk drawer. *Gross.*

After dusting off his rumpled shirt and slacks, he straightened the knot in his stained tie. "Sure, come in."

"This is Ms. Taylor. She sent in the FOIA request."

"Of course. Please, have a seat." He stood but didn't extend his hand for a shake, and Madison breathed a sigh of relief.

When he motioned for them to have a seat at the small table with four chairs, only Madison sat down with him. Jordan remained standing.

"I've been sitting all day," she said. Obviously, he could relate and nodded.

"First," he said solemnly to Madison, "let me say how sorry I am for your loss."

As he proceeded with the canned pleasantries, Madison watched Jordan, studying her moves. Casually, she leaned back on the edge of his desk, using her body to block his view as she attached a high-tech extractor to his laptop. Jeff was about to look over as Madison created a distraction.

Abruptly, she slammed her hand hard on the table. *Ow.* "Look, I have a right to see my brother's records. All of them."

It worked. Jordan stepped over to the dirtiest window known

to man. She needed a clean cell signal. With the grime across it, Madison wasn't sure that was happening. But even a weak signal would make it possible. The stronger the signal, the faster this would go.

"Ms. Taylor," Jeff said, "I understand your need for closure. But it's been ten years. Maybe it's just time to let it go."

"What did you say?" she snapped as heat traveled to her cheeks in record time. She was genuinely about to blow.

Jordan didn't move. Instead, she stood there and watched, an intrigued spectator with her narrowed eyes and lifted brow. She wasn't about to intervene. Or help. Jordan Stone was too busy staring, seeming to wonder what Madison was going to do.

In the moment, it was something Madison wondered too. Her emotions were all over the place, and between her strong urges to cry hysterically or hit this guy with a full-on freak-out, she sat there, wrestling for her self-control.

Shit. What do I do?

It was Crystal's voice she could hear in her head. Or more precisely, from the tiny audio feed coming from the arm of the glasses she wore.

"Madison, this kid is young and naive, and that's why we targeted him. You're still in the game. If you push him, he might grab a supervisor. Think of our discussion. Let him see what you want him to see."

Mark cut in. "Jordan's working fast. She's close. She needs another six or seven minutes, tops. Keep this guy distracted. Chat about anything. How about this? He's completely obsessed with getting swole."

Madison's eyes popped. *Uh, what?* Her continued silence prompted Alex to pipe up.

"Mark means he's into extreme fitness. He's aiming to someday be the next American Ninja Warrior. He seems to do anything and everything to build endurance."

That wasn't exactly news. Behind him was an impressive

display of medals and trophies for everything from triathlons to warrior competitions, but primarily 10Ks and marathons.

"Yeah, I know," she said aloud, cutting herself short, realizing she'd just replied to Alex.

I can't keep all these conversations straight. Where did Jeff and I leave off?

"You know . . . what?" Jeff asked, staring at her. When she stared back blankly, he began to stand and turn toward Jordan. "I'm sorry I can't be of further assistance—"

"I mean . . ." Madison gently motioned him back to his seat. "Yeah, I know. As in, I hear what you're saying. You're right. It has been a long time, and I should let it go. But it's hard. So very, very hard."

Licking her lips, she took an exaggerated deep breath. Predictably, his gaze fell to her chest and he slowly returned to his seat.

Pointing to the *I love me* wall behind him, she continued. "Especially this time of year, with folks ramping up for our hometown run."

That got his attention, though his eyes remained fixed. "Oh, your brother was a runner?"

"Yes," she said, enthusiastic to bring up something about the brother that she actually knew.

I might not have known everything about the secret life of Jack Taylor, but I've got this covered.

"Jack loved to run. I run too, but I could never keep up. Jack always said I needed to work on my breathing if I was going to get serious about long-distance running."

She followed with another deep chest-popping inhale for effect.

Eager to impress, Jeff launched into a full-fledged lecture on breathing techniques, how he built his cardiovascular stamina, and who knows what the hell else, because Madison zoned out almost immediately. In the eternity it took for Jordan to wrap up, Madison smothered several yawns.

"Well, I think we've taken up enough of your time," Jordan finally said.

Oh, thank God.

Madison leaped up on cue, reluctantly taking Jeff's icky hand. She used the move to pull his attention away as Jordan retrieved her device. All evidence of her hack into the impenetrable system had been removed.

Jeff swallowed Madison's hand in both of his. *Yuck.*

"Listen, if you ever want some running tips, I could meet you sometime. You know, to do a run and," his gaze drifted down again, "work on your breathing."

Eventually, his gaze caught the sparkling from her ginormous ring. "Oh, you're engaged?" He gaped at her as he dropped her hands.

"Yes," Jordan gleefully answered for Madison. "To a powerful tycoon with the thrusting power of a SpaceX rocket."

After a brisk clap on Jeff's back, Jordan scooted Madison out of the room. "This way," she said, rushing Madison down the corridor.

They cut right, stopping at a door devoid of any markings save for a small metal plaque engraved with ARCHIVE 5. Jordan attempted the handle. Like Jeff's, it was reinforced with a cypher lock, also non-working. She opened the door and they scurried inside.

Along the wall, Jordan found a light switch and flipped it, flooding the pitch-black room with bright fluorescent light. A small desk and chair next to the door held an incredibly old computer that seemed eerily undisturbed for some time.

In front of them, the vast space held row upon row of industrial metal shelving about six feet high, filled to capacity with boxes and binders. The rhyme and reason to their order could have been the eighth wonder of the world.

Madison deflated. "How are we going to find anything in here?"

Immersed in her phone, Jordan said, "Looks like the only items here are those that haven't made it to being digitally preserved. Budget cuts. Everything here is from the year of Jack's mission. The oldest records will be at the end, and the newest here up front."

"But what if Jack's were stored electronically?"

"They weren't," Jordan said. "There are some missions they'll never store digitally. Too many old-schoolers in senior leadership positions believe the best way to keep something safe is by keeping it far away from technology. Hard copies only. We can only hope they didn't destroy them. But our chances are good they didn't, because Stone is positive the mission was never completely closed out."

Jordan headed down the long expanse of a warehouse with Madison on her heels, glancing at the never-ending rows of shelves.

"You think they'd rather keep everything in an unlocked room than store them digitally?"

Jordan slowed down, studying the boxes. "You've heard that military intelligence is an oxymoron, right? Well, you're smack dab in the heart of the proof. Since the building itself is secure, folks get lazy. Securing each office gets old fast. And a lot of historians and archivists were never operatives or active duty. Having to unlock the door every time they return from taking a leak is too much of a hassle."

"Could the archivist be back at any moment?" Madison asked, worrying aloud.

Jordan sneered. "No. He's out today. Sudden case of stomach flu."

Finally, Jordan stopped somewhere in the middle of the room. She grabbed a box off the shelf and plopped it onto the floor. "Jackpot. Operation Firefly."

"Firefly?"

"Jack's last mission," Jordan said, flipping off the lid.

Her fingers flew through the contents, pulling out a file and checking the documents within, then tapping it back down only to move on. A bright blue one caught her eye, and she opened it wide on top of the box.

"Alex," she said, speaking to him through the mic in Madison's glasses. "In your statement, you mentioned that someone tried to enter Jack's hotel room, then left an envelope. Is this the guy?" She pointed to a small black-and-white photo paper-clipped to the corner of the file.

"Yes," Madison heard in her earpiece.

"Yes," she repeated aloud to Jordan.

"Hmm." Jordan hastily flipped through the papers. "The man you saw goes by the code name Roberto, as well as a half dozen other names, but little information is here other than that he owned a small jewelry shop and was a mule for the letterbox."

"Letterbox?" Madison asked.

Alex translated the reference. "A letterbox is a liaison. Receiving and passing messages, or items. It means Roberto was just another cog in the wheel. The real guy passing the info back and forth, the letterbox, remained anonymous."

"There's little else here," Jordan muttered under her breath, "except Jack did receive the package."

Madison reviewed the pages as Jordan rummaged through the box. "There's something else. Whatever he received was small. Very, very small. And platinum."

Jordan didn't break from her work. "Yes, but that makes it even more of an issue because it could be anywhere. Or long gone, perhaps. Whatever it was, it was extraordinarily valuable. A key of some sort. Perhaps to a code."

"How do you know that?" Madison asked.

"Here . . ." Jordan pulled open an envelope. She slid a few index cards out into her hand. "This is coder talk. What they were doing not only required the decoder, but also the item that needed to be decoded."

Jordan flipped them slowly, one by one, ensuring Madison's glasses recorded every piece. "It could be the access codes for major power grids, or nuclear launch sequences. Without a decoder, it might as well be your nana's recipe for caramel apple strudel."

How does she know about Nana's apple strudel?

"Practically worthless," Jordan said, for the first time showing signs of frustration. "But there is this . . ."

From the folder, she removed a single sheet of paper. It was Jack's military orders. Madison had never seen them before. The form was covered in blocks, each filled in with various bits of information on Jack, including his name, social security number, location of each assignment, and its duration.

Jordan pointed to the paper. "You're gonna want to hang on to that."

Madison's spy wardrobe seemed to be missing pockets, though Jordan's pantsuit had several, on both the blazer and the slacks. She handed it back to Jordan. "Do you mind?"

Jordan's eyes danced with delight. "Not at all," she said, neatly folding the page to the size of a credit card. With a single finger, she pulled open Madison's blazer and inched the folded paper between her breasts.

Transfixed, Madison watched and then winced, drawing in a sharp breath. *Oh. My. God.*

The issue wasn't Jordan's little move. It was that Madison couldn't help but watch. Meaning, so did everyone else in the team, via a close-up view of her cleavage captured by the microscopic camera in her eyeglass frames.

As she stammered, not sure what to say, Jordan smothered her mouth with her hand. From the faraway entrance, someone had just opened the door.

CHAPTER 33

MADISON

"Hello," a male voice bellowed.

Madison sprang to her feet and peeked through the small openings between the boxes on the shelf. The guard might be older, but by his large build and impressive height, he looked intimidating as hell.

Silently, Jordan reassembled the contents of the box and returned it to the shelf. Despite her swift moves, Madison managed to catch sight of Jordan's annoying little fingers snagging something from the box. Whatever she'd pulled out, she pocketed. But with the man's shoes tapping toward them, there was no time to say anything.

In a heartbeat, he was a few shelves away, hot on their invisible trail. Any second now, they'd be discovered. Frantic, she looked to Jordan for a solution.

Nothing.

Jordan stood there, completely relaxed, smiling as if she had no intention of moving from their spot. Bug-eyed, Madison shrugged, gesturing wildly for a response.

Not a one.

Maybe Jordan was planning to wield a kick-ass martial-arts

move on the man.

Should we bolt? Sneak away or outright run? Was this what Alex worried about? Would Jordan ditch me? Or worse, pin this on me?

Jordan was wearing a badge. For all they knew, she belonged here. What was Madison's excuse? Madison was the one to sign in, not Jordan. And it was Madison who had met with Jeff.

This is bad. Very, very bad.

Resolved to accept the number of ways this could go down, Madison was ready for anything.

Correction. Almost anything.

Jordan removed Madison's glasses and placed them high on the shelf. Unclipping Madison's hair, she fingered through to fluff the strands, laying them loosely about her shoulders, then mouthed the word *perfect*.

She can't seriously think I'm gonna seduce this guy. Not only is he fully armed, but he's also older than my dad. How about this? I'll bat my eyes, heave my breasts, and hand him Jordan's business card. I hear it's guard night at her place.

As the footsteps rounded the corner, Jordan grabbed Madison's shoulders and pinned her against the shelving. Madison's slight squeal was muffled by Jordan's full lips, and her body was smothered in a dizzying touchy-feely embrace.

Of all things, Jordan moaned, freely sliding her hands over the curves of Madison's butt. Shocked, Madison gasped.

Jordan's hand yanked her thigh up and around, wrapping herself in Madison's leg. Footsteps louder, the guard closed in.

Breast to breast, Madison couldn't think, and began echoing the seductive sounds of her impromptu lover, letting her hands wander Jordan's body in return, though much more innocently.

The guard's shocked gasp was loud and distinct, and Madison nearly laughed out loud as she heard him stumble backward and release a *good Lord* under his breath.

Determined, she maintained her calm . . . even as Jordan

touched her warm tongue to hers, invading her through her parted lips. Finally, the guard tiptoed away.

In the distance, the door clicked open and slammed closed, but neither she nor Jordan broke from the kiss. Her breath hitched again when Jordan rounded first base and headed for second.

Unless she stopped it, Jordan's hand was sliding its way across her thigh and up the back of her skirt. Even as Jordan filled her hand with the fullness of Madison's tense ass, she didn't pull away.

Instead, she replayed Crystal's words. Over and over and over again.

Don't react. Respond.

Don't. React.

Respond. Respond.

Respond.

For the moment, Madison allowed her body to be swept through a tidal wave of touching and kissing. And feeling.

Her mind cleared, allowing her to focus. A minute later, a single thought broke through.

Yes.

CHAPTER 34

ALEX

Alex could only sit and breathe as the group remained glued to the uneventful screen. The micro camera seemed to be sitting upside-down on a shelf, abandoned where Jordan had placed it, diligently recording every second of the boring wall across from it.

The microphone? That was another story. Thanks to the latest technology for unrivaled surveillance, the audio was crystal clear. It captured every moan and whimper, long after the footsteps of the guard had moved on.

Like his companions, Alex watched nothing but a blank screen, eager for a continuation of the video. Though certainly not for all the same reasons.

Crystal broke the almost silence. "I need a snack. Anyone else?"

Quickly, Mark and Stone followed, none making eye contact with Alex, who was too preoccupied to glance back at any of them.

He barely heard them leave. With his head swirling, heart racing, and cock standing tall like a redwood, he sat frozen. Settling his breaths, he waited. And waited. *And* waited.

After what could have been seconds, hours, or days, the trio returned with snacks in hand. The screen hadn't changed, and Alex hadn't moved.

No doubt, it was awkward as shit for them all. But he didn't care.

Eventually, the glasses were yanked from their spot and clasped in the ringed hand of Madison. After several steps, the glasses were flipped, staring up at Madison's face.

"I need a word with Jordan. Alone."

What the fuck?

Before Alex could say a word, the video was capturing the inside of a desk drawer, letting them all stare at a few paper clips and dust. Muffled voices could be heard, but not made out.

"I'm sure you can clean up the audio," Stone said helpfully.

Mark didn't make a move. As a happily married man, he knew the drill.

"No," Alex said calmly. His response was blunt. "Madison requested privacy, and we're giving it to her."

Madison had asked for his trust, and by God, he was giving it to her. But at the moment, his issue wasn't trust.

Madison had crossed a line. With her moans fresh in his ears, and that smudge of Jordan's signature red lipstick visible on her kiss-swollen lips, one thing was clear.

He'd be seeing her.

Soon.

But not fucking soon enough.

CHAPTER 35

MADISON

With the glasses secured deep in the desk drawer, Madison steeled her resolve, casting a nervous smile at Jordan.

"Look," she said softly, "I need to make one thing clear. Yes, you're beautiful and sexy, and can undoubtedly teach me a thing or two. Things that would probably make my head spin, and might be illegal in at least a dozen states. But just as Alex belongs to me, I belong to him. I'm completely his—mind, body, and soul."

Jordan cozied up to her. Locking a strand of Madison's hair around her finger, she let it slip though as she traced Madison's jaw and pulled her chin up. Her lips remained a whisper away.

"Maybe, just maybe, the bracelet does suit you."

They both smiled as Jordan took a step back, opened the desk drawer, and retrieved the glasses. She licked her lips as she slid them up the bridge of Madison's nose.

"She's all yours," Jordan sang to the audience, and sauntered out of the room as Madison trailed behind her.

Upstate New York

Madison was exhausted, grateful to have Paco once again perform the work of driver as they returned to the rendezvous point. The ride was quiet, leaving Madison to her spinning thoughts.

As the van pulled into the garage of the DGI bunker, the headlights flooded a very serious-looking Alex. Paco quickly killed the lights, but it was long enough for Madison to read Alex's face. His eyes held a hardness she was unfamiliar with, and that made her squirm.

They all exited the vehicle. Madison was last. Even with his arms uncrossed, she couldn't avoid the heavy weight of his stare. She could feel it. Feel him. Her heart pounded and her breath hitched as he held open the large metal door.

Jordan breezed by him, exiting the garage without a word, and Paco quickly followed. Madison tried making her way toward it, but he let the solid sound-proof door close behind the others, clanking loudly as it shut.

They were alone.

"Not so fast, Ms. Taylor," he rumbled low, stepping closer.

The warmth of his body was like the heat of the sun, and his dark stare stole her breath. The space between them was charged and electric. With barely a touch, she was backed against the door. In another step, his hard body pressed against hers.

Madison bit her lip, feeling the pressure of his solid dick. It made her grow wet.

The ball of his thumb pressed against her full lower lip. "I'm not sure this shade suits you."

After one hard swipe of his thumb, he replaced the missing lipstick with a rough, hungry kiss. She knew what he wanted. A taste. A taste of something he'd never known, and he'd never taste again.

With her lips parted, his tongue forced through, exploring in long, sweeping licks. Taking back the mouth that was his.

He unclasped the button of her jacket and her breasts spilled out. His desire was rough and raw. Commanding. Desperate. It left her soaking with need.

Every sensation was different. This wasn't the Alex she knew, but it was the Alex she wanted. Here. Now. Sexy as fuck and hotter than hell.

A *don't react* reminder was the last thing she needed. Her body was giving in, letting go, and responding all over the place. Big-time.

As his hands smoothed over all of her, he didn't miss an inch, careful in tracing and retracing every one of her curves. Only after several complete passes over every square inch of covered skin did he pause, letting his hand settle on the full weight of her breast.

He trailed hot kisses along her neck, across her cleavage, then back up to her ear. Sliding his fingers through her hair, he fisted it, tilting her head slowly to the side.

There, his hot breath cascaded across her neck. Her whole body shivered as he whispered, "If you did what I think you did, your hotness factor just flew off the charts."

He lifted her, and her legs wrapped around. Her arms held tight to his shoulders and neck, and he boosted her higher to hike up her skirt. Easily, his large hands cradled her ass, nudging her to spread wider.

Panting, she asked, "And what is it that you think I did, Mr. Drake?"

Reaching down, she yanked open his pants, releasing his stifled erection. Madison took him in both hands, gripping and stroking him lovingly.

He let out a pleasurable moan. Resting on the seat of his hands, she slid her panties aside, rubbing her aching core with his tip, getting his hardness ready and wet.

"What do I think?" Alex asked, and she whimpered as the tip

of his cock teased its way in. "I think you planted a nano-tracker on Jordan."

Sharply, his teeth tugged her ear, forcing her to arch back and take all of him at once.

"Yes!" Madison screamed, riding his length as he slammed himself hard and deep.

There, in the aftermath of her first deep-cover work, Alex staked his unyielding claim on her over, and over, and over again.

CHAPTER 36

MADISON

Having been fully frisked by her fiancé, ensuring every crevice and cavity was bug- and tracker-free, Madison walked inside with him. If Alex Drake was anything, he was damn thorough.

Jordan slinked over to Madison's side. "Your lip color seems to have vanished. Care for some of mine?"

Madison smiled, proudly wearing the rising blush of her cheeks as she huddled with the others around the small conference table. Dozens of printouts were strewn about, displaying the images captured by Madison's glasses. Her gaze traveled from sheet to sheet, studying the information on each page.

Stone shuffled a few around. "We're looking for two pieces—a lock and a key. From the way it looks, we have neither."

"Bullshit," Mark shot back. "My guess is you have one, and you need both."

Unconvincingly, Stone tried to object. "The operation was compartmentalized. I recruited Jack and gave him a broad-brush overview of the mission. But someone else, someone deep in the shadows, pulled him into whatever else he got caught up in. It eluded me then, and it's continued to elude me for the past ten years."

Exchanging glances with Alex and Mark, Stone sighed as his face filled with regret. "All I know is he was sent out to find something—find it and return it. But maybe . . ."

"Maybe what?" Madison latched onto Stone's hesitation.

He barely made eye contact. "Maybe he had different plans. Perhaps he was going to hold on to it."

Angry, Madison snapped, "Jack wasn't a traitor." Exhausted from the day and an inch from losing her shit on the man, she was relieved when Alex rushed over and caressed her shoulders. The gesture calmed her.

Stone waved a hand in apology. "No, of course not. I didn't mean that. I meant maybe he wanted to keep it out of harm's way. Like, he didn't trust the person he was supposed to retrieve it for. But Jack must have inadvertently tipped his hand. Asked a wrong question. Wondered aloud and made someone nervous."

"Finders keepers." Paco huffed, crossing his arms and shaking his head.

"Finders keepers?" Madison asked.

"A fairy tale," Jordan said, casually brushing it off. "A legend. A group of spy vigilantes who find and hold precious information, even from their own superiors and handlers, to prevent an uneven shift of power in the wrong direction. But trust me, government-issued spies aren't in it to break the sanctimonious bonds of big brotherhood. They have neither the financial resources nor the sponsorship to go it alone. It's all a bunch of glorified PR that makes espionage out to be altruistic."

Paco leaned to Madison with a mocking glance at Jordan. "Well, there have been cases of things miraculously turning up at just the right time, and in just the right hands."

Jordan glared his way. "Spies steal. That doesn't make them Robin Hood. Just like finding a few coins under a pillow doesn't mean there's a tooth fairy."

"No," Stone said, refocusing the group. "What this means is we need to focus and find the missing piece. The piece Jack had. And I'm quite confident it's not a tooth. It's either the lock . . . or the key."

Madison countered with a different possibility. "No, at some point, he would've had to have both. Known what he was in possession of. That's what made him dangerous. Otherwise, he wouldn't have been a threat."

Jordan glanced at Alex, then Paco. "You two were around him. Did he show you anything? Give you any hint of what he might be transporting, or perhaps how?"

Alex and Paco looked at each other and shrugged. "No," Alex said. "Nothing at all."

Next to Madison, Paco crossed his arms tight across his chest, no doubt memorizing the photos. He drummed the fingers of his left hand against his arm, a habit that let her know he was deep in thought. Again and again, his fingers rolled. Turning, he blew out an exasperated breath as she held hers in.

"What?" he asked as she stared at him.

Come on, Paco. Read my mind.

Giving her a concerned look, he said, "You look tired."

What? No. That's realization, not exhaustion.

Paco turned to the others. "Hey, I'm going to take Madison home. I'll come back after I drop her off."

"I can take her," Crystal said.

"No, I'll do it. I need some air," Paco said, his voice casual but insistent. Without saying more, he placed his hand on her back as he pushed her toward the door.

"Wait!" Madison stopped in her tracks, determined to explain. "No. I'm not tired." Her tone cracked a bit more than she'd intended. "I'm—"

Alex slipped his arm around her and turned them to walk her out.

"Hey," he said with reassurance. "No shame in it. Look, we've got a few hours of work to do here, and we get it. The day you've had would make anyone tense. It's completely understandable that you're emotional. Let Paco take you home. We'll just be a few hours longer."

With that, he scooted her out the door, placed barely a peck on her stammering lips, and handed her off to Paco. When the door shut, the clank of it locking behind them was just enough to raise her blood to a rolling boil, and she whirled on Paco.

"Paco!"

He drew in a sharp breath, hardening his expression. "Madison, do as you're told and get your ass in the car."

Furious, she marched to his Lambo. Paco's attempt to open her door was met with a *fuck you* glare.

She made a hasty grab for the door. "I can open it myself."

He held both hands high in defeat and moved around the car to take his place again as her driver. With a thunderous roar, he drove out of the garage, his smirk breaking into a full-blown belly laugh.

"What's wrong, *hermanita*? Don't you like it when Alex and I make you out to be the erratic, emotional little woman?"

Her irritation melted. It was all for show. "So, you know?"

"All I know is whatever you were thinking, you were about to let the cat out of the bag, and that's the last thing we want with these folks. Their entire livelihood revolves around how good they are at lying and stealing. Whatever you have, we need to keep it under wraps until they come through with their end of the bargain and restore Jack's military record. It's what you were promised, and what he deserves."

Despite her seat belt, Madison pulled herself over, hugging Paco's neck and giving him a hard kiss on his cheek. "So, now what? I mean, I might be wrong. It's really just a hunch."

Paco waved a dismissive hand. "I trust your instincts, and so does Alex. Whatever it is, you're probably spot on."

Thoughtfully, she considered how best to share her thoughts. "I'd like to wait until Alex is with us to discuss it."

"Okay, we'll wait a few hours. But I'm dying to know what you've got."

I seriously doubt that.

CHAPTER 37

MADISON

Manhattan

Although glad to be back at the penthouse, Madison wished this weren't weighing on her. Alex and Paco stood before her as she sat on the sofa, hugging a pillow tight to her chest as she stared at them. The men looked at each other, then back to her, their concern growing.

"Madison," Alex said, "whatever it is, we're in it together."

Sucking in a breath, she nodded. "You two should sit down."

They dropped onto the sofa on either side of her, squeezing her in just enough to make her smile. It worked.

"Go ahead," Alex said, nudging her gently.

"Jordan mentioned that Jack had been working with a very small amount of platinum."

Paco placed his hand atop hers. "Something that small could be anywhere. Mailed. Buried. Lost."

"Hidden," she said pointedly. "Hidden in plain sight."

"That sounds like Jack," Alex said, and Paco nodded.

Madison pulled in a ragged breath. "I think I know where it is."

Paco sat up. "Did Jack give it to you? Or to Dan?" If Jack was going to give it to anyone, their father would have been as likely as Madison.

"No." With all the care, warmth, and love she could muster, Madison gazed at Paco. The man who should have been her brother-in-law, but she had to settle for thinking of him as a brother. "I think he gave it to you."

Perplexed, Paco frowned. "Madison, I'm sorry. He didn't."

Gingerly, she brushed the ring on his pinky. "Did Jack ever mention James Zaharee?"

Paco exchanged a blank stare with Alex, and they both shook their heads. Considering Paco never forgot a name or a face, it was obvious he hadn't.

Softly, Madison continued. "Jack was obsessed with Zaharee since he was a child, marveling at his mastery of miniature writing." She lightly rocked Paco's pinky ring back and forth.

Paco pulled off the ring, lifting it before them in his palm. "I see where you're going with this, but I've checked. I've studied this ring every day since he gave it to me. The design is common. There are millions of rings with the identical insignia. And there's nothing engraved on it."

Smiling, Madison clasped her hand around his, enclosing the ring delicately within his fist. Shaking her head, she said, "Jordan said Roberto had a jewelry shop. That makes sense with the ring, but jewelers are also skilled engravers. And whatever he was supposed to deliver was platinum and small. Really small."

She rubbed Paco's hand. "The reason Jack was obsessed with James Zaharee is because he loved the Declaration of Independence. And, well, Zaharee was most famous for writing the entire Declaration of Independence," she pushed out a breath, "on a grain of rice."

Alex wrapped his arm around her. "You think Jack had the ring engraved with the information? On something that small?"

She nodded. "I'm positive he did and kept it somewhere he

was sure it would be safe, even if he couldn't keep it secure himself. He could have had it laser engraved on platinum, and then encapsulated into, well, pot metal. Because the melting point for platinum is much higher than that of pot metal, or even gold, it could be heated later, like melting the chocolate away from the macadamia nut. The nut stays perfectly intact, with all its ridges preserved. Then, when he needed to retrieve it—"

Paco yanked his hand back from her before jumping to his feet. "No. Hell no. Madison, it's the only gift I have from Jack. It's my engagement ring, and all I have left of him."

Pacing, Paco slid the ring back on, clasping his hand protectively to his chest. He looked back at both of them. "If you think I'm melting it down in the insane hope that there's a piece of engraved platinum in it, you've lost your damn minds."

Alex stood to meet him, placing a reassuring hand on his shoulder. "Hey, we're not forcing you to do anything you're not ready for. Not at all. But Jack was killed because of it. And you know better than anyone that we can have it replicated exactly, to the tiniest detail. We can even duplicate whatever's in it, so it has the identical weight and feel."

Gently, Madison squeezed Paco's hand. "But there's no hurry. None. Not as far as I'm concerned." She stood and wrapped her arms around him, hugging him hard.

"But . . ." Alex pocketed his hands. "You know none of us will get a moment of sleep until we find out what this is all about. Which is no skin off my nose, because I don't sleep anyway."

With a heavy sigh, Paco returned Madison's squeeze. "And it's the only ticket to Jack's status being fully reinstated." He yanked Alex over as well, linking them all in the tightness of a family bear hug.

Alex said, "Well, that and perhaps Jack's orders that Jordan slid into Madison's ample bosom."

They held the hug and chuckled as Madison lightly swatted him on the ass.

CHAPTER 38

MADISON

Three days later

IN THE COMFORT of Alex's office, Madison watched as Paco studied his ring in the light, seeing its brilliant gleam. "It's too shiny," he said, disapproving of its sheen. It was the first time he'd tried on the remade ring.

For a moment, Paco twisted the band, scrutinizing it as it moved. Though the identical combinations of nickel, copper, and brass had been used, remolded, and stamped to exacting detail, it was clear the patina of age was gone, making the ring look shinier and new.

"Well, a few days of cheap bar soap should dull it down," he said, slipping it back on, flexing his finger as he admired the fit.

Madison looked lovingly at the way it molded to his skin, and smiled at him. Smiling back, he adjusted his tie, signaling he was ready to move on.

"Well?" Madison linked her arm through his, glancing at the ring as she laid her head on his shoulder.

He sucked in a deep breath. "Yes, *hermanita*. It feels right. It's still the ring from Jack."

"Good," she said.

With a kiss to her forehead, he asked, "How's the decoding going?"

"Slow," she said with a frustrated frown.

"Hey." Alex waved them over to his desk, where he'd been painstakingly capturing the inscriptions from the platinum bead that sat in his palm.

No one could know about this, so Alex decided to handle the work himself. With several specialized instruments, he had the code. But it was still no good without the decoder.

"I think I've got an idea," Alex said. "We're not going to give Jordan or Stone the original. Like Paco's ring, we'll replicate it, but with just the slightest tweak to the code."

"How?" Paco asked. "How would you do it without them knowing?"

"Code breaking is my next favorite pastime next to Madison." The man was born to make her blush. "There are repeaters within the code. Like anywhere I see something that resembles an *a*, I replace it with maybe an *m*, but the rest of the code stays intact. It's subtle, in case they've seen this code before, but they won't be able to crack it. Whatever this is supposed to unlock, it won't work."

"Why would we want to do that?" Madison asked.

Alex smiled. "Because we can't just hand them the real one. Until we know what it unlocks, we hand over a dummy."

"But they said they don't have whatever it is this will decode," Madison said, feeling a little silly reminding him.

"Bald-faced lying at its finest," Paco said, replying for both himself and Alex.

Alex set the little bead of platinum in a specially designed box, closed it, and set it down. "You were right, Madison. Jack must have had both pieces at some point. I'm betting Stone has the other one. Smart people don't devote this kind of time and energy when the odds aren't stacked in their favor."

Madison thought about Jordan. "What about the images from my glasses? Jordan took something out of that box when she thought I wasn't looking."

Alex agreed. "Oh. You mean this?" He handed her a printout. In the image, Jordan was clearly holding an access card, one Madison had never seen.

"What's that?" Madison pointed to a small fleck of gold along the bottom of the card. The head looked like a lion. But somehow the image was blurred, with the bottom strangely resembling a fish tail.

"That's definitely a Merlion," Paco said, having sufficiently squinted and leaned in for a look.

He seriously needs to just rip off the Band-Aid and buy a pair of reading glasses already.

Alex raised a brow. "It's the official symbol of Singapore. And I know that access card."

Madison suspected he not only knew it, but probably had a hand in making it.

Smiling, Alex took her hand and squeezed. "Well, beautiful . . . ready to make a deal?"

Taking Paco's hand with her other, she held her breath and nodded. "Yes," she quietly blew out.

Alex grabbed his cell, again dialing the number.

"Insurance services." A man's voice answered, one it seemed Alex didn't readily recognize, though traces of a Latin or French accent could be distinguished from just the two words.

"Yes," Alex said, smiling at Madison's noticeable confusion. "I'm interested in getting an appraisal on something valuable. Some might say it's priceless."

"Hold, please."

The elevator rendition of "Moon River" had Alex and Paco singing along. Madison giggled until the line reconnected. In an instant, they were silent.

"We can have an adjustor at your property in fifteen minutes."

Whispering to Madison, Paco asked, "What's with them and the fifteen minutes?"

"Actually," Alex said, "I'm at my place of work. DGI headquarters in Manhattan. My suite."

Both Madison and Paco flashed him a silent *Are you sure?* Smiling, he nodded.

After only a moment of silence, the man replied. "Yes, sir. Fifteen minutes. DGI. See you there."

Once the call disconnected, Alex explained. "They're done with their games. Once they have what we give them, I doubt they'll stick around. You know what that means?"

Paco grinned. "Operation Shadow commences."

CHAPTER 39

MADISON

STANDING in front of the floor-to-ceiling window of the isolated DGI conference room, Madison lost herself in staring at the clouds in the sky, haloed with shards of sunlight breaking through.

Is real closure possible?

Before she could tackle the itchy hives working their way up her arm, she stalled with the approach of steps.

"They've arrived." Alex squeezed her shoulders. "Ready?"

She turned toward him with the slightest nod. "Ready," she whispered, then headed to the conference table, about to take a seat.

"What are you doing?" he asked.

"I'm—"

"Sitting in the wrong seat. Remember? Jordan was intent on speaking with you. This is your meeting." He urged her toward the leather executive chair at the head of the table, holding it out for her. "This is your seat. Mark and I are just eye candy."

Sitting, she looked over at Mark, who shot her a calming wink. "Well, one of us is," he teased before slipping on his glasses.

He picked up the small box on the table that held the grain-sized bead of platinum. "You think they'll come through?"

Bearing his weight on his hands, Alex leaned on the table. "I'm betting they already have."

"And what about us?" Madison couldn't help wondering if skirting their end of the deal would only leave them burned.

"I promise you we will, but only after we know what the real intent and impact is. We have to make sure the information Jack gave his life for is in the right hands."

A knock at the door pulled Mark to his feet, joining Alex in standing. Madison moved to hop up as well, but Alex gently pressed her shoulder, urging her to remain in her seat.

Jordan entered first, making her way past Alex and barely acknowledging him. Her sights were set on Madison.

Stone, on the other hand, didn't seem to care where he sat. He took the first open seat next to Mark.

Jordan's piercing stare met Madison's bashful eyes. A flash of heat was already climbing Madison's neck, but she played it cool, not hiding or acknowledging it at all.

Don't react. Respond.

She embraced the blush, which seemed to satisfy Jordan.

"So," Jordan said, "you have something for us?"

In a sense, Madison had come to understand Jordan. Her fervent gaze wasn't infatuation, and it wasn't a game. Madison had become her new object of interest, and she was studying her. Trying to catch a tell—a deception. Trying to see if Madison would slip her a fake.

Instead, Madison focused on Jordan's lips. Replaying images of their encounter, she let raw emotions flood her thoughts, turning her deception to desire.

Her body responded quickly. Her pulse spiked. Her breathing became erratic and quick. Her lips felt full, needing the swipe of a lick.

"No," Madison said, her voice slightly above a whisper, yet

housing all the power. All the control. "First, you have something for me."

Jordan nodded, pulling a large manila envelope from her Hermès messenger bag. Along the top, *Madison* was scrolled with a lavish heart over the *i*.

Thankful, Madison gave her an appreciative nod and opened it, reading the paper inside once and then again. The letter was from the Human Resources Command, United States Army, and stated the following:

Ms. Taylor,

It has come to our attention that the military records for Jack Taylor may be erroneous, based on information we have received from a third party. To expedite the correction, please send a copy of any documents you may have to substantiate his military service to the address below. Once received, we will provide written confirmation of the correction.

The mild lift to Jordan's lips was so slight, only Madison could read the subtle smile. It surprised her how disarming this vixen could choose to be. It felt sincere.

Jordan didn't have to give her Jack's orders when she found them in the archives. But she did. Appreciation welled in Madison's eyes, and she let Jordan wipe away a tear that escaped.

Unable to speak, Madison mouthed *thank you*.

"Anytime," Jordan said, enigmatic to the end.

Madison gave Mark a nod, who handed the small box to Stone. Not bothering to open it, he placed it in his pocket, then stood.

"Gentlemen, and Madison, perhaps we'll have the pleasure of working together again. Someday."

They all stood, and Alex gave him a confident reply. "I'm sure we will. It's a small world."

Before Madison could move to the comfort of Alex's arms, Jordan cut in between them, her trademark wicked expression in place. The vixen was back.

Flipping a card between her fingers, she said, "In case you ever need me."

Now used to Jordan's touch, not that she had ever imagined that reality, Madison remained still as Jordan dragged the card across her collar and down her blouse.

Enjoying herself, Jordan took her sweet time tucking it into what seemed to be her favorite hiding spot. She pulled Madison in for a hug, whispering in her ear. "See Alex?"

Madison caught the intensity of Alex's expression, and glanced down at his pants. She murmured back, "Mm-hmm."

"Are his pupils dilated?"

She let out a long *yes*, unable to contain her own devilish grin.

"You're welcome." Jordan softly sighed with a cheek-to-cheek kiss. Releasing Madison, Jordan made her way to Stone, taking his arm as they headed out the door.

Shifting on his feet, Mark said, "I'll see them both out." They left, and he shut the door behind him.

Alex stalked closer, sweeping his darkening gaze over her. Hiding her smile, she bit her lip and coyly averted her eyes.

"You know," he said as his fingers dipped into her blouse. They lingered, brushing her nipple before capturing the small piece of cardstock. Slowly, he fished it out, tracing it up her neck to her chin, lifting her beautifully blushing face and summoning her gaze to his. Disappointed, he grumbled, "I never got Jordan's digits."

Madison's giggles stretched on and on as she melted into the warmth of his tender kiss.

CHAPTER 40

MARK

MARK WATCHED as the waiting driver held open the back door of the black Bentley sedan for Jordan and Stone. Once they were seated, he shut it and moved quickly to the driver's door.

He diligently tried to avoid Mark's scrutiny, keeping his chauffeur hat low and his dark glasses high in an obvious effort to conceal his face. But he couldn't hide everything.

For example, Mark noticed the sunglasses the chauffeur sported were $3,000 Ray-Ban Aviators in 18-karat gold. He often wore a pair himself. As the man's hands locked around the steering wheel, Mark was thankful he didn't wear gloves. It gave him so much more insight into who he was dealing with.

On his right hand was no ordinary ring. The emerald-eyed golden panther was the talk of social media and celebrities, a signature piece of the internationally renowned jewelers Cartier.

Before Mark could catch too many more glimpses into the Jordan Stones and their "chauffeur," the car rolled away.

He made a call. "Over to you."

CHAPTER 41

STONE

ONCE INSIDE THE CAR, Stone sat back as the driver carefully removed his sunglasses. Unamused, the man turned back, digging his elbow into the armrest. "Why am I always the fucking chauffeur?"

Behind him, Jordan leaned forward, wrapping her arms around the leather seat until she connected her hands across his chest. "Because I love seeing you in this outfit."

"Don't sweet-talk me, Jordan. The two of you deliberately kept me out of this one. I'm still pissed."

As well he should have been. He was, after all, the third to round out the team. He had been the man in the suit in Puerto Rico, the reason Paco Robles joined that mission in Italy. And why, to this day, Paco remained by Alex Drake's side.

"We all have our weaknesses," Stone said, hoping he came off more patriarchal and less condescending.

"It was for your own good," Jordan softly added, her tone sincere.

"And for the good of the mission," Stone said, which earned him a huff. It was cause enough to remove the small box from his jacket pocket. "Fear not, *P*, your luck's looking up. We're heading east, and you and Jordan will be the happy couple this go-round."

Pierre Roca, or *P*, adjusted the rearview mirror to speak with Stone more directly, though he seemed content enough to keep Jordan's arms wrapped against him. "And what will you be?" he asked, lifting his voice with hope and the thrill of possibility.

Stone didn't mind that it was annoying. *P* needed a break. "I'll, um, be your butler," he said, at which point *P* and Jordan laughed with delight.

Stone was happy too, but inwardly. He loved having them this close. Outwardly, he ignored them, prying open the box and studying it.

"And that?" Jordan asked, curious about the fate of their recent acquisition.

Stone thoughtfully considered the miniscule chunk of metal, gliding the tip of his finger over it carefully, even reverently.

"I don't know yet. We'll keep it, perhaps. I won't decide until after this trip. It will give us an opportunity to revisit an old acquaintance . . ." His tone tensed. "One who obviously knew more than he ever let on." Frowning, he snapped the box shut and slid it back into his pocket.

Jordan released *P* to sit back and take Stone's arm. "And that's why you'll forever be the King of the Keepers."

Loosely, he concealed the sense of pride that welled within him.

Jordan returned her attention to *P*, wrapping her arms around him again before sliding her tongue to the tip of his ear. Stone pretended not to watch as she gave it a sharp bite. Letting out a deep moan, *P* followed it with a naughty chuckle.

At the very least, they should get a room.

Stone settled back, pulling a pair of reading glasses from his breast pocket as he scrolled through his phone in a weak attempt to mask his irritation. But the woman was half a second from jerking *P* off. Even Stone had his limits.

"Jordan," Stone said coldly, "you never seem this giddy when you play my wife. Why is that?"

"I'll tell you why," P said as he kissed her hand, then started the car. "Because you can't truly appreciate her remarkable talent for repeatedly ramming an eight-inch strap-on up your ass."

P and Jordan held their breath, awaiting his response.

Without skipping a beat, Stone sat back and scrolled through his phone, simply acknowledging the statement with a weak, "Touché."

They roared with laughter until Jordan slid back in her seat as well, buckling up and preparing for the ride. Legs crossed, she slid off one shoe and turned to Stone, rubbing her foot softly against his shin. "So, what are you so engrossed in?"

He turned his phone to show her Madison's image lighting up his screen.

"A little young for you, isn't she?"

"And a little sweet for you." Stone pursed his lips before catching Jordan's eye. "Do you think she deceived us?"

Jordan considered it, slumping back in her seat. It took a moment for a smile to warm her face. "I don't know," she mused curiously.

Stone stared at the phone, memorizing her image. "Neither do I. But she's interesting. And," he took a breath, "she reminds me of Jack. Confident. Sincere. Barely on the brink of realizing her true potential. With the soul of a Finder . . ."

When his despondent words trailed off, Jordan placed her hand over his, giving it a tender squeeze. "I like her," she said, unusually sentimental in that moment.

Stone looked at her, then at P's reflection glancing back, his eyebrow raised.

"So do I," Stone admitted quietly.

He took one last look before clicking off the phone and putting it away.

"Perhaps our paths *will* cross again." After a contemplative moment, he added, "I'll have someone keep an eye on her, because you never know."

CHAPTER 42

※

PIERRE

P READJUSTED the rearview mirror to its original position, again able to see the traffic behind him as he prepared to pull away. Taking another glance in it, he smiled.

The quiet flash of gray should have remained camouflaged in the distance, but to *P*, it was the beacon he'd been waiting for. Despite the drab dot of a helmet well masked amongst the vibrant Manhattan backdrop, nothing could hide it.

Or him.

P chuckled under his breath, finding the disguise as effective as using a busy Parisian street to hide the Eifel Tower.

Taking in an energized breath, he smiled. His faith was renewed. No matter how Stone and Jordan discouraged him, his carpe diem had finally arrived, and this time, he would sure as hell be seizing it.

Come on, Robles. Move your ass.

CHAPTER 43

PACO

Paco kept a sharp eye on the darkly tinted Bentley as it pulled away from DGI. His Ducati 1299 Superleggera would easily catch up. Though not a showpiece like its Panigale V4R cousin, the Ducati was exactly the high-performance motorcycle for this job. Anything else would draw too much attention, and the last thing he needed was attention.

Unlike the brightly painted showstopper that suited the average collector, this bike had been superbly converted. Carbon fiber subdued its color to a bland tone, and the added exhaust cutout valve quieted its telltale rumble. The fifty-thousand-dollar piece of stellar machinery was sure to be unnoticed by all.

He slipped on the high-tech helmet, switching on the heads-up display. He could clearly see the location of the Bentley moving along a 3-D city grid, but the display didn't obstruct his view. If anything, it enhanced it.

The tracker Madison had placed on Jordan would signal for a full ten miles, letting him seamlessly fall back to avoid detection.

"Call Alex," he said aloud. The auto-system placed the call.

"Got them?" Alex asked without even saying *hello*.

"Yup. Tracker active. Signal strong. I'll let you know what I find out. And tell Black this new helmet of his kicks ass."

Black would be Davis R. Black, or Richard to his friends. Alex loved every opportunity to collaborate with the CEO of Black Technologies on cutting-edge work.

"I thought you'd like it. Test it to the max so we can let him know what enhancements we need, but for the love of God, be careful. Don't crash." They both knew Paco's penchant for high-speed maneuvers.

"Worried about me? Aw, old age is making you soft."

"Well, I'm worried, all right. That helmet's worth a small fortune."

Underwhelmed, Paco let out a light laugh. "Thanks. I'll keep that in mind. Asshole," he grumbled in jest.

Alex shifted his tone. "Seriously, take care. Keep me posted."

"Will do."

Alex ended the call, and Paco keyed up his playlist before merging into traffic. Nothing like a little "Don't Stop Me Now" by Queen to set this chase in motion.

CHAPTER 44

ALEX

ALEX ARRIVED at their penthouse apartment a few hours after Madison, a little apprehensive about the discussion to come. She'd seemed intent on leaving DGI, though it seemed like a lifetime since she brought it up.

At the depressing thought of not seeing her every day at work, he missed her already. But it wasn't a line. Her happiness was his obligation, and his daily vow to a departed friend.

Ping. It was a text alert from Paco.

PACO: *They're on a Gulfstream. First stop Paris. Drum roll for the final stop.*

ALEX: *Singapore.*

PACO: *Bingo. We lucked out. They left their entire manifest with their final destination.*

ALEX: *Have our folks in Singapore keep an eye on them until you can catch up.*

PACO: I'll head out first thing tomorrow. I've got the 787 lined up. If they lollygag in France, I'll beat them. Worst case, I'll trail them by a few hours. If nothing exciting happens, I'll be home in a week.

ALEX: Sounds good. And let me know how the master suite of that new Dreamliner is. At nearly three hundred million, the toilet in that jet better be solid gold and self-wiping.

PACO: If you're asking for shit pics, I'm gonna need a raise.

ALEX: Hey, this is a professional corporate text, not Snapchat. Peddle your fetish photos elsewhere.

PACO: And let me know how it goes with Madison.

ALEX: I will. Be safe.

Alex set down his phone and headed into the living room. A long silver box was set on the soft chaise with an inviting red ribbon that caught his eye. "Madison? What's this?"

She called out from the bedroom. "A gift from Jordan. For me. She left it in my office."

Suspicious and alarmed, Alex was on it in two quick strides. Narrowing his eyes on the box with the hinged top, he couldn't tell if it had been opened.

Inspecting its size and weight, he determined it was just about right for a long-stemmed rose, but could contain anything. Even, in a worst-case scenario of epic proportion, explosives. He handled it with care.

"Madison, I'll be back. Before we open it, I need to have it checked out."

Box in hand, he prepared to head back to DGI to get a good look at its x-rayed contents, but Madison blocked his path.

"Too late," she said as she stepped toward him. With her long legs encased in a scandalous pair of fishnet stockings tucked into glossy high-heeled riding boots, it was clear he wasn't going anywhere.

Beneath her buttoned competition riding blazer was a braless goddess whose gorgeous breasts were taut against the stretchy fabric, begging to be released. She'd finished the look with a pair of black lace panties, a glimpse of them teasing him from beneath.

When Madison took a few steps closer, he completely forgot about the potentially hazardous box that might hold dangerous explosives that could wipe them all from the face of the earth. In this moment, it was the last thing on his mind. He dropped it, letting it slip from his fingers to land carelessly at his feet.

He took a quick look down to notice it had flipped open. The empty box was neither a threat, nor his immediate concern.

Alex recognized the item in Madison's hand. The gift. A braided black leather riding crop that would probably need a few baths in bleach before Madison's delicate fingers should have handled it. He breathed out a small sigh when he saw the tiny gold sticker and realized it must be new.

Delighted, Madison tapped the tip of the crop against the palm of her hand. "I believe you dropped the box, Mr. Drake."

"God, please tell me I'm getting punished for it," he said as he loosened his tie.

Her giggle was light and carefree, and eased his tight lips to a playful grin.

Half joking, he asked, "Did Jordan just become your new best friend, or mine?"

Madison prowled toward him, pressing against him as he sat on the chaise. Sliding herself onto his lap, she teased his mouth with the tip of the leather. He could only lose himself in the moment for so long before reminding himself of the gift giver.

Madison, this could be bugged, he mouthed.

She giggled, leaving him with a smile and a suggestive dismount. "It's not," she said with pure glee.

He stood too, letting his own half smile meet hers. "How do you know?"

Madison brushed his lips, conjuring his moan. She retrieved a small silver card from her pocket and placed it in his hand.

Recognizing the handwriting, he read the note out loud. "It's not bugged. Have fun, J."

"Satisfied?" Madison whispered.

He grumbled low. "Not half as satisfied as I'm about to be."

Alex cradled her cheeks, nibbled her lips, and took his time taking long, sweeping tastes of her before tearing himself away.

Resting his forehead on hers, he said, "You're the only woman for me, Madison Taylor."

"And you, Alex Drake, have an appointment."

"An appointment?" He pocketed the card, captivated and curious.

Her lips were a whisper from his, and she had a naughty glint in her eye that spiked his pulse. His gaze washed over her as he returned her grin.

"I believe it's time for my riding lesson," she said softly, handing him the crop. She turned away, sashaying down the hall. "Come along, Mr. Drake."

The braid of the crop felt natural in his grip. Different. New.

His hungry gaze followed her, enjoying every step of her walking away. His ninety-nine percent angel was showing off every bit of her sizzling-hot one percent, plunging a flaming red arrow deep inside his heart. The devil in him longed for her heat.

"Indeed, it is, Ms. Taylor." Briskly, he smacked the crop against the palm of his hand and chased after her.

In their bedroom, Madison waited, leaning against the bed. His glance floated down her body, taking in every arc and angle, finally landing at her shiny black boots. "Are those comfortable?"

She nodded. "Mm-hmm."

He arched a brow. Decisive, he said, "Good, because you'll be keeping them on." He traced the end of the crop along her inner thigh, commanding her. "Turn around."

Once she obeyed, he bent her forward on the bed.

He ran the tip of the crop on a lazy trail up the back of her leg, gliding along the underside of her ass and swiping her core. She moaned. He tore off his clothes and removed his tie. It felt like an eternity since he'd been inside her. The last time was too rushed.

At the sight of her—bent over, wanting, waiting—he pumped himself hard, dredging up every bit of his self-control. As much as he wanted to bury himself balls deep in her tight walls, tonight was for her. If he had his way, every night would be for her.

He placed the length of his thickness along the crack of her soft, round ass before leaning to her ear. "You're beautiful, Madison. You have no idea what you're doing to me."

"Then show me," she begged.

"In my own time," he said, giving her ear a terse nip. Her sexy squeal went straight to his cock.

He caressed the firm flesh of her butt before slowly tugging her panties off as he whispered, "Perfect."

Admiring her firm ass and slick core beneath, he slid the crop against her hip, then let the rod rest along the small of her back.

"Give me your hands," he growled.

Obeying, she lowered her hands down the sides of her body, presenting them to him. He moved them into position, palms against her butt. Stretching the elastic lace of her undies wide, he secured her wrists by looping each end to the waiting crop.

Satisfied with her restraints, he told her, "Don't move. Not a muscle."

With that, he moved her hands, using her own fingers to spread herself for him. Expose herself so he could take in her round ass, soaked lips, and tight hold in a glance. Giving herself over completely, just as he'd always do for her.

He dragged two fingers along her, painting her pretty pussy

with her own sweet dew. As soon as she bucked back, craving more, he gave her ass a smack.

"You're not going to move until I tell you to come. Understand, Madison?"

"Yes." She breathed out the word, panting hard.

Alex dropped to his knees with soft, sensual kisses along her cheeks, letting his stubble graze against her thighs, and enjoying each tortured whimper she released.

But she obeyed. She didn't move.

"Good," he said before slicing his hot tongue through the plump folds of her core.

He forced a thick finger inside, and her shudder was instant.

He gave her ass another smack. "Not yet, beautiful."

Moaning, Madison writhed in place.

"Is this what you want?" Alex asked, circling her clit with the pad of his finger. "Do you want me to make you come?"

"Yes," she begged. Her body quivered, and she cried out, "Please."

Fisting his cock, he invaded her with his tongue, feeding on her cunt, lapping up her wetness and fingering her with his other hand. The walls of her sex shuddered with need.

He pressed a second finger in her soaked pussy, and she rocked with him. "Now, Madison. Come for me now."

Alex let her ride out the wave against his hand, slowing his pace as she peaked and floated down. He wasn't done, but he was finished with her restraints. He released her wrists, giving each a tender kiss.

Lying beside her, he moved her on top so she could mount him, because her outfit was perfect for it. His dick was hard against the heat of her wet center. Unconstrained, he shoved every inch of his thick length in to the hilt.

"Yes," she cried. Rocking with his thrusts, she adjusted to his size, sliding herself from the tip of his shaft clear to the base. Owning him as much as he owned her.

"Fuck, Madison, you're so tight."

He reached for her blazer, releasing the buttons one by one, letting it fall from her shoulders and drape along her arms. He pinched her nipples and caressed her breasts. She was breathtaking.

The soft waves of her hair were silky against his hands, and more of her softness brushed against his touch. As her head fell back, her body arched, and her mouth parted to take in deeper breaths with each penetrating thrust.

"Just like that, Madison. Just like that," he said, losing himself in the glory of her, watching as she chased her climax faster, spreading her thighs wider to take in more as he bucked back.

He gripped her hips, driving himself further. Deeper. Madison leaned back, gripping the solid muscles of his thighs, barely grazing his skin with the tips of her nails before timidly shying away.

"No," he said, his voice gruff and stern.

Grabbing the crop, he placed the tip of it to her chin, coercing her eyes to his. She nearly stopped, like that was fucking happening. He gripped her ass, driving himself in, forcing her against his seeping cock, working her back to his pace.

"Never hide what you want from me, Madison." His dark eyes and hoarse timbre commanded her. His hips reignited, ramming her mercilessly. "Do it."

Madison skimmed her fingers along his thighs, sucked in a breath, and raked her nails against his skin.

Alex hissed, arching his back. It was everything. Everything he needed. Everything he wanted. This was Madison. She was his, and he was hers.

"Now," he said, splitting her wide, filling her, and pumping all he had deep inside. She collapsed upon him, crying out as her body shook and her tight core milked him hard.

As their breathing calmed, Madison nestled in his arms, laying her head on his pounding chest. Tenderly, he brushed his fingers across her shoulder, through the long, lush strands of her hair and down to the small of her back.

Disappointed, he found her tension still there, in tight knots along the softness of her back.

"Penny for your thoughts?" he asked, his voice gentle.

"Hmm . . ." She trailed a finger across his chest, lazily drifting it back and forth. "I was just wondering when I might be able to take these off." She bent her knees, casually swinging her boot-laden legs in the air.

He laughed. "In three days." When her skeptical glare challenged his playful expression, he looked down at them again, reconsidering. "Two and a half?"

Rolling her to her back, he made his way down her body one tender kiss at a time. He unzipped the first boot, sliding it off along with its stocking, and worked his massaging fingers into her tight calf.

"Anything else on your mind?" he asked.

Her gaze broke away, staring across the room. Moving from Swedish to shiatsu, he worked her muscles harder, and she moaned with relief. "Your hands are unbelievable. If this whole billionaire CEO thing loses its luster, you've definitely got options."

He caught her playful glance as he kissed the inside of her thigh. "So do you, beautiful. Lots of options at your sexy little fingertips. Listen, if you're worried about leaving DGI . . ." Her wide eyes met his, her angst apparent. "Don't."

Alex removed the other boot and stocking, repeating the process along her leg. "How about this? Stay. Just until you decide on your next move. You'll know the right opportunity when it comes along. And there's a lot more to know about DGI. We do a lot of work with vets. Our robotics center is located next to a VA medical center. I'd love to introduce you around. It's . . . been a while since I've been there."

He drew in a deep breath, ready to battle another demon or two for the woman he loved.

She cupped his cheek, sweetly laughing as she caressed his jaw. "Well, I'd say that sounds right up my alley." Her fingers combed through his hair. "You're the love of my life, Alex."

"And you, Madison, are the love I never thought would happen. The happiness I never imagined, or even thought I deserved."

He pulled her hand to his lips.

"Other than you and me being together, nothing else matters. If you want to be part of DGI, then you're going to be a fucking part of it. I didn't build this company by giving a rat's ass about the court of public opinion, and I'm not about to start. But," he gingerly caressed the small of her back, holding her close, "if your dreams are taking you down a different path, I'll still be the man by your side, every step of the way. You've given me a gift, a life far beyond what I dared to even hope was possible. So, mark my words, Ms. Taylor. I won't settle for anything less than you being over-the-moon ecstatic on a goddamn daily basis."

He kissed her again, taking in a deep breath and loving the smile his lips left on hers.

CHAPTER 45

Three weeks later

Madison tapped her fingers, eager as her phone attempted the FaceTime call. It was more than a little frustrating to watch it click over to voice mail.

Unavailable?

She checked the time and did the math in her head. Five in the morning in New York should be five in the evening in Singapore. Scrolling through her text messages, Madison verified the time and date. And she had accounted for the shift in time zone.

As she reread his last text, she squealed with the announcement of an incoming call. Eagerly, she tapped to accept it.

"I'm sure you have an excellent reason for refusing to FaceTime me, Mr. Robles."

"Well," Paco said, keeping his tone casual. "I can't FaceTime right now because I'm . . . um . . . sunbathing."

"And?" Madison drew out the word.

"And let's just say I don't like tan lines."

Slapping a hand over her open mouth, she couldn't mask all her girlish giggles.

"Well, then don't pan down," she said. "Come on, I need to see your face. You were only supposed to be gone a week. For those of you playing along at home, that's seven days. We're now blazing past three weeks and heading for four, and a month without Paco is a month without sunshine and Starbucks. Seriously, I need my Paco fix!"

In the small span of silence, it was obvious her pleas were falling on his diamond-studded deaf ears.

"Don't worry. I promise you'll see me soon, *hermanita*. But what's going on today? How's it been working with the VA and the robotics team?"

She didn't mean to sigh. Especially in the face of him calling her his little sister.

Paco picked up on her angst. "Let me guess, Goldilocks. That bed's nice and all, but your frisky little feet are dangling over the edge and anxious to move along. And quit giving me that look. Seriously, those wrinkles aren't going to Botox themselves."

Even though he couldn't see them, her furrows melted, but it didn't wipe away all of her gloom. "God, what's wrong with me? I'm being handed one silver platter after another, and all I'm dying for is a plastic tray of all-you-can-eat from Golden Corral."

"Girlie, I've got you. We'll meet up at the chocolate fountain. And don't call me God. Your Royal Highness is my absolute limit. I'm not a deity. I just look like one."

"I'll bet you do with all that *au naturel* exposure."

"But if we're heading to a buffet when I return, I'd better hit the gym. Actually, I could head there now."

Cutting the call short? Already?

"Wait. Before you go." She quieted for a moment, hesitant to make her request. But Paco's quirky mind reading was as sharp as ever. As she struggled for words, a text popped up.

As always, he made her grin. It was a picture of Paco wearing a traditional *baju melayu* suit. The buttercream silk suited him perfectly, and it draped him like a second skin, custom tailored to perfection. His smile was brilliant, and he looked as though he was posing for the cover of *GQ Singapore*. Behind him was a giant stone sculpture of what he'd called a Merlion. Its surroundings looked like an oasis across the globe.

"There," he said. "Is that what you need? Now you're seeing me."

"Worst loophole ever." She held the phone a little tighter as she fawned over the shot.

"I promise, I will see you very, very soon. Listen, I'm running late. I've got a big night ahead—"

"Of course you do," she teased. "New York nightclubs are in their twenty-third day of mourning your departure. Their vigil continues."

"As it should. And I know you have a big day ahead." His tone was knowing and suggestive.

"I shouldn't be surprised that you know about the meeting, but just how much do you know? Alex won't tell me a thing except to show up in his office at four sharp."

"Well, I would tell you, but it will take more time that I have. I really have to run. My sunblock has faded in all the wrong spots."

"How inconveniently convenient."

But she couldn't end the call just yet. Not like that. And if there was one thing Madison Taylor could count on, it was that Paco would burn and blister to a disturbing degree before he'd hang up on her.

Softly, she said, "This thing today. Whatever it is, I feel like it's important. To us. To our family. And I don't want to do it without you. I know the time difference, but can I FaceTime you from the meeting, so I can see you? Really see you? I mean, it'll definitely cut into your beauty sleep—"

"I promise you, no matter what, you'll see me." His words were tender and sincere. "But I really have to go. Talk soon. Love you, *hermanita*."

"Love you too."

Though her days were now filled with learning the ins and outs of Drake Robotics, today was different. Madison had called it quits early with the prosthetics team to hurry back to DGI.

Setting foot in the skyscraper was vibrant. Thrilling. Like coming home. It was nothing like when she'd left all those weeks ago.

Her early arrival was intentional. The meeting with Alex wasn't for another half hour, but it gave her a chance to revisit her old digs. Her first real office. Her energy was off the charts, and she bubbled over with exhilaration.

Smiling, Madison hopped into her familiar leather desk chair and fired up her computer. Immediately, a message popped up, making her grin from ear to ear.

ANONYMOUS: *Hi.*

She let out a little sigh at the nostalgia the message evoked. *I'm so head over heels in love with you.*

MADISON: *Hi back at ya.*

ANONYMOUS: *I'm taking an employee morale survey.*

MADISON: *Really? Because the president of the morale committee used that line on me months ago.*

ANONYMOUS: *You don't say? How'd that turn out?*

MADISON: *Oh, you know. Totally marrying the man.*

ANONYMOUS: *So, you're saying it works. Then I'd better get back* to business. What Starbucks beverage would make you happiest right now?

His question made her smile. *Hmm, an extra creamy Alex Frappuccino would sure hit the spot.*

MADISON: *I'm going with an oldie but a goodie. Iced matcha latte with almond milk.*

ANONYMOUS: *You sure? They've got a ton of coffees. And an exotic collection of iced teas.*

MADISON: *Iced matcha. I'm positive.*

I may not be able to make a career choice, she thought, *but the least I can do is pick a drink.*
Madison glanced at the clock on her desktop as footsteps approached.
That can't be the matcha. It's only been a minute.

MADISON: *Gotta go. Someone's coming. I feel like a kid waiting for the ice cream truck, with the sweet sound of tinkling music miles away. #waiting4matcha. Love you.*

The footsteps stopped as she finished typing.
"I love you too," Alex said with his captivating voice and charming grin. In he strolled, carrying a tall green cup of her favorite drink. "One iced matcha latte with almond milk coming up."
He set the drink on her desk and leaned in for a kiss. She locked her arms around his shoulders and pulled him in.
"Now that's one hell of a kiss," he said, stealing another one.
Suspicious of his remarkable accomplishment, she eyed the

drink. "Wait, how's that possible? You messaged me, and I only just said what I wanted."

He whipped out his phone. "DGI app. And Paco's not the only one who can read your mind. I am about to marry you, after all. I'd like to think I know you on a deeply intimate level."

"And what would have happened if I'd decided on something more spontaneous?" Her eyes lit with the challenge.

Alex sat back on her desk, casually crossing his arms as his brows lifted. "Well, it's all very logical. There are technically over eighty thousand combinations of Starbucks drinks."

Intrigued, Madison sat taller.

"Now, you prefer almond milk, so that narrows the field. And you only drink hot beverages first thing in the morning . . . basically, nursing them until they turn into cold beverages. Field further narrowed."

Her subtle smile transformed to a wide grin as he continued.

"And although they can do any number of custom drinks, you pretty much stick to basic menu offerings, especially with iced drinks. So, after all is said and done, we're really down to about thirty-one possibilities."

Madison drew the straw to her lips and sipped, waiting for the rest of his deductive reasoning, but he stopped. "Okay, so we're at thirty-one. How did you get from thirty-one to one insanely perfect iced matcha latte?"

"Telepathy?" he said.

"If it were telepathy, you'd be naked." Suggestively, she sucked the straw between her lips.

"Hey, I have to have some trade secrets up my sleeve." He kissed her forehead. "So, four o'clock sharp. My office. Not a second early or late."

Sure. Nothing ominous about that.

"Four o'clock sharp," she whispered in agreement as he leaned over for a sweet farewell kiss. "And I thought we said no more secrets?"

He headed out, saying over his shoulder, "Trade secrets don't count."

Watching that man walk away, Madison sipped her drink and smiled as she imagined him naked.

And in slow motion.

She'd just returned to her screen when another alert popped up. She clicked the message. It was from Fred, the head of IT.

> *FRED: Hey, you're online. You need to get to the break room a floor down ASAP! Someone left THIRTY iced coffees in assorted flavors. If you can't, let me know what you like, and I'll grab it before the masses gets wind of this manna from heaven.*

Madison calmed herself, preventing the consequential creamy matcha goodness from spraying out her nose.

> *MADISON: You're such a sweetie, but I'm good. The manna delivery man hit me up earlier.*

> *FRED: As long as you're covered.*

She passed the remaining time catching up on emails, clearing out a few tasks, and soaking up every minute of being in the moment. Her smile re-emerged with every scrumptious sip.

Trade secrets, indeed.

∽

Madison eventually made her way to Alex's office, careful to check the time. Sucking in a deep breath, she was ready to FaceTime Paco.

At the exact time—not a minute early or late—she knocked.

Someone knocked back. Before she could knock again or try the door, her phone rang.

Paco!

She accepted his FaceTime request. His face filled the frame as he waggled his brows, and she burst out laughing.

"It's two minutes after four your time," he said. "Why aren't you in Alex's office yet?"

Madison hushed her laughter as his fabulous eyebrows launched its own little variety show, dancing with wild exaggeration. "I can't believe how happy I am to see you, Paco. And I tried, but it sounded like a bizarre game of knock-knock."

Paco stayed in the frame when a voice boomed from behind him.

"Did you try the password?" the man shouted.

Dad?

Wait. Dad's in Singapore?

A round of raucous laughter broke out from behind Alex's office door. Without knocking, Madison opened it. As soon as she did, she froze, captured in that state of over-the-moon ecstasy that Alex had raved about.

CHAPTER 46

MADISON

Stunned, Madison couldn't believe it. There they all were, laughing from their seats around the conference table. As soon as they saw her, they stood.

Her father, Paco, and Alex were on the far side, with Mark and Jess on the other with a man she didn't recognize nearest. The stranger was seated next to the head of the table, a seat, she guessed, that had been saved for her.

Madison quickly made the rounds of hugs and kisses, while holding on to her confusion as much as her joy. Paco was her first hug.

"Sunbathing, huh?" she asked with a grin.

He gave her a coy shrug. "I was technically in the sun."

"Where?" she asked, drawing out the word.

"Basel. I needed a quick stop before New York to pick up some goodies for everyone."

Dan proudly displayed the watch on his wrist. "See what I got?"

Paco lifted his wrist as well. "Matching Patek Philippe watches."

Her loving gaze locked on her dad, who was tickled pink to

have a twin adornment to Paco's. Without a doubt, he hadn't the slightest clue that it probably cost more than his house. He and Paco were together. Nothing filled her heart more.

Having greeted all but one, she pulled away to meet the mystery member of the party. The silver-fox Patrick Dempsey lookalike sported a deep blue suit and golden two-toned tie. She couldn't help but think he looked familiar.

Unworried, she wrapped her arms around him. "I don't know who you are, but you're in such good company, I have to give you a hug," she said firmly.

He laughed as he returned the gesture. "Well, I'll take it, young lady. I'd say it was icing on the cake for today, but I think that's still to come." He motioned for her to take her seat, and they all sat. "It's great to meet you, Madison. I'm Bill Charles—"

Congressman Charles?

"—and Alex and I go back quite a few years. Before this whole DGI world-domination bit, for sure. We met when I was using my GI Bill to get a law degree. Alex willingly took the aid of a struggling law student to help with some contract writing."

Alex chimed in. "A stellar lawyer who would work for a few bucks and some home-cooked meals. Let's just say it was definitely the Casablanca beginning of a beautiful friendship."

Bill placed a hand on hers, giving it a gentle squeeze before proceeding. "Alex reached out to me and shared with me what happened with your brother. I'm so sorry for your loss, but I'm just as sorry for his. He was stripped of a status he was entitled to, and as a vet, that just . . . well, I won't pelt you with expletives, but let's just say it didn't sit well with me. So, while you were working with Army Records, I was digging into a few other things."

He released her hand, reaching for the glossy black folder on the table before them, and slid it to her. Flipping it open, she saw it had a few documents on one side, and a small envelope tucked into the pocket on the other.

Madison reached for her father's hand, and he scooted closer to take it. They exchanged a teary gaze before carefully studying the contents.

The first letter acknowledged Jack's length of service at the time of his death, reinstating his active-duty status posthumously. But it was the second that brought on the rush of tears.

She handed the fancy document to her father, who shared it with Paco. This was no letter. It was a certificate.

> *To all who shall see these presents, greeting:*
> *This is to certify that*
> *The President of the United States of America*
> *has awarded the*
> *PURPLE HEART*
> *Established by General George Washington*
> *at Newburgh, New York, August 7, 1782*
> *to*
> *Second Lieutenant Jackson D. Taylor*
> *United States Army*

Dan's face dropped to his hands, and Paco squeezed his shoulder for support. Everyone understood, and each and every one was a mess of tears.

Madison swiped helplessly at her cheeks. *For all their planning, no one thought to bring a box of tissues?*

Mark found one quickly and passed it around.

It was then that Madison noticed the boxes. Medals undoubtedly filled them, but no one reached for them. They couldn't. Instead, they just focused blurry eyes on the certificate.

Madison took a deep breath and tried to move on. Again, she took to the folder, but seemed to be staring at an identical certificate. She removed it, her blurry eyes struggling to see the words, then she gasped aloud. This was no copy.

"Oh my God," she blurted, and shot a glance to Paco. She jumped up and hugged him. Hugged him hard but couldn't speak.

Dan grabbed the certificate. In half a second, he was doing the same thing, wrapping his arms around Paco and blubbering like a baby.

Not knowing what was going on, Paco caressed Madison's back tenderly. "Hey, there now. What is it?"

She pointed, and Paco looked down to see the second certificate lying next to Jack's. They were virtually the same, with the distinctive difference in two lines, indicating who it was issued to.

Staff Sergeant Paco J. Robles
United States Air Force

Madison wiped his cheeks, tending to the slow stream of tears Paco hadn't noticed.

"There has to be a mistake," he said. "I didn't lose my life in combat."

The congressman spoke up. "That's not the only reason the Purple Heart is awarded."

Alex nudged Madison and Dan back, letting Bill take center stage for the moment ahead.

"Your wounds and concussion were the result of a terrorist attack—one that happened while you were part of a military mission. There's no mistake. You're a deserving recipient."

Congressman Charles stood and opened one of the boxes on the table before him before removing its contents. "I am honored to formally present you with this Purple Heart for your bravery in service to our country." He held the medal as Paco stood, then pinned it to his lapel. As he shook Paco's hand, Paco blinked silently in amazement as tears streamed down his cheeks. "Thank you for your heroism, Staff Sergeant Robles."

When the congressman stepped back, Madison and Dan

immediately rushed over to envelop Paco in hard hugs. They held each other for several minutes, finally releasing him to let Alex give him a handshake and a hug. Paco wrapped his arms around Alex, resulting in both men exchanging pats on the back.

Soon, they all returned to their seats, and the congressman rested his clasped hands on the table. "But it doesn't end there."

He tapped at the last of the contents. A small envelope still in the folder. With trembling hands, Madison removed it and emptied its contents. In her hands was a check.

"I don't understand," she said, dabbing at her nose and eyes with the fresh tissue Alex handed her. She searched Congressman Charles's face for the answer, and he began to explain.

"Because Jack died on active duty and in combat, he was entitled to certain benefits that were never paid out. These are those benefits, with a small amount of interest."

Madison looked at it again. Though far from a million dollars, it was still a whole lot of money. Much more than she'd ever expected, though she never really expected anything. She handed the check to her father, who shoved it back.

"Dad, this is yours," she insisted.

"No, jellybean, it's yours. In case you hadn't noticed the last time you were home, *somebody* has been keeping me swimming in checks."

Madison smiled at the inside joke. All these years, her father had been sitting on millions of dollars in uncashed checks, every last one of them signed by Alex Drake.

Thoughtfully, she studied the check, then considered Paco. Jack and Paco might as well have been married, and the money should rightfully go to his spouse.

"Don't even give me those puppy-dog eyes, girlie. I've got more than enough for the rest of my life."

The last thing Paco meant was money, though the man had enough to buy a small island or two. Or eight. She heard his meaningful words loud and clear and followed his fingers as they brushed the Purple Heart on his chest.

"You don't have to decide this minute," Jess said, her words full of wisdom and promise.

"Still not giving me the answers, huh?" Madison asked, recalling their conversation on the road trip to the Adirondacks.

"Nope." Jess grinned. "Although, I'll bet that would make a nice little bit of seed money for a certain one-eight-hundred-passion project."

The others didn't understand the inside joke, but waited as Jess and Madison enjoyed a tear-filled moment.

"Actually," Madison said, "I think that's probably perfect."

"What is?" Dan asked, wrapping her in his arms.

Madison faced him with a big grin, glistening eyes, and for the first time in a decade, a surge of hope. The hope that she could finally move past her grief. Take her love for Jack and catapult it to a whole new level.

"This," she waved the check back and forth, "is perfect. It's Jack's past and my future. And our legacy," she said with a tender glance at Paco and her dad.

"This is the beginning of a new nonprofit to help families of fallen service members." She took the check in both hands, seeing all the boundless potential in the small piece of paper. "The Jack Taylor Foundation."

The words had barely escaped her lips before the congressman chimed in. "I'd like to match that amount."

"Me too," Mark said.

Alex jumped in. "Me three."

"Nope. No check writing from you, Mr. Drake," Madison said.

"Why not? I swear, my check will clear," he joked.

"Because you've been writing checks to the Taylors for long enough."

Alex scrunched his face with exaggerated offense. "Seriously, my money's no good here?"

"Your money? No. Well, at least not now," Madison said, adding, "But your *here* is good here."

Alex's indignation transformed to confusion. "Huh?"

"Your *here* is good here. Here. DGI headquarters. I'm gonna need an office, and this might be the perfect place. You've got a lot of unused resources in these sky-scraping digs. Perhaps you could donate a small piece of the DGI pie? An office or two for me and whomever else I can rustle up to volunteer?"

She gave her father an adoring look, and he shot back a wink of approval. "And supplies," she said to Alex. "Seriously, your supply room could use a bit of a cleanup."

Frowning, Alex maintained his pout. "You've got it. Anything you need. But I'd still like to donate a few bucks to this foundation."

In Alex Drake terms, a few dollars could easily mean a few hundred thousand or a few million.

"Not a cent. At least, not until I figure out what I'm doing. And as for the two of you," her gaze darted between Mark and the congressman, "you have my sincere thanks, but I'll hold your IOUs for the moment."

She snapped the check between her hands. "First, let's just see what I can do with this. This is where it will start. This way, Jack is the *foundation* of the Jack Taylor Foundation."

"And you have one hell of a kickass mentor to help ensure that goes as far as it possibly can," Jess said.

Madison nodded at Jess. "That I do."

Congressman Charles checked his watch. "Unfortunately, I'm needed across town." He stood and extended his hand to Madison, who took it in both of hers. "And my IOU can be collected anytime, Madison. Anytime at all."

She jumped up to wrap another hug around his neck, this one much tighter than the first, before returning to her seat. The door closed behind the congressman, and Madison smiled at her friends and loved ones left around the table.

"Okay," Paco said, "I don't know about you all, but my oncoming jet lag is only slightly offset by being absolutely famished. And if you don't figure something out quickly, I'm taking Madison up on her offer for some chocolate-fountain fun."

Confused, Mark and Alex squinted at each other.

Madison and Jess watched with excitement, shouting in unison, "Food challenge!"

The air filled with chatter about themes and menu items. Soon, they agreed that Paco's place was centrally located and should host the festivities. It was even better that he'd become the B&B for Dan.

They paired up, with Paco and Dan agreeing to get the charcuterie and champagne ready for everyone's arrival. Mark and Jess would head to a different store than Alex and Madison, and all would meet back at Paco's in an hour.

∞

As the elevator opened to the DGI garage, Alex and Madison strolled toward the lone luxury car left in the empty subterranean space. His fingers wove through hers.

"Madison, I want to give you something. An engagement gift. And . . . it's a little fancy," he said with a pre-emptive apology as he let her into the car. He made his way to the driver's side and sat but didn't start the engine.

"Alex, you've already given me more than the Publisher's Clearinghouse."

"Then one more piece on the pile won't make much difference," he said in that adorable tone that absolutely melted her.

Watching her, he waited for the smallest inkling of approval. She gave it in a big, beautiful kiss.

"Good." Stealing another kiss, he whispered, "Close your eyes."

He slipped a velvety box into her hand. Even with her eyes shut, she knew it had to be a particular familiar shade of blue. "Okay, take a look."

Opening her eyes, she opened the elegant box. Her sharp gasp filled the air. "Alex . . . I don't know what to say."

The box was brilliant with the sparkle of diamond earrings, their light dancing with every subtle shift of her hand. They perfectly matched her engagement ring.

"I wanted you to have a pair since your last ones were swiped from under your nose by a dastardly thief."

"Hey, that's my brother you're talking about. And technically, I gave them to him."

Madison loved that Paco conned them from her right off the bat. Since that day, she'd never seen him without them. She flipped down the visor, admiring her reflection as she put them on.

Alex stroked her cheek. "Well, I'm hoping these are very much to your liking. That you feel like they're truly *you*, because, and I say this with all the love in the world . . ."

She turned to him, suddenly concerned. "Because what?"

He took her face in his hands, caressing her cheeks with his thumbs.

"Madison, in all seriousness, if for whatever reason you don't like them . . ." His eyes tracked hers as he took a deep breath. Solemnly, he shook his head before whispering, "I'm not taking one for the team. A diamond-studded cock-ring is one thing. But I am absolutely, positively not getting anything pierced."

Madison watched this handsome man with the lickable dimple return to the task of starting the car. "So, now there are conditions on our love?"

"Damn straight. I draw the line at piercings. Besides, you have conditions too, with the whole 'no check writing from you, Alex,'" he said, mimicking her in his best falsetto.

She threw back her head with a laugh. "Not forever. Just not now. Which is more than you're giving me, since, apparently, piercings have made its way to your hard-limit list."

"Trust me, you don't want anything to snag on the way out. Speaking of lists, we need to figure out what we're picking up at the store. I'm in the mood to kick some best-friend butt tonight. Team Drake's taking home the trophy." He gave her a naughty glance. "And speaking of trophy . . ."

"Let me guess. If you win big, I'll win big too?"

"Without a doubt, you'll be taking first. Repeatedly."

"Why do I have a feeling I'm going to see your trophy either way?"

"Because you, my determined little sex kitten, have a remarkable way of keeping your eyes on the prize."

He took her hand to his lips, giving it a reverent kiss. He wove their fingers together and rested their joined hands on his thigh.

As they drove off into the sunset, Madison marveled at the prize of a man sitting next to her. He did more than restore her brother's military record. He had Jack and Paco officially recognized as the heroes they always were.

And all this time, Alex Drake had been like a son to her father, generously giving what he had and asking for nothing in return.

True, the earrings, like the bracelet and ring before them, were masterpieces. But they paled in comparison to Alex Drake himself—the man who'd blown into her life with a snide remark and a splash of spiked coffee. The man who'd lovingly labored every day since then to slay his demons and steal her heart.

Next to her sat the man she was destined to love forever. The man she was going to marry.

As they took off into the glowing kaleidoscope of a bustling New York evening, Madison knew that together, they could take on whatever life threw at them.

They'd thwarted a building full of occasional busybodies. Danced with a dangerous group of ex-spies. And in the midst of it all, they treaded dangerously close to what was sure to become

Manhattan's event of the century—their wedding. And let's not forget the spur-of-the-moment pop-up food competition.

Life was throwing Madison and Alex one racy adventure after the other, and they were ready to face it all. Her smile spread wide as she admired their interlaced fingers and squeezed a little tighter.

Bring it on!

Because hand in hand, they could tackle anything. Together, they could take on the world.

~

Thank you for reading *Burned*! Alex and Madison have more adventures ahead. (And, don't forget Paco!) *Ready for answers?* **Get FINDERS KEEPERS Now!**

Keep going to read the first few chapters.

~

Join Lexxi's VIP reader list to be the first to know of new releases, free books, special prices, and other giveaways!

Free hot romances & happily ever afters delivered to your inbox.
https://www.lexxijames.com/freebies

~

If you loved Burned, here's another military love story.

For Jake Russo, abandoning the past became his only future. It should have been his burden alone. But he had one cross to bear. Watching over Kathryn Chase . . . in secret.

Her unangelic guardian paying back a debt.

Available on All Platforms! **Get FALLEN DOM now!**

Looking for another sexy billionaire? Meet Davis R. Black … aka Richard. Some know him as a tech mogul. To Jaclyn, he's the King of the A-holes. Which is why this billionaire is hiding *his* in plain sight. Check out the first book in the Ruthless Billionaires Club.

Available on All Platforms! **Get RUTHLESS GAMES now!**

FINDERS KEEPERS

AN ALEX DRAKE NOVEL

PROLOGUE

ALEX

Alex Drake stood before a full-length mirror, eyeing every detail of his new three-piece suit. Normally, his custom tailoring would be done in the comfort of his penthouse home. Today, Alex and his best friend were meeting with his tailor in his office—a grand executive suite at the top of his skyscraper in the midst of Manhattan.

The look was flawless. A tad more formal than he preferred, but with a reluctant nod, he approved. This wasn't just a suit. Frowning, Alex lifted the lapels of his suit jacket to inspect the vest.

Though comfortable, the weight was much heavier than any normal vest. *It's battle armor.*

When Paco stepped beside him, Alex admired his friend, who was wearing a new suit of his own. "Looks good."

"Good?" Paco huffed. "No, not good. Good is professional and worldly. Boring as shit. We're totally rocking it like James fucking Bond. You killed it again, Josh."

Satisfied, the tailor happily took the compliment and gave them a smile before departing.

Alex's throat tightened by a heavy knot of nerves. He nodded again, sighing to himself.

"A three-piece suit is perfect." Paco caught his gaze in the mirror, his tone confident and reassuring. "Don't worry. Good things come in threes. The number is mystical, magical, hence the rule of threes. It amplifies the intensity of everything. Luck. Power. The Jonas Brothers."

"I'll settle for luck."

Paco lifted a brow. "I'll settle for the Jonas Brothers."

A soft ping sounded from Alex's phone, but he ignored it.

"Not getting that?" Paco asked, a curious smile on his face, but Alex's only answer was a shake of his head. "It could be important."

"It can wait."

Paco didn't ask more, and Alex sure as hell wasn't getting into it. Obviously, Paco recognized the assigned ring tone. *Jordan Stone*.

Talk about a mystical enigma. With legs up to her eyeballs and a penchant for sin and seduction, Jordan Stone was in a class all her own. Alex never knew where he stood with her. *Or with Madison*.

Coming on strong with Alex was one thing. But when it came to his fiancée, nothing was off limits for Jordan, and she made no pretense about it. She liked Madison and would take any and every chance to cop a feel or steal a kiss. *But why?*

And why the three of them to begin with? The three Jordan Stones.

A decade ago, his Jordan Stone, aka *Jordan*, lured him with her wicked ways. And her tongue. Resisting her would have been pointless, but giving in was his undoing.

At the same time, Madison's brother, Jack, was meeting with a much older and supremely powerful man—Jordan Stone, or simply *Stone*. The mastermind recruited the sharp West Point grad with a patriotic song and dance, seducing the all-American guy to do more for his country than his country could do for him.

It cost Jack his life. And left everyone who cared for him devastated in the aftermath.

And then there was the third Jordan Stone—Paco's recruiter, and perhaps the biggest mystery of them all. Where that man with no alias was concerned, Paco left no *stone* unturned. Literally.

On paper, the operative didn't exist. All Paco ever learned about him was that the man died on a mission years ago. Unsettled, Paco continued investigating.

It was one of many things Alex and Paco had in common. If there was an unsolved puzzle, leave it to them to obsess over it.

"Hey. Where'd you go?"

Seeing the worry in his best friend's eyes, Alex forced a smile. "Nothing. Just thinking about threes."

Nodding, Paco gave him a bigger smile. "I know what you mean. Siri," he boomed.

"Siri here."

"Play *Sucker*." Singing along, Paco hip-bumped his boss before busting out all his club moves.

Embarrassed, Alex pinched the bridge of his nose. Sternly, he said, "Paco?"

"What?" Paco gave him an innocent look. "You've got to get out of your own head for a hot second. Nothing does that like letting loose with Kevin, Joe, and Nick."

Shaking his head with an inescapable laugh, Alex avoided the next butt bump by checking his watch. "Oh, look at the time. Airport in two hours."

The reminder was hardly necessary.

Paco killed the music, rubbing his hands together enthusiastically. "When the real party starts!"

CHAPTER 1

MADISON

Madison glared at the sexy stud of a man standing before her. With his arms crossed, he blocked the steps to his transatlantic jet with his solid build.

"No girls allowed." Alex Drake was standing his ground, scoffing at the conventions of political correctness despite his high-profile position. His defiant eyes let her know he meant business. And his telltale smirk showed just how much he loved it.

Hands on her hips, she pushed back. "Is that so?"

An immediate divide was occurring right there on the tarmac of Teterboro Airport. The blurred lines of beauty versus billionaire became irrefutably clear. Men versus women.

Standing on one side was Alex Drake, founder of Drake Global Industries, or DGI. But he stood alone as the other men chuckled, abandoning him as they boarded the jet.

His best friend and cutthroat rival, Mark Donovan of Excelsior/Centurion, was the first to ditch his bestie. And then there was Davis "Richard" Black, CEO of Black Technologies. He threw an apologetic glance at his new fiancée, Jaclyn, who stood in solidarity with Madison.

Alex stepped closer.

Confused, amused, and throwing him the prettiest pouts in all the state, the women stood aligned. Jess Bishop, the sassy, no-holds-barred wife of Mark, might have married the man, but never took his name. She locked arms with Madison as she'd done dozens of times.

Apparently comfortable in the immediate girl power they shared, Jaclyn Long, COO of billion-dollar conglomerate Long Multinational, took Madison's other arm. Though she and Madison had only just met, their obvious alliance was unflinching.

Take that, Alex Drake.

Rounding out the bonds of sisterhood was Paco Robles. A politically astute man who could easily dissuade a take-no-prisoners battle of the sexes, he held his ground with the women. His stance clearly screamed, "I'm not Switzerland."

"That's so." Alex checked his watch. "And it's time to say goodbye." Possessively, he swept Madison from the arms of her comrades and kissed her until her body practically melted into his.

"Wait." Alarmed, she lowered her voice. "You're seriously ditching us?"

"Yes. The boys are heading to Singapore without you." Postponing an explanation, he kissed her again.

"What?" Her brows knitted in disbelief. "I can handle the risks, if that's what you're worried about. I know what to expect, and I'm ready for it."

"Are you?" he asked. In an instant, worry crossed his face.

The question had been asked and answered dozens of times. But as much as nobody wanted Madison that close to certain danger, there was no way they were going to Singapore without her.

"Yes," she said firmly, reassuring Alex as best she could. Impatient, she asked, "And why did we all pack if you were ditching us?"

Paco stepped closer. "Because I wanted to surprise you, and this was the perfect cover. Ladies, our jet is right over there."

"*Our* jet?" Madison turned to him with a worried frown. "So the big macho men are heading into the storm, and we're relegated to the sidelines?"

Et tu, Paco? Et tu?

Looking back at Alex, she asked, "And where exactly are *we* going?"

Her fiancé released a frustrated huff as he gently stroked the pout of her lower lip with his thumb. "Look, this wasn't my idea. Begrudgingly, I support Paco's wishes. Besides, it gives the team time to get everything set up before you all join us. And I'm sure as hell not forcing this on you. I know Jess wants time with Mark, and we all know that Richard and Jaclyn would like a few days to get, uh, reacquainted. So I'll leave it up to you. You're all welcome to join us as we head to Singapore. Or . . ."

"Or . . ." Paco drew out the word for effect, aiming his enthusiastic charm at Madison. "We can head to Paris where a dozen of your girlfriends are already waiting to kick off your bachelorette party."

Wide-eyed and squealing, Madison looked at the ladies who were now as excited as she was.

"I'm always down for a chocolate croissant," Jaclyn said.

Jess grinned. "Being constantly surrounded by Mark and all my brothers, I'll never turn down a girls' getaway."

Inwardly delighted, Madison conceded. "I guess the big macho men *are* leaving without us."

Without another word, Jess and Jaclyn hurried across the tarmac to the luxurious France-bound jet, chattering excitedly about what they wanted to do first when they arrived.

Madison would have bolted too, but Alex wrapped a tight arm around her as he walked her to the jet at a leisurely stroll.

"Hey now," he said, "let's get a few things straight. This is going to be a very calm, sophisticated, sedate girls' getaway. Maybe some spa time and pampering. A glass or two of wine." As they stopped at the bottom of the stairs to the jet, he kissed her hard and ended with a stern warning. "And no exotic dancers."

Smiling, Alex released her, swatting her playfully on the butt as she booked it up the stairs.

Paco joined her at the cabin doorway and called out to Alex with a big grin. "Spa time. Overflowing booze. Strippers galore. Got it!" He saluted sharply.

Narrowing his eyes, Alex shouted back over the roar of the engines. "It's mighty convenient that you're one of the girls when we could really use you."

Madison and Paco exchanged a devilish look before he shouted back.

"The lines have been drawn. Queens rule!"

With that, they ducked inside and the stairs closed behind them. The jet bound for fun and excitement in the City of Light taxied, and from her buttery-soft leather seat, Madison watched Alex through the small window until the plane took off.

CHAPTER 2

ALEX

Drake Global Industries
Singapore Headquarters

Despite the oversized conference table, Alex sat just one chair from Mr. Chang, whose first name was nearly impossible for most Westerners to pronounce, a consequence of one too many *x*'s in the mix. So for most, he went by the easier moniker *Jeff*.

Unchallenged by Mandarin, Alex never had an issue with Chang's first name, but both men naturally gravitated to calling each other by their last names. They shared an easy camaraderie, two men who'd separately climbed the ranks of wealth and status through the valley of corporate warfare, one low crawl at a time.

Their respect was instant, and to this day, was very much shared. Which made an adversarial spin on their relationship impossible. But it was fun to try.

Alex tapped a finger to the polished mahogany table. "You've been keeping secrets, Chang."

Chang's humble grin was always endearing, but he didn't disagree. "We all do, Drake."

Casually, Chang poured the tea into traditional undersized cups. They each admired the swirl of steam lifting from their oolong before taking a sip.

Giving Alex an inscrutable look, Chang said, "You'll have to be more specific."

Smiling, Alex enjoyed this. Mirroring his expression, so did Chang. The game was well understood. Love was love, but business was business. Chang nailed it. Their livelihood and security were only as good as the secrets they locked away.

From his inside breast pocket, Alex extracted a small plastic card. The crest on the bottom made the random, ordinary keycard distinctive and specific—a golden Merlion, the symbol of Singapore.

With an indifferent glance, Chang shrugged. Undeterred, Alex slid it closer to his counterpart.

Picking it up, Chang flipped it back and forth. "It's an access card. The design is still widely used today across a vast range of companies. Corporate empires. Hotels. We've even used it, I don't know, ten . . . twelve years ago, perhaps."

"That's the right time frame," Alex said under his breath.

Chang's company, now known as DGI Singapore, wasn't new when it entered the DGI fold. It was an acquisition, the first of many that had grown Alex's corporation worldwide.

Grasping at straws, Alex asked, "Back then, was it connected with any special project? Military, or something covert? Dangerous?"

The uncertain fog in Chang's eyes lifted, replaced with a glint of recollection. "Ah." Clasping his hands, he leaned in. "Do you believe in ghost stories, Drake?"

Assuming Chang was referring to the mystery surrounding Jack's mission-related murder a decade ago, Alex schooled his features and relaxed in his chair, crossing an ankle over his other knee.

Jack being Madison's brother wasn't the only reason Alex was deeply invested in this conversation. The attack had nearly cost him and Paco their lives, and devastated the Taylor family in the aftermath. They all needed answers, and he prayed that Chang had something of substance to offer.

"Well, my life's been haunted by this mystery for a decade, so let's go with yes."

Nodding, Chang lowered his voice, unusually careful with it being just the two of them in the room. "I think you're looking for *Yōulíng Láng.*"

"*Yōulíng Láng.*" Alex repeated Chang's pronunciation perfectly. The phrase barely challenged his repertoire. Aloud, he translated the meaning of the two words. "Ghost wolf?"

With a somber nod, Chang looked on with regret. "I don't know much. We don't keep records . . . intentionally. My first encounter was as a soldier. My team was deployed to find an operative that had gone missing." His head dropped. "And we did. We found our man."

Alex poured him more tea, empathizing with the pain his friend was dredging up. "You don't have to—"

"You need to know what lies ahead." Taking a breath, Chang continued. "The torture our man went through was extensive. Unnecessarily so. This wasn't a matter of mere information extraction." Chang's eyes locked with Alex's in somber understanding. "And it was only a few miles outside the city. How do you say it? The bastard had balls."

Retrieving the card and tapping it on the table, Alex asked, "Why does this card make you think it was the Ghost Wolf?"

"Over the years, I've seen his handiwork. I've chased him the way people chase Bigfoot or the Loch Ness Monster, in my spare time, and very careful about the resources I throw at the search. Because . . ."

Prodding him, Alex asked gently, "Because?"

Chang blew out a long breath. "Because people who look too hard become the next victim. I don't believe in ghosts, but I believe in the Ghost Wolf. I can tell you this much—his attacks happen all over the world, usually targeting operatives moving very valuable information. And there's always an access card, one you can't trace, wiped down and left with the body. Be careful, *tóngzhì*." *Comrade*. Warning punctuated his words. "To the Ghost Wolf, it's a game. A deadly one."

Thinking of Madison, Alex took a calming breath, hiding his anxiety. "Thank you, my friend."

CHAPTER 3

MADISON

Paris, France
The Eiffel Tower

MADISON STARED down at the note. Strangely, the penmanship had become familiar.

EIFFEL TOWER
NOON
ALONE
PS: I KNOW THE COLOR OF YOUR PANTIES

Grimacing at the last line, she stuffed the note back in her purse. *No, she doesn't. Does she?*

With each passing minute, Madison's apprehension ticked higher. Over and over, she scanned the crowds. Nothing. Then she tilted her head back, viewing the metal weaving of the iconic structure in front of her up to the sky.

Should I go up? Hang out down here? Wave my hands in the air and holler like I just don't care?

Frustrated, she checked her phone. Fifteen minutes after twelve. *She's late, and I'm out of here.*

Determined, Madison hailed an approaching cab. When it stopped at the curb , she quickly hopped in. Not knowing a bit of French, she fished through her bag for the business card to the hotel. The car rolled away before she could find it.

"Don't worry, Madison. I know where you're going." The sultry voice was as taunting as ever.

A dramatic entrance. Of course.

Madison looked up, meeting the driver's eyes in the rearview mirror. "Jordan. If you wanted me to hop in a taxi, why not put it in the note?"

"Because if I take the mystery out of our relationship, how would I ever steal your attention?" Jordan's words were laced with suggestion. "Besides, I had to do some dry cleaning for both our sakes."

Confused, Madison checked her outfit, but then caught sight of Jordan rolling her eyes in exasperation in the rearview mirror.

"Civilian translation? I needed to make sure nobody was following either of us. If someone were following you, watching you adorably check the time with a frantic glance about, they'd realize you'd been stood up. Hailing a cab to head back to the hotel would be a natural response. Further watching would be a waste of their time."

Madison eased back into her seat. "Whose time? Other than you, who's following me?"

Jordan gave her a small smirk. "Someone who's about to make your life a whole lot harder."

Madison didn't respond, hoping her silence would encourage Jordan to disclose more.

"No." Jordan slowly blew out a breath, somehow reading Madison's mind. "We need to convince the puppet masters that you're a pawn, and you play that part so much better when you're in the dark."

Mindful, Madison kept her tone steady and cool. "Then why warn me at all? Won't that ruin your element of surprise?" Her added jazz hands for effect came out ineffective, as Jordan didn't even look.

Without acknowledging the question, Jordan changed the subject, her tone now uncharacteristically serious. "Your party's this evening, but when will someone start missing you? Calling to check on you?"

Of course Jordan knows about the party. If she knows about my panties, details about my party are hardly a national secret.

Madison shrugged. "I don't know. Everyone's busy prepping for tonight. I slipped away because they think I'm at a spa."

"You're not far off. My company can be very relaxing. Just give me a chance." Playtime apparently over, Jordan refocused and continued. "So that leaves the ever-protective Mr. Robles. It should take him about ninety minutes to miss you, and that gives us plenty of time. I'll need your phone."

Not bothering to protest, Madison handed it over. If Jordan wanted to hurt her, nothing was stopping her. As they sped away from the city, Madison decided to sit back and enjoy the ride.

I wonder if she'll kill me if I pester her with "How much longer till we get there?"

Hopefully soon.

Not killing me. Getting there.

Huffing, Madison pouted in silence. *Phoneless rides are boring and inhumane.*

∾

Ready for answers? **Get FINDERS KEEPERS Now!**

ABOUT THE AUTHOR

Lexxi James is a best-selling author of romantic suspense. Her feats in multi-tasking include binge watching Netflix and sucking down a cappuccino in between feverish typing and loads of laundry.

She lives in Ohio with her teen daughter and the sweetest man in the universe. She loves to hear from readers!

www.LexxiJames.com

Printed in Great Britain
by Amazon